DANGEROUS
MASTER

Books by Tawny Taylor

Dangerous Master

Darkest Fire

Decadent Master

Wicked Beast

Dark Master

Real Vamps Don't Drink O-Neg

Sex and the Single Ghost

DANGEROUS MASTER

TAWNY TAYLOR

APHRODISIA

KENSINGTON PUBLISHING CORP.

www.kensingtonbooks.com

A special thank-you to Sierra Summers.
Girl, you are the best!

1

It was heaven. Glorious, nude male bodies as far as the eye could see. Limbs entwined; muscles stretching and flexing; hard, thick cocks gliding in and out of pussies, mouths, asses.

Mandy Thompson's job had taken her to all sorts of places, from the presidential suites of Michigan's finest five-star hotels to rat-infested hellholes in the most dangerous pockets of Detroit. But never a place like this.

Until tonight.

A tray of full champagne glasses balanced on one hand, Mandy stood in the doorway, her gaze meandering around the space, sliding from one beautiful male body to the next. A sigh slipped from between her lips. "Damn, I love my job. I am *so glad* I took this case."

"I told you, you wouldn't regret it." Sarah Gray, her best friend, adjusted her corset before leading her down a narrow walkway that skirted the perimeter of the room. "Just remember, you can't get so carried away that you forget everything I taught you."

Easier said than done. Although Mandy was professional

enough to realize the danger of forgetting where she was, why she was here, and what could happen if anyone made her.

To everyone but Sarah, Mandy was a waitress, paid to tote around trays of champagne.

To Sarah, and to her client, Allison Clark, wife of Mr. Andrew Clark—two-timing trust-fund baby—she was one of the best private detectives in Metro Detroit. Discreet. Thorough. And as tenacious as a bulldog.

Sarah and Mandy made a full circle of the room. Only twice was she stopped by thirsty guests. Then they headed outside, down the main corridor, and into a second spacious room, this one set up as a bondage dungeon.

Sarah stopped in front of a scene featuring a gorgeous man, nude with the exception of an itty-bitty G-string that strained at the seams. He was strapped spread-eagle to a wooden cross. But it wasn't the rippling muscles, pulled taut beneath oil-slicked skin, or the hard penis testing the construction of his G-string that made Mandy feel warm between the legs. It was the look of rapture on his tanned face. It was sexy beyond imagining. It was enough to make her cream her panties.

"Now *that's* how you tell if you're doing things right," Sarah said, her voice a little on the breathy side.

Her own voice husky, Mandy said, "It's no wonder you spend practically every free minute at places like this." Shifting the tray to hold it in front of her body, she leaned back, letting the wall support her. The drywall felt cool against her burning skin. It was a very welcome sensation.

Sarah gave Mandy a little nudge. "I have a feeling you will, too, even after you're done with your case."

"Maybe. Speaking of the case..." Mandy pushed off the wall, forcing her gaze from the man on the cross. She closed her eyes for a moment, trying to visualize the man she had been hired to watch. It wasn't easy shoving aside the memory of the man on the cross, but she did it.

Late thirties. Blond hair, wavy and cut about collar length.

Andrew Clark, one of Metro Detroit's richest men, was said to be submissive and prefer male doms and sex partners. He had talked his wife, Allison, a former topless dancer, into signing a prenup. She wouldn't get more than ten thousand dollars in the event of a divorce, unless she could prove infidelity.

Why a gay man who'd married a woman to pacify his father would think a document would be enough to protect him was beyond Mandy. But it was good for his soon-to-be ex.

And good for Mandy's bank account, too. Despite having steady work that paid well, it was getting lean. Lately, she was shelling out hefty money for her grandmother's care. Her maternal grandmother, a woman who wore the "feisty Irish" tag with pride, Grandma Dougherty was the only family she had left, and Grandma Dougherty was the most important person in the world to her. Mandy would live in a cardboard box to keep that woman in the home she loved.

"Do you see Mr. Jones?" Sarah asked, using the code name they'd agreed upon before leaving her apartment.

"Not yet."

"If he isn't in one of these two rooms, he's probably in one of the private suites upstairs." Sarah gave Mandy's arm a tap. "Let's go around to the other side to make sure."

"There are private suites?" Hefting the tray, Mandy sighed. "This isn't going to be easy."

"Like I told you, Mr. Jones isn't much of an exhibitionist. You're probably not going to catch him bent over a horse, a sweet boy fucking him in the ass."

Mandy had seen a picture of Andrew Clark, aka Mr. Jones. Seeing a hot guy fuck him in the ass would be a sight to behold. "Now, that was fodder for one hell of a dream." Fanning her face with her free hand, Mandy motioned with a tip of the head, indicating a nearby scene. The dom was drop-dead, traffic-stopping, panty-dropping gorgeous, and the sub, a man who was younger than him, maybe in his midtwenties, wasn't far behind him in the looks department. "What is it with this party? Every single male is beautiful. I've never seen so many good-looking men in one place in my life."

Sarah shrugged. "Couldn't tell you. But it's one of the things I find most appealing about Zane's parties." She nudged Mandy in the side. "Finally."

"Is it Mr. Jones?" Mandy followed the direction of Sarah's gaze.

"No, it's my subs."

"Did you say 'subs'? As in, plural?" Mandy located a pair of men in their late-twenties, both wearing jeans that fit them like second skins and tank tops that did a lot of good things for their pecs, shoulders, and arms. "Those two?"

"Uh-huh." Sarah gave Mandy a grin, then turned on the charm as the pair sauntered up to them. "You're late." She was still smiling, but there was an evil glimmer in her eyes. Mandy had a feeling those two were going to regret being late. Then again, maybe not. "I have a suite. Let's head back."

"Ladies first," one of the two men said as he gave Mandy the once-over.

Mandy raised her tray. "I'm not playing today. I'm working."

"Too bad."

She was almost sharing that sentiment. Almost.

Keenly aware of the man's lust-filled eyes on her, Mandy gave Sarah a little wave. Sarah and her wonder twins headed in one direction while Mandy headed in another. In the congested main hallway, someone tapped her on the back. She carefully turned to face the back-tapper.

Ohmygod.

The man was too freaking beautiful to be real. His face was the stuff of dreams. His body, of wet dreams.

"Hi." Mandy swung the tray around, assuming he wanted a glass of champagne.

"No thanks." His voice was a deep baritone. It made her nerves prickle, in a good way.

"Okay." Confused now, she gave him one of her brightest smiles. "Can I help you?"

"I guess that depends." His gaze meandered up and down her body. If she wasn't so incredibly attracted to this man, she might've been irritated by his obvious staring, or embarrassed. As it was, she was getting warmer, particularly between her legs.

Aware of how damp her panties were becoming, she tightened her thighs, pressing them together. She reminded herself she wasn't at this party to make new friends. She was there to collect proof of her client's husband's infidelity. "Depends on what?" she asked, infusing her voice with a more professional tone.

His perfectly arched brows lifted slightly. He extended a hand. "I'm Zane Griffin."

She knew that name.

He was, essentially, her boss. She'd been hired by an agency to work at this party, at his party. And if she wanted to make sure she was hired to work future parties, she had better make a good impression.

She placed her hand in his. "Amanda Thompson." His grip was firm. He didn't let her hand go. Now more nervous than turned on, she slightly shifted the tray balanced on her other hand. "You said I could help you?"

Something she couldn't quite read flashed in his eyes. "Yes." He finally released her hand. She placed it under the tray, which was getting a little heavy. He took the champagne from her and set it on a nearby table. "I saw you. In the dungeon."

Immediately, Mandy recalled what the agency representative had told them when she'd first arrived. There was to be no alcohol served in the dungeon. And there she was, toting champagne into the dungeon. Her face burned. "Ohmygosh, I'm sorry. I totally forgot. My friend, who is a guest, was showing me—"

"It's okay," he interrupted. "I'm not making myself clear." He straightened ever so slightly, which made him look that much more intimidating. "It's true—there should be no alcohol served in the dungeon. But that's not why I wished to talk to you."

"Oh, okay." Mandy tucked her now-empty hands behind her back.

"I need someone to work in my private suite. To serve some very special guests there. I wanted to ask if you'd like to be that someone."

This was exactly the opportunity she needed. With any luck, Andrew Clark would be one of those "special guests," and she'd have her evidence by the end of the night. All she needed was one photograph of him either being penetrated or penetrating another person, male or female, to collect her paycheck.

"I would be honored."

"Excellent. This way." Zane Griffin, aka Master Zane, as Sarah called him, placed a hand at the small of Mandy's back and steered her toward the sweeping staircase in the front foyer. Up she went, propelled by his touch, aware every second of the heat of his hand, even through the material of her white cotton blouse. At the top of the stairs, he turned her into the first room. They entered through a pair of French doors into one of the most opulent master suites she'd ever seen.

Immediately inside the French doors was a lounge area, with several cozy couches. A porn film played on a huge flat-screen television hung on one wall, the sound replaced with some sultry jazz playing over unseen speakers. Here and there, flickering candles created soft ambient lighting. On the floor lay a thick rug. It looked like some kind of animal fur. Mandy could imagine lying on that rug, nude.

Zane stopped in the center of the room.

Mandy hung back, closer to the door. "This room is gorgeous."

"Thank you." His gaze locked on Mandy's face, Zane slowly circled the perimeter. "I designed this space." He stopped in front of a painting of a nude woman, hanging over a deep mahogany dresser. He looked at it, and his features softened slightly. "Every piece has a special meaning to me."

"I can tell." Something pulled her deeper into the room. One moment she was standing just inside the door, and the next she was beside Zane, looking up at the painting. The artist had used oils. Mandy could tell by the layered shading and texture. "This painting is very nice. I tried my hand at painting figures in college. It's definitely not my forte."

Zane turned, facing Mandy. Now she felt small and vulnerable and uncomfortable. He was big. Really big. And his body was powerful, his arms thick, his shoulders heavily muscled. If he wanted, he could easily swoop her off her feet, cart her to the nearest bedroom, and . . . do whatever he wanted.

She almost wondered what that might be like.

He leaned close enough for her to catch the slightest scent of cologne, trapping her between his body and the dresser. "Amanda, you know what will be happening in this suite, don't you?"

"I have some idea." The image of this man nude flashed through Mandy's mind. She shifted back, putting as much space between her body and his as she could. It wasn't enough. Not by a long shot.

"You won't be bothered by what you'll see, will you?" He caged her body between his arms, his hands resting on the dresser's top.

"No." But she sure as heck was bothered now. She'd figured

this case would be a little awkward, maybe a bit uncomfortable, but she hadn't seen this coming. "I'll be okay." Her voice sounded so small. There could be no way he'd believe her.

Mandy wouldn't have believed it was possible, but Zane leaned closer still. If she inhaled too deeply, her tits would probably touch him. She didn't inhale...at all.

"My guests, particularly in my personal suite, must have absolute privacy. You may not tell anyone who you've seen here. Nor are you permitted to take any photographs or recordings. As if he knew she had a hidden camera in her skirt pocket, he slid a hand over her hip. It stopped right on the spot.

Mandy swallowed. She'd been made. Already.

Zane was holding her gaze hostage. That wasn't making her feel any better about being caught red-handed with a camera. "What's this?" His hand slipped into her pocket. But instead of going right for the camera, he let his fingertips graze her leg through the thin fabric of the pocket's lining. The intimate touch made her quake. She wanted to shove him away. She wanted to smack him across the face. She wanted to run out of this place and never come back.

She didn't do any of those things.

But neither did she answer his question. She figured he already knew what it was. And even if he didn't, he would soon enough.

Who the hell was this little chit, bringing a camera to his party? The agency had promised to do a background check on every person they'd sent. This little minx with the tumble of brown waves cascading over her shoulders, the cool gray eyes, and the lush lips had been cleared. But it seemed she shouldn't have been.

What was she up to?

Zane knew he should throw her out on her ass. *Should.* So why couldn't he get himself to do it?

He inhaled deeply, thinking the lungful of air would help him gather the strength to show her the door. Or at least release her and take a step back. It didn't. Instead, that inhalation carried her scent deep into his nostrils, deeper still, until he could practically taste her.

She was scared.

But that wasn't all she was feeling.

Thanks to his heightened senses, he could tell she was ready. To fuck.

Her pussy was wet for him. And damn if he didn't want to shove his cock inside her slick heat and find out how tight and hot she was.

He slid his hand, still deep inside her skirt pocket, around to the back of her thigh and pulled her hips flush to him. He checked her eyes. The pupils were dilated, but her lids were narrowed in defiance.

Damn, she was fun.

"Sir, I'm here to do a job. Not to be a...participant."

Her voice lacked conviction. She wanted this, wanted his touch. Wanted his cock. She wouldn't admit it, not with words. But her body couldn't lie.

He curled his fingers around the camera.

Her eyes widened.

"Who are you?" he asked.

She lifted her chin. "I told you my name."

"Yes, I know. But *who* are you?"

Those pretty eyes narrowed again. "I'm the waitress you hired, that's who."

"Sneaking around with a camera." He pressed the object against her thigh. "Are you a reporter?"

She didn't answer.

He pulled the device out of her pocket and, backing away slightly to eliminate the distraction of her intoxicating scent, took a look at it. It was tiny, just under three inches by one inch. If not for the person who'd reported seeing her holding something suspicious, he might never have known she'd carried it in. Somehow she'd made it past his security team. They'd been trained to detect stuff like this.

He'd have to talk to them later about their failure.

He took a closer look at the device. It was a video camera, sold primarily for security use. "Are you a cop?"

She worried her lower lip. "No."

A spark of anger buzzed through his system. He dropped the camera on the floor and crushed it with his heel. Dammit, he didn't need this shit. Didn't need someone poking around, looking to make trouble for him, for his guests.

But...she mesmerized him.

More than any woman had. And although she was pretty, he couldn't say exactly what it was about her that made him so hard and tight and hot all over.

He caught her chin in his hand and tipped her head back. "If you ever bring a camera into one of my parties again, I'll make you regret it for a long, long time."

"Is that a threat?" she snapped.

Damn, she had balls.

"No, it's a promise." Not allowing himself to smile, he stepped back, motioning toward the door. "My security team will escort you off my property. Good-bye, Amanda Thompson." He pulled his phone out of his pocket, hitting the button to call Phillips, the man in charge of his security team.

She had the nerve to glare at him. "I don't need an escort. I can see myself out."

"Oh, no, you can't," he said through gritted teeth.

If only she knew how close he was to dragging her back to his bedroom and giving her what she wanted. The guard was for her sake, not his.

The beast inside had wakened.

2

Five minutes later, Mandy slumped into Sarah's car and fished her cell phone out of the glove compartment. Because phones were not permitted at the party, Sarah's phone was in there, too.

There was no way for her to get in touch with her.

And, of course, as luck would have it, Sarah had the car keys.

As a result, Mandy was stuck waiting outside until Sarah decided she'd had enough of the Wonder Twins. That could take hours.

Luckily, it was a pleasant early summer evening. The sky was clear, the cool air scented with the sweet smell of lilacs. Mandy dug around in Sarah's car, scoring a pen and an unused bank deposit envelope. She scrawled a note on it for Sarah, positioned it on the steering wheel so she'd see it, shoved her phone into her pocket, and headed out, walking down the long, winding driveway toward the main road. Her destination: the coffee shop she'd spied as they'd driven in. It was still relatively early, not quite ten. She hoped the shop would be open as late as the one by her house. She'd kill at least a half hour. After that, she hoped she could find a bar where she could sit and nurse a margarita or two.

Three hours later, her phone, set on vibrate, buzzed. Sitting in a pine booth at a sports bar roughly a half mile from the party, Mandy hit the button, answering the call.

"Hey, girl, where are you?" Sarah's voice was cheerful, as always. "I'll come pick you up."

"I'm at Sammy's. It's down the street, on the right-hand side."

"Be there in a few." Sarah ended the call.

Mandy paid her tab and headed outside to watch for Sarah. Her friend's car zipped up to the front of the building a couple minutes later. As Mandy slid into the passenger seat, Sarah gave her an apologetic look.

"Sorry. I didn't realize you'd been kicked out."

"It's okay." Mandy gave her friend what she hoped was a reassuring smile. "I'm capable of keeping myself out of trouble for a few hours. How were the Wonder Twins?"

"Wonder Twins?" Sarah echoed as she pulled her little Fiesta out onto the street. "Oh! I get it now. They were good. Thanks. What happened to you?"

"Zane Griffin found out about my camera. I don't know how. It was way too small to see. Someone must've told him. But who?"

"Wow, that's strange." Sarah's features twisted into a look of confusion. "Nobody but you and I knew about it. You got through security with no problem."

"I know. Someone must know I'm on a case. And they must've assumed I was there to collect information."

"Did Zane approach you about it, or did he send one of his goons?"

"No, it was Zane."

Sarah visibly tensed. "What was that like? That man intimidates the hell out of me."

"It wasn't pleasant." That statement was partly true.

"I bet."

"Needless to say, I won't be coming to another of his parties." Mandy let her head fall back against the headrest and closed her eyes, the stress of the night setting in. "Dammit, I was hoping tonight would go better. I'll have to find another way to catch Clark in the act. The bastard's careful. Careful isn't good."

"You'll do it. I have faith in you."

"Thanks. That makes one of us. Maybe I'll get lucky and another case'll land on my desk while I'm working this one. I need something easy so I can get paid. Like a married man who likes to meet his girlfriend up at the Red Roof Inn."

Sarah patted Mandy's knee. "You know I'll help you any way I can."

"Yeah, I know." Mandy gave Sarah what she knew had to be a wilted smile. "Thanks."

"Find out who Amanda Thompson is," Zane said to Phillips. "I want to know everything about her—where she lives, what she does to pay her bills, what she does in her free time. She's up to something. Has to be an undercover cop or private detective. Maybe a journalist. Somehow she made it through the agency's background check."

"Got it." Phillips pulled a small notebook out of his pocket and scratched her name in it. "Do you have more than a name?"

"We have the plate of the car she came in, though I'm guessing it isn't her vehicle. She didn't carry the keys, right? You said your team saw her walking up to the coffee shop?"

"Yes, that's correct. Her friend picked her up at Sammy's."

"Okay. That's it. Thanks." Ready to work off the tension coiled through his body, Zane excused Phillips. No sooner was Phillips gone than Zane's mind flashed back to that moment when he'd had Amanda Thompson caged between his arms. It had taken everything in him not to crush her mouth under his and drink in her flavor. How he'd wanted to strip off her clothes, tie her to his bed, and torment her until she begged for his cock.

That was what she'd wanted. It was what he'd wanted, too.

It was what he wanted now.

He closed his eyes and unzipped his pants, wrapping his fingers around his cock and giving it a few slow pumps. Damn that felt good, but it wasn't nearly enough. He wanted a tight, wet cunt. Her tight, wet cunt. Or maybe her ass.

His teeth sank into his lower lip as he pictured her on his bed, bent over, her round ass pink and warm from a spanking. Her pussy would be dripping with her juices, the air heavy with her perfume.

He stroked himself faster, imagining it was her hands closed around his rod, stroking him to completion. He could imagine her full lips pursed, her tongue moistening them, preparing them to slide around his cock.

His balls tightened. His muscles pulled into painful knots.

He stopped stroking and opened his eyes.

He needed to fuck. Now. He needed a partner who would be willing and able to take it hard and fast. He knew exactly who that partner would be.

His blood simmering, he went out to the orgy. His gaze found his first choice right away. Bruce Reeves was currently on his knees, driving his cock into some woman's hungry mouth. Her saliva coated his condom-wrapped rod, easing its way into her throat. Bruce's unclothed body was hard and tight, his suntanned skin glimmering with a light coat of sweat. But on his face was an expression of pure boredom.

Zane had the perfect cure.

He walked around the back of his chosen partner and hooked his fingers, dragging his fingernails down Bruce's back.

Instantly, the muscles under Bruce's skin tensed, pulling into defined bulges. Goose bumps coated Bruce's back and shoulders. His thrusts shortened, becoming faster, more jerky. Finding some lube next to Bruce's knees, Zane coated his fingers, parted Bruce's ass cheeks, and tested his anus. The ring of muscles relaxed, and Zane's fingers slid deep inside.

Bruce groaned.

Zane bent over at the waist, whispering into Bruce's ear, "I'll make you feel better than you've ever felt. But only if you do as I ask."

"Yes, please," was Bruce's response.

"Your cock is mine."

Bruce yanked it out of the woman's mouth. Hard and thick, the sheath coated with a glistening blend of the woman's saliva and some flavored oil, his cock twitched.

"Take off that condom and follow me."

"Yes, master." Bruce disposed of the condom in a trash can positioned next to the door and followed Zane upstairs, to his suite.

Zane closed them inside, then turned his attention to his partner. The taut skin stretched over Bruce's well-muscled body glittered in the flickering candlelight, the tiny droplets of sweat sparkling, making him look almost otherworldly. But the thick hardness of his shaft and the hunger in his eyes made him look 100 percent human. Zane slid his hand behind Bruce's head, gathering a fistful of Bruce's hair and pulling, extending Bruce's neck. The pulse beating at his throat was a temptation Zane found nearly impossible to resist.

Growing warm as his hunger for the blood pulsing through Bruce's body spiked, Zane dragged his tongue down the column of Bruce's neck, relishing the taste of salt and man and need. His nostrils filled with the scent of sex, of cum, the smell heightening his hunger. Zane reached around Bruce's body with his other hand, grabbing a handful of hard ass, and pulled

Bruce flush against him. Their erect cocks, his covered by his clothes, Bruce's not, ground against each other. His fangs lengthened, the pain only adding to his building arousal.

The pulse under that thin layer of skin pounded in his ears. His mouth flooded with saliva, and his mind and body focused on his one need. To feed.

Not yet.

Zane released Bruce's hair, cupping his cheek instead, and plunged his tongue into Bruce's mouth. He drank in Bruce's flavor, savored the hint of pussy he caught on Bruce's lips, the slight tang of cum on his tongue. The fingertips of his other hand slipped into the crevice between Bruce's ass cheeks, their progression aided by a slick combination of perspiration and lube.

Zane's tongue stabbed into Bruce's mouth, and his fingertips glided down, working their way to Bruce's anus. Bruce's skin warmed under his touch, his breath escaping his nose and mouth in short bursts. He trembled, and a groan of hard male need filled their joined mouths. Zane drank it in, pulled it deep inside, letting it stir his own need.

Zane broke the kiss and shoved Bruce back. "On your knees. There." He pointed at a spot on the floor, at the center of the room where the bearskin rug lay in front of the empty fireplace.

Bruce moved like a panther, his movements sure, graceful. He lowered himself to the floor at the precise spot Zane had pointed to. A slight tremble worked through his body as he waited.

Zane went to the cupboard. Inside, he found some lube and a handful of condoms. He carried them to his waiting submissive. The lube was all he needed. His body did not sustain disease of any kind, neither viral nor bacterial, and thus there was no concern about STDs. But to protect his identity, he kept up appearances, using condoms during most of his sexual encounters. But not with Bruce. Bruce knew what he was.

Standing before Bruce, Zane made an adjustment. His balls were snug and high, his cock straining against his pants. Thanks to that little exchange with Amanda Thompson, he had no patience. He didn't want to play. He wanted to fuck. Fuck hard and fast and come. And then he needed to feed. But he was determined not to take any shortcuts, cheating his partner out of the pleasure he deserved.

Setting aside his own needs, Zane walked around to his submissive's back. He dragged his fingernails down Bruce's back, creating a series of red welts that traveled the length of his torso, ending just above his ass cheeks. He repeated the motion again and again, until there were only narrow patches of tanned skin between the deep burgundy stripes. With each set added, Bruce's cock jumped. His balls tightened. Precum dripped from the ruddy head.

"Stand," Zane commanded. "Now turn to me." Zane took the submissive's cock in his fist. With his other hand, Zane fondled his balls. "I'm going to suck you until you're begging to come." He gave Bruce's cock a hard squeeze and licked his lips as a droplet of precum seeped from the slitted opening. "I'm going to lick away every drop of cream you give me. And then I'm going to fuck you harder than you've ever been fucked before."

The submissive's eyes rolled in his head. "Yes, please," he whispered.

Zane pulled on his submissive's cock, using it like a lead as he walked to a chair and settled into it. Then he put his hands on either side of his partner's hips and pulled them toward him, taking his cock into his mouth, relaxing his throat so it could slide deep. He set the speed and depth of his submissive's thrusts, forcing him to fuck his mouth hard, deep, fast. And when he trusted Bruce to keep that pace, he let one of his hands slide around to his ass to find his anus.

When Zane's lubed finger slid inside the tight hole, Bruce's cock jerked inside his mouth. Zane added a second finger, stretching Bruce's anus, preparing it for him. Bruce's breathing grew shallow and quick, his movements jerky. Zane added a third finger, and Bruce let his upper body fall forward, catching himself on outstretched arms, his hands braced on the back of the chair.

"More," Bruce whispered breathlessly. "Oh, damn. More."

Zane crammed his fingers inside Bruce's hungry hole and swallowed Bruce's ample precum, his every sense alert to his partner's body. He could feel the heat radiating off Bruce's skin. The scent of pleasure-pain filled his nostrils, so sweet, so intoxicating. His ears filled with the music of his partner's gasps and groans and the slurping smack of his lips and tongue. Just as Bruce was about to come, Zane shoved at his chest, forcing him back.

"No. On your knees."

Bruce trembled as he dropped to his knees. Zane handed him some pillows, positioning him so his ass was up high, at just the right angle to take him to the hilt. He spread some more lube around the ring of muscle, added a little inside, and entered him in one long, slow thrust. They both shuddered at the pleasure, and their voices carried around the room as they sighed with relief.

"Yes, more, please," Bruce murmured, angling his body into a better position.

Zane passed him the lube as he slammed in and out of his ass. "Take your cock in your hand. Stroke it." He was close. Damn close. So close, he didn't give a damn about anything else.

"Yes, thank you."

"Come for me. Come, dammit." Zane's body was on fire.

His blood was burning. His cock was so hard, he gritted his teeth against the pleasure and the pain. His balls were about to explode. And a searing hunger tore through his whole being. "Come now!"

Beneath him, Bruce shook. He shuddered and quaked and moaned. Then there was a fraction of a second of silence and a long exhalation. "Yessssss."

A picture of Amanda Thompson flashed through Zane's mind, and his balls contracted. His cum blazed up his shaft, exploding from his body in white-hot bursts. Dizzy from the intensity, he drove into Bruce's ass, filling it with his seed. He lowered his body, until his chest was resting against Bruce's back. He licked a path around the side of Bruce's neck, opened his mouth, and bit.

Bruce's scream pierced his ears as the first mouthful of blood flowed over his tongue.

3

This was getting old.

Mandy had spent the last few weeks pretending to be a new submissive at a local bondage club, while watching mostly naked men and women of all ages, shapes, and sizes be chained up, tied down, spanked, paddled, flogged, and caned. At first, it was pretty damn sexy to watch. But gradually it lost its appeal. She just could not understand why they did it. What purpose did it serve? How could they mistake pain for pleasure?

She needed to wrap up this case and move on. She'd put in hours upon hours and had nothing to show for it. She was beginning to think her client was never going to get the proof she needed to win her case. And she was going to lose her reputation as the bulldog of Detroit.

Mandy yanked at the creeping hem of her miniskirt and shimmied through the thick crowd gathered at the far end of the public dungeon. This place wasn't the best for her purposes. There was a no-penetration rule in place, and that rule was strictly enforced. There were security guards ensuring that nobody stepped out of line and that all play was safe and consensual. Her hope was that she'd score an invitation to a private party somewhere else, a gathering like Zane's.

Zane.

She'd thought about him a time or two since that night. He'd popped up in a dream every so often. In those dreams, he did things to her that she never would have guessed she'd like. She'd wakened in the middle of an orgasm more than once.

No man had ever done *that* to her before.

But, and this was a *big* but, he was more than she could handle—outside of a fantasy. She reminded herself of that fact every time one of those dreams had her second-guessing herself.

If only he wasn't so...darkly dominant. Intimidating. Fiercely gorgeous.

A pleasant buzz of energy zapped through her body as she pictured his face in her mind. What a face. What a body.

No, she wouldn't wish him to change, not at all. It was that dark dominance, that sense of danger, that made him so damn sexy. He was the ultimate bad boy.

Someone tapped her shoulder.

Thinking it was Sarah, who'd scampered off to talk to a fellow dom, she spun around.

It wasn't Sarah.

"Hello," Zane said.

"Hi." Mandy's mouth went instantly dry. He was here. Zane. God, it was him. And he was looking just as good, if not better, than he had in her dreams.

He leaned over and murmured in her ear, "I've been watching you." She wasn't sure how she felt about that. "And I know what you're doing," he added.

"Do you?" She wanted to get away from this man. No, she didn't. She wanted to lean in closer, draw in his scent, and feel his heat burn over her body.

He slid an arm around her waist. "Come with me." Not

waiting for her to decide whether or not she wanted to, he started weaving through the crowd, pulling her along. She followed. Her mind screamed silent warnings. But her feet kept going. They left the dungeon, following a long, dark corridor that ran behind it. They stopped at the end.

He turned her so she was trapped between the wall and his bulk. She tried to decide whether she needed to scream for help or listen to what he wanted to tell her. She looked up into his dark eyes. They looked intense but not terrifying.

No, she wouldn't scream. Not yet.

"What do you want?" Her voice sounded small. She felt small, too. He was so tall, so big. And, more than that, he gave off a powerful presence, an energy that made her feel powerless and vulnerable.

"You like to watch. It makes you wet."

"Um." A gush of heated cream dampened her panties. He was right, in some respects. She would much rather watch than participate.

He leaned closer, closer still. His breath was sweet, his body warm. "Watch me."

A shudder swept through her body. Hell yes, she'd like to do that. But...but...He lowered his mouth to hers, brushed his lips across hers. The door behind her swung open, and she practically tumbled into the room. He grabbed her upper arms, steadying her as she regained her footing. Her gaze lifted to his. Dark eyes locked to soft blue. Mandy's heart did a funky *pitter-patter-thump* in her chest.

Zane motioned behind her. "Won't you have a seat?"

"I shouldn't."

Zane tipped his head slightly. "Shouldn't, but you want to. You will."

She'd say one thing for this guy—he didn't lack confidence. "No, I don't think I will." She twisted her body to break out of his loose hold. She saw then what was behind her.

A man, nude. A gorgeous man. Kneeling. Head tipped down. Hands resting on smooth-skinned thighs.

Was that... ? Could it be... ?

His face was hidden, but she was almost positive Zane's waiting submissive was none other than Andrew Clark.

Hot damn!

She smiled up at Zane. "On second thought, maybe I will accept your invitation. Thank you." She let Zane escort her to the comfortable-looking couch positioned along one wall. She sank into the soft cushions, swung one leg over the other, and plunged her hand into her jacket pocket.

Her camera was gone.

Damn. How? When?

Zane gave her an evil grin as he shut the door, trapping her inside the room with him. "Were you looking for something, Amanda?"

"Nope." *Bastard.* That was the second camera he'd taken from her.

"Good." He sauntered to the minibar in the room's corner. "Drink?"

"Water's fine."

He opened a bottle of Perrier and poured a glass, adding a lemon slice before taking it to her. Their fingertips grazed as he passed the glass to her. Her face went instantly hot as his sharp eyes studied her. "Enjoy."

She had the distinct impression he wasn't talking about the water. "Thanks." She sipped while he searched the contents of the cabinet sitting along one wall.

He picked a leather flogger from the cabinet and went to his submissive. "What makes you hot, Amanda?" Zane dragged the dangling leather straps over the submissive's shoulders. Mandy's gaze slid from Zane's face to the sub's body. His skin was coated in goose bumps, his muscles visibly tensing underneath. "Is it just the sight of flesh?"

Mandy's pussy clenched. That was a part of it. Particularly when that flesh was so freaking beautiful. "Maybe."

His gaze locked on hers. "I don't think that's it at all."

"Then why don't you tell me?"

Zane flicked his wrist. The tails struck the submissive's back. Mandy flinched. The submissive didn't. Her heart started hammering against her breastbone. The submissive remained perfectly still, stone-statue still. Mandy had no idea how he did that. Zane's eyes narrowed ever so slightly. "Or is it the pain that makes your pussy wet?"

She shook her head. "No, it's definitely not that."

Zane struck the submissive a second time. Mandy felt her face burning up.

"Are you sure?"

"Positive." Her fingers curled around the edge of the couch cushion.

"Your pussy's wet now."

That it was. But not because she was watching some poor man get whipped. She wasn't sadistic. Only sadists would get hot from that.

Mandy shrugged.

Zane flogged the submissive a third time, a fourth. He motioned for Mandy to come to him. She didn't move at first. But when he motioned a second time, she came closer. "Look. At his face," he told her.

Mandy had to squat down to see the man's face. Sure enough, it was Andrew Clark's face she was looking at.

Andrew's pupils were dilated so wide, she could barely see the ring of color circling them. Andrew's chest was rising and falling faster than normal, and his neck and chest were flushed a deep crimson.

Of its own will, her gaze dropped to his cock. It was thick and hard and its tip glistened with precum. A silver metal cock ring circled his penis and testicles, sitting flush to his pelvis. She couldn't seem to look away.

"Do you like his cock?" Zane asked.

She liked it okay, but she sure as heck wasn't going to touch it or anything. "Um, sure."

Zane stooped behind her. He was too close. Her nerves were zapping and buzzing. "Do you want to touch it?"

The object of their conversation twitched.

Her mouth dried up. "No, thanks."

"Do you want to suck it?"

Andrew's cock twitched again. The flared head visibly swelled a little more.

"No, thanks. I'd rather just watch." Mandy started to stand. Zane stopped her with a hand on her shoulder.

"Stay there." That was a command. An order.

"I think it would be better—"

"I said, *stay there.*" Zane bent over her shoulder. His breath puffed in her ear. Her body tingled. "Watch."

She thought about telling him to fuck off and leave. If the guy kneeling in front of her hadn't been Andrew Clark, she probably would have. She was so not liking this bossy asshole dom thing. But she decided it would be a good thing if she played along for now. If Zane invited her into another one of these private sessions with Clark, she'd have another shot at getting her pictures. The trick would be concealing the camera better.

She gnawed on her lower lip and settled into a comfortable position on the floor.

"Look at her," Zane said to his slave as he straightened up. "She's watching you. She's hungry for your cock."

Andrew's dilated eyes found hers. His lips parted slightly, his breathing visibly speeding up.

"That's what you want, isn't it?" Zane circled around the back of Andrew.

"Yes, master."

Zane bent over his slave, leaning close to him. Zane's eyes found Mandy's. His lips curled into a seductive smile. "You want her to suck your cock down her throat." A very different image flashed in Mandy's mind, of Zane standing nude before her, his cock thrusting into her mouth.

Andrew visibly trembled. "Oh, yeah."

Zane flogged him again. "You want to shoot your cum down her throat."

Andrew licked his lips. His eyelids were heavy, the deep red stain coloring his neck creeping up to his face. "Yeah."

Zane struck him again, and Andrew shuddered. "You want to grab her hair and fuck her mouth."

Was that what Zane wanted? Mandy's empty pussy clenched as a wave of warmth surged through her body.

"Oh, yeah." Andrew's teeth gritted. His skin shimmered as a coating of sweat slicked his shoulders, his back, his stomach. He was going to cum. Just from being flogged? "More, please. More."

Zane's wrist flicked again, again. And with each strike, Andrew's body became tenser, hotter, his cock harder. And, thanks to Zane's sharp-eyed gaze catching her reaction every time, Mandy became more breathless, dizzy, and tight all over. "Come now!" Zane demanded. "Catch it in your hand."

Andrew closed his fist over the head of his cock. His head fell back. His whole body quaked and then spasmed. He roared as his fist filled with his come.

On the verge of coming herself, Mandy watched. At Zane's dark look of satisfaction, a flood of slick warmth soaked her panties. That was nothing like she'd expected. It was strange and unsettling and bizarre. And freaking hotter than hell.

Zane pushed Andrew's head to the side and dragged his tongue up the length of his neck. "Very good. You have pleased me." He walked around them, stopping directly behind her. He leaned over her shoulder. Painfully aware of his heat, Mandy shivered. "Did you enjoy that, Amanda?"

"Y-yes," she said, her pussy warm, her panties sodden, her senses überalert. She inhaled deeply, smelling Zane and Andrew. Man and cum and sex. God, it wouldn't take more than a stroke or two to send her over the edge.

Where was her rabbit when she needed it?

"Very good. I'm not finished with you." Zane helped her to her feet, and she staggered back to the couch. Meanwhile, Zane and Andrew sat and talked quietly. She drained her glass and stood, prepared to leave them alone. Zane gave her a don't-go look and held up an index finger.

Andrew nodded, said one last thing, then gathered his clothes and left.

Now she was alone with Zane. All alone. And he'd said he wasn't done with her.

What did he have in mind?

He sauntered over to her with a loose-hipped swagger. He didn't sit. "Who's your client?"

Okay, so that wasn't what she'd expected. She threw one leg over the other and crossed her arms. The position only added to the ache between her legs. "I'm sorry, I can't tell you that."

"I'll find out."

Mandy shrugged.

Bending at the waist so his eyes were level with hers, he pinched a lock of her hair between his finger and thumb. "I could get you banned from every club in the state."

She wondered if he was bluffing. "For what?"

"None of them look too kindly on people bringing cameras into their establishments. All I'd have to do is show them this." He pulled her camera from his pocket.

She believed him. "You got me. I did sneak a camera in here. And I brought one into your private party. And you know I'm working as a private investigator. Still, you invited me in here. Why?"

"So I could get this from you before you used it." He toyed with the camera, a long, tapered finger tracing its length. She could almost imagine him touching her like that, his finger tracing down the hollow of her stomach.

Her brain was turning to mush. She struggled to think, to respond, to say something. "That's all? You tricked me into coming in here with you just so you could pick my pocket?" Then a moment of clarity came to her. "Wait, you had the camera before I'd even come into this room. I know you did."

His fingers curled into her hair. He bent down, until his nose was in the crook of her neck, and inhaled. So much for clarity. So much for her brain. "Maybe you're right." His teeth rasped her neck. "Maybe I wanted to punish you."

4

This woman was tormenting him. In a bad way. In a good way. Good and bad. And damn if she didn't deserve to be punished for what she'd done, both intentionally and unintentionally. His body was on fire. He needed to feed, but Bruce wasn't there and he was in no condition to go find him. Why? Because his cock's throbbing was far more agonizing at the moment than the hunger burning in his belly. He wanted to fuck Amanda. No, he *needed* to fuck her.

She was wet.

She was ready.

But he couldn't take her now.

He fought to rein in his baser urges as he nipped her neck, drawing the scent of her need deep into his lungs. He could taste her arousal in the air, could imagine her wet pussy folds glistening as he parted them to slide his tongue inside her.

His cock, already so hard it hurt, twitched. How he longed to tear off his trousers and shove his cock into her lush mouth, to lick her pussy until she begged him to take her.

Soon.

He nibbled on her ear and smiled as a coat of goose bumps puckered over her shoulder. He loved to watch her body react to him, to his look, his touch. He could only imagine how she'd react to his kiss. Her breasts were rising and falling swiftly, the points of her nipples poking at the smooth material of her top. He imagined pulling one of them into his mouth and drawing hard on them.

"W-what are you going to do?" she asked, her soft voice breathy.

"What do you think I should do?" His fingers still wound in her hair, he moved down her body until one of those little visible peaks was directly in front of his mouth. He looked up into her dilated eyes. "Should I torment you until you beg me to stop?"

Her lips parted. Her eyes widened. But she didn't speak.

He took that as a yes and closed his mouth over her covered nipple, capturing it between his teeth.

"Oh, God." Beneath him, she arched her back like a cat, pushing her breast against his face.

He flicked his tongue over the hard tip, up and down, up and down. Releasing one hand from her silken hair, he found the other nipple and pinched it between his finger and thumb.

She slammed her hands on the swell of his shoulders, curling her fingers and digging her nails into his flesh. The pleasure-pain only amplified his need.

"I'm going to punish you until you can't take any more." Taking his cue from her reaction, he pulled her shirt up, exposing her tits to his hungry eyes. Damn, those were two of the most perfect tits he'd ever seen. His mouth filled with saliva. His blood boiled in his veins.

"Ohmygod," she muttered, her eyelids fluttering closed. "This is crazy."

"Is it?" He couldn't deny himself for another second. He lowered his head and flicked his tongue over one pink nipple, taking his first taste. Yet another wave of excruciating carnal need blazed through his body, the intensity clouding his mind. He pulled her nipple into his mouth, suckling deeply, drawing the flavor of her skin into his throat. But that only made the agony more unbearable.

Just who was punishing who?

"Ohhhh…nooooo." She locked her arms, forcing him back. Her nipple slipped from his mouth with an audible pop. Their eyes met. Hers were full of desperation and lust and confusion. "I can't."

"Can't what?" He licked his lips, savoring her flavor still clinging to them.

"Can't let you do this." She pulled her shirt down. But those hard little points poked at the clingy black material. "I'm not… your type."

"How do you know?"

"Because I don't…" She hesitated. She licked her lips. He liked the way she did that, could see that pink tongue of hers swirling around the head of his cock. "You know I'm not here to learn about D/s. I'm not a submissive. I'm pretending."

She wasn't pretending. Not earlier. Not now. "Are you sure about that?"

She lifted a visibly shaking hand, pointing at the flogger he'd used on Clark. "I'm sure that if you hit me with that whip, I wouldn't orgasm."

He felt himself smiling at the thought of flogging her. "Maybe not yet. But you could learn."

A deep red stain swept up her neck. She fiddled with her hair, using clumsy hands to gather the long waves away from her pretty face. "No, no. I couldn't."

He didn't want to talk anymore. "Close your eyes."

"Why?"

"Because I said to."

"But I told you—"

He cut her off by crushing her mouth under his. She wriggled beneath him for one, two, three seconds, her mouth tight. But by the fourth second, she stopped struggling. Her lips parted, and he slipped his tongue inside her, tasting her, exploring her sweet depth.

He could kiss her forever.

She sighed into their joined mouths, wrapped her arms around his neck, pulling him to her. His body sank until it rested on top of her soft curves. Her heat warmed him. Her breath soothed him. Her sweet flavor devastated him. All he could think about was taking her, keeping her, protecting her.

Amanda's tongue found his. They stroked, they explored, they battled, and, as the kiss deepened, they conquered. One of Amanda's hands skimmed down his arm, following it to the wrist before slipping between their bodies and brushing over the throbbing bulge at the front of his pelvis. She gasped.

"You see," he whispered against her lips. "You are my type." He rocked his hips forward, pressing his engorged rod against her palm. The light rasp of the material over his erection made him shudder.

"But—"

He silenced her again, this time by grazing his teeth over her collarbone. "Haven't you ever considered the possibility that punishment could be pleasurable?"

"*Pleasant* punishment? What would be the point of that?"

"I'll show you." He levered back, his hips still thrust forward, shoved his hands under her shirt, and slid them up to cover her breasts. "I'll show you how pleasant torment can be." His palms rasped the turgid peaks. "I'll take you to the edge of control." He pinched them, just hard enough to make her tense up all over. Then, when she relaxed slightly, he rolled them between his finger and thumb until she was tight and trembling.

"I . . . I don't know."

"Don't let fear hold you back." He pushed her top up under

her chin. "Your tits are beautiful. If they were mine, if you were mine, they'd always be uncovered." He weighed her breasts, one in each hand. "Perfect." He took one nipple into his mouth, alternatively suckling and flicking his tongue back and forth over it. Then he moved to the other one, doing the same thing. As he inhaled, the scent of her cream teased his nostrils. The sound of her little gasps and moans of pleasure tormented his ears. The taste of her skin tortured his taste buds. It was going to take every bit of the discipline he'd honed over the years to hold back. But he'd do it. Somehow.

"Now, close your eyes," he commanded, knowing she was ready.

This is crazy.
What am I doing?
Oh, God, don't stop.
Currently sprawled on the couch, Mandy didn't know what she was thinking. Or what she wanted. Or what she didn't want. Or what she feared.

All she knew was what she felt.

Need.

Hunger.

Lust.

Desire.

Desperation.

Lust.

Confusion.

Lust.

No man had ever made her so hot, so horny, so freaking confused in her life. What his touches did to her. What his kisses did to her.

Sweet Jesus, he knew exactly how to use his mouth, his hands, and his words to make a girl go crazy.

Was he right? Did she secretly long to be dominated? Would

she like being punished? The mere thought of closing her eyes and waiting for the sting of the whip made her feel a little dizzy.

She couldn't.

"I said, close your eyes."

Her pussy clenched, yet another gush of cream soaking her panties.

Or could she?

She closed her eyes, as he had asked. Correction, as he'd commanded. He was a dom, and he'd used a strong, domineering tone. And that tone had made her hot. She liked it. A lot. She also enjoyed several other things about this man, like the way he moved, with a fluid, feline grace. And the way he looked at her, his eyes dark, the flicker of something thrilling and dangerous shimmering deep within their depths. She'd never been a sucker for the bad-boy type, but here she was now, trembling, on the verge of orgasm, letting a very bad boy fondle her breasts.

"Take off your shirt."

Considering the flimsy knit material was shoved up under her chin, it wasn't such a big deal taking it off. But if he asked her to take off her skirt or her panties, she'd have to refuse.

He pinched both nipples, and she saw stars behind her closed eyelids. He rolled them between his fingers and thumbs, and she bit her bottom lip, trembling at the pleasure. To her dismay, he released one of her nipples, but he didn't leave it neglected for long. With his tongue, he took slow, languid licks, the movement reminding her of a cat. The hand that had formerly been on her right breast was slowly sliding down her stomach. Lower, lower it inched. And with each small movement it made, the tension in her body wound tighter.

He was heading for her pussy. She just knew it.

Anticipation of his touch between her legs had her gasping, her back arching away from the couch, her hips thrusting up into the air.

"Has anyone ever taken you to the edge, Amanda?" He pressed against her pelvis, forcing it back down.

"No."

"Good. I'm glad I'll be your first." The satisfaction in his voice made her body burn that much hotter. His hand jumped from her lower abdomen to her thigh, skipping the parts of her anatomy that needed his touch most.

She didn't want to think about that right now. All she wanted was to feel, to enjoy and experience. But a little voice was nagging her, whispering words she didn't want to hear.

You don't know this man. He could hurt you.

You're acting like a slut.

What if he does something you don't like?

Will he stop if you tell him to?

You're not this kind of girl.

He nipped that spot on her neck again, the one that made her pussy spasm and made that voice shut up. His hand crept higher, sliding to the inside of her thigh, and her empty pussy started clenching and unclenching, a throbbing heat pulsing through her body. It stopped moving.

Damn.

"Touch me," she mumbled, arching her neck to provide him better access to the magic spot.

"I am." He squeezed her boob to illustrate. But his other hand, the one she was hoping would move higher, was still stuck in the same place, inches away from her throbbing center.

"No, you know what I mean."

"Tell me." He brushed his lips over hers, the soft caress stealing her breath. "Tell me what you want." He kissed one eyelid, then the other. It was a sweet gesture, unexpected.

"Between my legs."

"What's between your legs?"

He was going to make her say the words, manipulative bastard.

"Touch my pussy. Please."

"Is it wet?" He scattered little kisses over her upper chest.

"Yes. Very."

"Hot?"

"Burning."

A fingertip grazed the thin fabric covering her labia. The touch nearly sent her over the edge. Her back coiled into knots. Her lungs deflated. It was one small touch. That was all. But it was more devastating than any she'd ever experienced. "Mmm-mmm." He lifted his finger to his mouth. "Open your eyes." When she opened them, he flicked his tongue over the tip of his finger, and she sucked in a gasp. She could swear she felt his tongue dancing over her clit. "Sweeter than honey."

She pressed her thighs together and rocked her hips back and forth, trying desperately to rub away the ache in her pussy. It was getting worse by the second. She wanted something big and hard inside her, needed it. Badly.

He kissed her, and she tasted herself on his lips, his tongue. She slid her tongue into his mouth, pulling in his flavor. She hooked her fingers, digging her nails into the rock-hard muscles of his shoulders, and opened her thighs wider. "Touch me again," she said into his mouth. "Please."

His finger slipped under the satin crotch of her panties, and in the next heartbeat, the sound of the fabric tearing echoed through the room. Her thighs stretched wider. She lifted her hips off the couch again.

Would he fucking touch her? Again? Harder this time? Please?

"Are you suffering yet, Amanda?" he asked as he slowly kissed his way down her body.

Oh, yes, he was going to eat her pussy.

She curled her fingers into his hair, filling each fist, and pushed him lower. "Hell yes."

"I'm going to make you suffer more."

"Please, no."

"Oh, yes." Now kneeling at her feet, he pressed her knees apart, splaying her thighs as wide as they would go. He blew a stream of air over her swollen tissues, chilling them. The unexpected sensation sent a shiver quaking up her spine. She tried to pull his face into her, but he clamped his hands around her wrists, jerking them out to the sides. "Who is in control, Amanda? You? Or me?"

She knew what he expected, and she was more than happy to answer as he wanted, knowing she would be rewarded. "You are."

"Put your hands up over your head and don't move them."

"Okay." She rested her clenched hands on the top of the couch cushion and braced herself for bliss.

Bliss came in the form of a light flicker over her clit.

She shook from head to toe. "Ohmygod, yes."

"You've been waiting for that, haven't you?"

"Yes."

He did it again, and once more, she trembled all over. Her inner walls clamped tight, and a gush of cream coated her labia, preparing them for the penetration she hoped would come soon.

She had never been so wet, so ready for sex.

The third time, he added a single fingertip, slipping into her tight canal as his tongue danced over her clit, and she almost came. Something inside her snapped. She didn't give a damn about anything now but what was going on between her legs. She sucked in a deep breath, stretched her thighs even wider apart, and said, "Please, fuck me."

"Mmmm," he said over her clit. The vibration buzzed through her entire body, from the soles of her feet to the roots of her hair. "Mmmmm..."

"I'm going to die." She tried to thrust her hips up again, but he held her down, applying pressure to the tops of her thighs.

Then he pressed not one but two fingers into her hungry pussy and she screamed. Just as the first wave of her orgasm was about to wash over her, he jerked them out.

"Noooo." Her eyelids snapped open.

Zane was sitting back with the world's most wicked smile on his face. "See now?"

Breathless and dizzy, she shook her head and tried to slap her knees back together. He stopped her. "See what?" she asked, her teeth clenched.

"Was that punishment not pleasant? Did I lie?"

She snapped her jaw shut and jerked her hands down to cover her burning pussy. "Is this just a game to you?"

He wedged his body between her knees and caught her wrists in his fists, slamming them back up against the top of the couch. He leaned in until his mouth was almost touching hers. Dammit, did he know how to tease a girl. "No, this isn't a game, Amanda. None of it." He released her wrists and straightened up, and suddenly she felt small and vulnerable. His gaze flicked over her body. He licked his lips.

She pulled her knees closed, clamping them against his legs to hide her swollen tissues. Her arms slid down her body, crossing over her breasts.

He shook his head. "Those tits should never be hidden." He moved away from her. "A drink?"

"No thanks." She scrambled for her shirt, which was hanging over the arm of the couch, yanking it over her head and pulling it over her still-tingling nipples. While he poured himself a glass of Perrier, she pushed to her feet, her focus on the door.

"Don't leave yet."

"I need to go."

Swiveling, he gave her a look she couldn't quite read. He extended a hand, offering her a full glass of water. "You should stay for a few minutes. We need to talk."

"No. Can't." Feeling her face flushing, she tottered to the door, pulled it open, and stumbled out into the hallway. He didn't follow her. Thank God. She took a few moments to get herself together. Once she was fairly certain she wouldn't trip or stumble from being so wobbly kneed, she headed down the hallway, through the main dungeon, and out into the still, cool evening. She pulled in some much-needed fresh air as she made her way to her car.

That was...

There were no words to describe tonight.

As she flung herself into her car, she realized that they hadn't talked about him turning her into the security staff at all the local dungeons. Would he?

Did she care?

Maybe it was time for a career change.

5

"She was wearing a red spandex bodysuit, a clown wig, and some Elton John sunglasses when she disappeared," the petite woman sitting in Mandy's office said matter-of-factly.

Mandy scribbled down the description. "Was it Halloween?"

"No." Blushing, the woman added, "Grandma Belton became a little eccentric after her stroke in '02. She said she's been given another chance at life and wants to live it to the fullest. I say she's enjoying a second childhood and to hell with what people think. Whatever the case, her eccentricities make for some fun at family gatherings."

"I'm sure they do."

Dabbing her teary eyes with a tissue, the client sniffled. "She shot the turkey last Thanksgiving."

"At least it was fresh. I've heard fresh turkey is much better than frozen."

"No, it was already dead. It was already cooked."

"Oh." Mandy scribbled down *Possibly armed and dangerous.*

"The giblets landed in Dad's hair."

"Oh, dear."

"Dad's hair was blown clear across the room by the blast."

A very bizarre image of flying giblets and toupees flashed through Mandy's mind. Changing the subject, she asked, "Did your grandmother have any medical conditions that might contribute to her disappearance? Schizophrenia? Dementia? Alzheimer's?"

"No. Her mind was as sharp as a tack."

"Did your grandmother have any friends nearby?"

"Yes."

That was encouraging. "Do you have their names?"

"I have the names and phone numbers of over a thousand people. That doesn't include her friends at Thursday night Bingo, or her Facebook and Myspace friends. All total, Grandma had over ten thousand friends."

Yep, it was time for a career change. Mandy couldn't even score a simple missing-person's case. Why couldn't this one be a case of a dementia patient who'd wandered over to a neighbor's house, mistaking it for her childhood home?

"We've reported her missing to the police, but they aren't doing much at all. I'm really worried about her. You will take the case, won't you?"

"Yes, I will." Mandy asked a few more questions about the missing elderly woman with the unique fashion sense, then thanked her granddaughter, accepted the list of "friends" and a photograph of Grandma Belton, and showed her visibly worried granddaughter to the door. Alone once more, Mandy sank into her chair and closed her eyes.

Sarah came bouncing into her office a few minutes later. "So, what's the new case? Another cheating husband?"

"No, missing person."

"Cool! Give me the deets." Sarah flung herself into the chair that the client had just vacated. She snatched the photograph off Mandy's desk. "What's with the hair? And the clothes. Is this a woman? She looks kinda like Johnny Depp's Mad Hatter."

"Yes, it's a woman. Her name is Ruby Belton. And she's a tad on the eccentric side."

"*Tad?* More like a ton." Sarah returned the photograph to Mandy's desk, then flung one leg over the other. "Of course, you're going to let me help, right?" Sarah had been hired to answer phones, handle paperwork, deal with all those pesky little details Mandy tended to either neglect or fuck up—like plane reservations. But Sarah much preferred undercover work to filing. Not that Mandy could blame her. She did, too.

"Of course you can help. But this case isn't going to be anywhere near as much fun as the Clark case."

"Why's that?"

Mandy slid the list of names and phone numbers across the desk. "The missing person is eighty-three. And she isn't into domination and submission."

"Most aren't." Forehead crinkled, Sarah skimmed the list. "What's with the list?"

"Those are her closest friends."

Sarah gave her a raised-brow look.

"You get to call them all today."

Sarah's expression soured. "All of them?"

"As many as you can."

Sarah stood. "What're you going to do?"

"I'm going to e-mail the other nine thousand." Powering up her laptop, Mandy grumbled, "What had ever made me think being a PI would be glamorous?"

"It was that stupid movie, *Charlie's Angels.* You wanted to be Drew Barrymore."

"Stupid is right." Mandy glanced at the clock. She had four hours to kill before she headed back to Twilight, the bondage club, to try to catch Clark. Knowing most spam filters would tag an e-mail going to nine thousand people at once, Mandy opted for writing one master e-mail and then sending it to each person individually.

Oh, the joy.

Sitting in the limo, the windows heavily tinted to protect him from the weak sunlight, Zane double-checked the address. The building's front entrance faced south. Not the best situation for his kind. But fortunately, the day was overcast, heavy gray clouds blocking much of the sun's dangerous radiation. With a hat, a pair of sunglasses, an umbrella, and a trench coat, he'd make it through the front door without a problem.

He pulled the hat on, flipped the collar of his trench up to cover his neck, shoved the glasses on, and readied the umbrella. "I'll call you when I'm finished," he said to the driver.

"Very well, sir."

He opened the umbrella, ducked from the vehicle, and, trying not to look too conspicuous, strolled to the door. Inside the tiny building—a nineteenth-century storefront that had been converted into an office—he closed the umbrella and removed the glasses, even though he was fully capable of seeing with them on. A familiar face greeted him at the front desk.

"Zane?" Sarah said, plunking the phone on its cradle. "How can I help you?"

"I'm here to see Amanda Thompson."

"Of course you are."

"I'd like to discuss a professional matter with her."

"Sure." Sarah picked up the phone, then, without dialing, put up an index finger and dashed through the door behind her. She returned a few minutes later, smiling. "Mandy will see you now."

"Thank you." His footsteps echoed in the small space as he headed toward the back of the reception area. He found Amanda's office to be small but professional, decorated tastefully in mostly neutral tones, the furnishings aged, weathered, but beautiful.

Amanda stood the moment he entered. "Zane, how can I help you?" Her face flushed a pretty shade of pink as she motioned to the chair in front of her desk, then hurried around him to shut the door.

Zane watched her flit back to her desk as he settled into the chair. Memories of the time they'd spent together at the club and in his suite played through his mind. His dick got hard. His balls tightened. "I would like to hire you."

She eased into her chair, eyebrows scrunched together. "I'm sorry, but I'm a little overbooked at the moment."

Mandy tried to pretend she wasn't completely freaked out about Zane's surprise visit. She couldn't work for him. Not after...after what had happened at Twilight this past weekend. Not a chance. But she wasn't going to tell him that. Better if he thought she was too busy to take on a new case than to admit how that experience had shaken her. How it had challenged the way she saw herself, her sexuality.

"Overbooked?" Zane leaned forward, pulled a wallet out of his pocket, withdrew a stack of cash, and set it on her desk. "Are you sure?" He gave her that look, the same one that he'd given her last weekend.

The effect was exactly the same.

Her face became blistering hot. Her blood pulsed through her body in audible bursts. Her panties became soaked.

Yanking her gaze from his, she glanced down at the money. That was a hundred-dollar bill on top. And who knew how many underneath it. The stack was tall. Potentially, she could be looking at thousands of dollars.

"A retainer," he explained.

Thousands of dollars could sure come in handy. Her gaze leaped to the tray of unopened bills she'd been trying to pretend didn't exist. The rent was due in a week. The electric and gas, too. Thanks to her grandmother's recent medical bills, she barely had enough in her bank account to cover her own obligations, plus Sarah's salary. She wasn't expecting much action on the Clark case anytime soon. He was much more careful than she'd anticipated, and every time she'd found him, Zane was there, and had taken her camera.

And the new case...well, she hadn't taken much of a retainer, only fifty dollars. She didn't have the stomach to ask for more. It was the kind of case she took because it was the right thing to do, not because she expected it to pay much.

"Why do you feel you need my services?" she asked, shifting in her seat. Could he tell how uncomfortable she was? She checked his face. If he could, he was doing a good job pretending he didn't.

"I'd like you to join my security team."

"But I'm not a security specialist."

"But you are. You've managed to dodge not one but two security systems...or have there been more?"

Her face got hotter. She didn't answer.

"That's what I thought." Zane shifted forward, moving closer to the desk. "I need you to stop people like you from getting into my parties."

"But...it's a bit of a conflict of interest for me."

"Why's that?"

"There are times when I need access to certain people and places, like your parties...." And she knew for a fact he'd never let her step foot in his house again if she didn't take the job. But if she did, she'd be faced with one hell of a dilemma. How could she get Clark on infidelity without breaching her contract with Zane?

No matter how she looked at it, this was a lose-lose proposition for her and a win-win one for him.

Zane raised one well-manicured eyebrow. She knew what he was thinking.

"I won't have access to your parties if I don't take the job, will I?"

He shook his head. "If your subject is doing something illegal, I might be convinced to assist you. However, I cannot and will not get involved in any investigation that would invade my guests' privacy. Again, if there hasn't been some sort of illegal activity involved. I am tolerant of many things, but kidnapping, murder, drug trafficking, prostitution, et cetera, aren't among them."

"Then you aren't going to be able to help me. In this state, infidelity isn't a crime."

Zane's smile was one hundred percent wicked. "No, it isn't."

This man was evil. Dangerous. And downright infuriating.

Zane stood. "Thank you for your time." He extended a hand. Mandy reluctantly accepted it. When his fingers curled around her hand, a wave of sensual heat whooshed through her body.

How could she possibly work for a man who made her feel so off-kilter? Who made her think of a million weird and wicked things she'd like to do to his body? Who gave her wet dreams every night?

"You'll let me know by tomorrow?" he asked, giving her hand a slow pump up and down.

"Um, sure." She uncurled her fingers, but he didn't let go.

"Very good. I'm having a party this weekend. I need to get my security team in place." He finally released her hand, but his gaze still held hers captive as he picked up the stack of money and set it in her palm. "Will you be returning to Twilight?"

Clasping the money, she thought about lying. But what

would be the purpose? She shoved the money into her pocket. "Yes. Tonight."

He nodded. "I'll see you there."

She didn't take a full breath until he was out of the building. No sooner did she hear the dull thump of the lobby door swinging closed than Sarah came rushing in, flinging herself into the chair.

"What did Zane want? You've got to tell me!"

Fingering her burning face, Mandy pretended to be super-busy. "To hire me," she said, shooting for a carefree tone but failing miserably.

"*Hire* you?" Sarah's expression twisted with confusion.

"Yes, apparently he was impressed by the fact that I was able to sneak a camera into his party last weekend."

"Ah, so he wants you to come work for him to make sure nobody else can do the same thing. Kinda like the companies who hire hackers to plug their security leaks."

"Yes, exactly like that."

"So, are you gonna take the job?"

"I don't know."

"Why not?"

"Because..." Mandy didn't know how to finish that sentence. She hadn't told Sarah about what had happened between her and Zane at Twilight. She hadn't told anyone.

"The guy gives me the creeps, too," Sarah said, standing. "But I've seen his clothes. And I know what he drives. I'm guessing he'd pay a lot of money to keep hidden cameras out of his parties."

Mandy shoved a hand into her pocket. Her fingertips found the crisp bills tucked in the bottom. "I have no doubt about that."

"You should do it."

"But if I do, I won't be able to get Clark. Or anyone else at his parties."

Sarah shrugged. "How much is Clark's wife paying you?"

Not as much as Zane would. That was for sure. "I can see where you're going with this—"

"Did you just say last week that you'd love to have something steady? Something that would generate a more level stream of income?"

"Yes, but—"

"This is the perfect setup." Exuberantly, Sarah flung her arms around Mandy's neck, gave it a bouncy squeeze, and released her. "Just think, you can work his parties on the weekends and pick and choose the cases you want to work during the week."

What Sarah said made a lot of sense.

"No more worrying about when the next case will come in."

That part would be nice.

"Not to mention, you'd be sure to get me invited to every single party he has...right?"

"Ah, so that's why you're so happy."

Sarah beamed. "What can I say? I'm no saint. I'd pimp you, if it meant I'd get a lifetime membership to the Zane Club. Did you see the male guests at that last party?" Mandy nodded. "I mean, did you really *see* them? They were all fifteens, on a scale of one to ten."

"There were a lot of very good-looking men."

Sarah snorted. "You're funny, Mandy. 'Good-looking'? That's the understatement of the century. When's his next party?"

"He mentioned something about this weekend."

"Hot damn!" Sarah extended a hand while eyeballing the clock. "It's my lunch hour. Can I have my paycheck? I'm gonna do some shopping. Need to buy a few things—"

"Wait a minute. I didn't say I'd take the job yet."

Sarah donned her dom face. "If you don't take the job, I

swear, you'll regret it." She grinned. "But it won't be because of what I did."

Mandy pulled Sarah's check out of her drawer and handed it to her. And before she could say one way or another, Sarah bounded out of the room.

6

"**Y**ou'll never guess who's at Twisted Hearts!" Sarah whispered into the phone.

Sitting at her desk, fuming over the fact that Sarah's lunch hour had lasted for nearly two hours now, Mandy pressed her cell tighter to her ear and grumbled, "Who?"

"Andrew Clark!"

Mandy tucked her phone between her shoulder and ear and signed the rent check sitting on her desk. "Great. Is he fucking anyone?"

"No, of course he's not. This is a store, not a motel."

"Then what's the big deal?" she asked, pulling the check out of the book and folding the carbon copy up to reveal the next blank check.

"The big deal is the ginormous dildo he's buying."

Mandy scribbled the name of the electric company on the first line of the check and sighed. "Sarah, so what?"

"He's gotta use that thing sometime."

"Yeah. And it's not going to help our case. There's no judge who's going to award our client a judgment because he fucks himself with a hunk of rubber."

"I wouldn't say that." After a beat, Sarah added, "He's not shopping alone."

Mandy set the pen down. "Well, you could've said that sooner. Male or female?"

"Female. Young. Hot. And dressed like a stripper."

"Follow them."

"Will do." Giving a little giggle, Sarah signed off.

Mandy, not willing to take any chances that Sarah would lose Clark, grabbed her purse and keys, dashed outside, locked the door, and dove into her car. She got within a half mile of the sex-toy shop when her cell phone rang. She hit the receive button. "Sarah? Where are you?"

"I lost them."

Mandy bit back an expletive. "Where'd you see them last?"

"On Ford, heading east."

"There are at least a dozen motels on Ford. What were they driving?"

"A black car."

"License plate?"

"I . . . uh, didn't get it."

"Make? Model?"

"I dunno. I'm guessing domestic. Midsize . . . ?"

Head slap. "Did you get anything?"

"A name."

"Great, what's the name?"

"Brittany."

Another head slap. "Brittany? I'd be willing to bet there are hundreds of strippers named Brittany in this town alone."

"Sorry. I did the best I could. They were tearing out of the parking lot by the time I got to my car. I was lucky to have followed them as long as I did."

"Start hitting each hotel on the south side of the street. Do you have a picture of Clark with you?"

"No."

"Okay. Scratch that. You go back to the office. I'll hit the hotels, see if Clark checked in with his new friend."

Sarah sighed. "I really did try."

"I know." Mandy smacked the turn signal and maneuvered into a dumpy parking lot next to one of the town's seediest no-tell hotels. "Thanks, hon. I'll see you later."

"Bye." Sarah sounded disappointed as she signed off.

Mandy instantly felt like crap.

She swung her car into a parking spot, threw the shifter into park, and cut the engine. She dug a picture of Clark out of her purse as she hurried up to the front desk.

Inside the depressing cinder-block structure, the lobby was dim and dank. The dingy front desk was empty. A thick wall of Plexiglas reached from the counter up to the ceiling, a small indentation in the counter allowing the exchange of cash between the hotel customer and the clerk.

Mandy hit the little bell sitting on the edge of the counter. A moment later, a tired-looking man with deep purple circles under his eyes and no more than a wisp of white hair covering his gleaming scalp tottered out of a door, taking his place behind the counter.

"Yeah?" he said, looking over her shoulder.

She glanced behind herself, then at him. "Hi, I'm looking for someone." She slid the picture down the trench in the counter, the back of her hand scraping against the bottom of the thick Plexiglas.

He didn't pick up the photo. "Yeah? So?"

"Did this man check into this hotel?"

"Are you a cop?"

"No."

"Then I don't hafta tell you nothin'."

Cursing under her breath, Mandy dug into her wallet, extracted a five, and shoved that into the trench, too.

The guy gave her a what-the-hell-is-that look.

She added another five.

He raked the cash into his fist, picked up the picture, took a quick look. "Nope." He shoved it back under the safety glass. "Good luck." The money disappeared into his pocket.

"Thanks." Knowing she'd need more than luck, Mandy headed back out to her car. If she had to give every hotel clerk on this street ten dollars to answer one question, she'd burn through at least a hundred dollars.

Deciding she'd try a few more, she started her car. Maybe for once, Lady Luck would be smiling down at her.

So much for Lady Luck. The bitch.

Figuring all hope was lost, Mandy headed home to get dressed. As she wiggled her ass into yet another tight skirt, she wondered whether it was even worth going to Twilight tonight. If Clark had enjoyed his romp with the stripper this afternoon, would he be in the mood for another sexual escapade tonight? He might be worn out.

Then again, he might be a sex addict, looking for his next score.

She supposed anything was possible.

Yanking down the creeping skirt so her ass cheeks didn't hang out, she scampered to her closet for a pair of hooker heels. Then she tottered to the door, grabbed her purse and car keys, and headed out into the warm evening.

She was überconscious of the way she looked as she clacked down the walk to her car. If only her complex had attached garages! She spied Mrs. Wentworth in 2D staring out her front window. She figured she'd be reported as a hooker before her car had left the lot.

Sure enough, as she cranked the key, she caught sight of three other ladies from the Social Security set peering out their windows, too. It was official; her squeaky-clean reputation was in the toilet.

She turned on the stereo as she maneuvered the car out of the lot.

Screw them all. She was who and what she was, and what she did was none of their damn business.

She sang at the top of her lungs with the radio as she drove the short distance to Twilight. At traffic lights, she did some car seat dancing, too, to Lady Gaga. Upon arriving at the club, she parked the car and took a deep breath.

God, she was nervous. And she knew it wasn't because of Clark.

Zane knew she'd be here.

Zane probably expected her to have a camera hidden on her.

But that wasn't what was making her jittery. It was the thought of seeing him again. He wasn't expecting an answer to his proposal yet. But she had a feeling he was going to do what he could to convince her to say yes. She knew from experience he could be a *very* convincing man.

After a quick makeup check, she wobbled up to the building and checked in. Tonight she was carrying a cigarette-lighter camera. She passed through security with no problem. If Zane had warned them, they hadn't found the camera.

Inside, she circled around the perimeter of the main dungeon, giving her eyes time to adjust to the dim lighting. She recognized several faces but didn't see Zane or Clark. She decided to take a stroll down the hallway leading to the private suites.

There. The tall guy in black. Was that Clark, heading into the last room on the left? Mandy hurried after him, hoping she'd catch him before he was closed inside. She was within reach when someone snagged her arm, jerking her around.

"Where are you headed in such a hurry?" someone asked. The voice was male but not familiar.

She twisted to look behind her. Didn't recognize the face. But it was a very handsome one. His hair was dark brown, on the long side, wavy, sexy. His face was breathtakingly gorgeous. White teeth flashed brightly against his deeply tanned skin. He was big, almost as intimidating as Zane. He clamped a large hand around her upper arm. "Come with me."

"Am I in trouble for something?" she asked, stumbling as he pulled her off balance.

Someone else caught her other arm and pulled in the opposite direction.

"She's with me."

Mandy knew that voice. Zane.

The other guy stopped walking, thank goodness. She wouldn't be torn in two.

A highly charged stare-down followed.

"I said, she's with me, Sorenson," Zane repeated through gritted teeth.

Mandy was getting a little buzzed on the testosterone in the air. Either that or she was just übernervous her cover was about to be blown.

Sorenson released her. "Fine."

She didn't take a deep breath until he was out of sight.

Zane dragged her into the last room, the one she thought she'd seen Clark duck into, and shut the door. Sure enough, Clark was there, in the center of the room, kneeling, nude, and sporting a hard-on.

"Sorry for interrupting," Mandy said, her gaze hopping from Clark to a tense-looking Zane and back again.

Zane didn't speak right away.

"Who was that?"

"Rolf Sorenson. His brother runs Twilight. You need to stay away from him."

"Oh."

Zane extended a hand. "The camera."

"If I give it to you, will you return it to me before I leave?"

He lifted his brows. "Of course."

She squinted her eyes at him. "In *one piece* this time?"

His lips quirked into a lopsided grin. "Only if you promise I won't ever see it again."

"You have a deal." She extended a hand and shook on it. Then, when he gave her a meaningful look, she said, "We're still talking about cameras, aren't we?"

Still gripping her hand, he tipped his head. "Are we?"

"Yes. Cameras. Nothing else. Yet."

"Very well." He extended the hand that wasn't holding hers. She set the lighter camera in his palm.

He scrutinized it. "Very nice." In his pocket it went.

"Yes. And *expensive*," she grumbled.

"I'll keep my word if you'll keep yours." He patted his pants pocket, the motion drawing her eye down.

My, that was quite a bulge he had front and center. If he didn't shove socks down his pants, he was very, very well endowed. Her imagination went wild for a brief moment, picturing Zane nude. It was a glorious picture.

Don't go there. You'll never be able to work for the man if you do.

Too late.

She heard herself sigh. "I guess I'll be going now." There was no point sticking around to watch Clark scene with Zane. She had nothing to capture the proof. No camera. No video. And clearly Zane wasn't going to let her bring a camera into any future sessions with Clark or with anyone else, for that matter.

Why did I even bother tonight?

Zane leaned in. He was close. Very. Normally that kind of

crowding made her feel uncomfortable. But not with him. "My submissive had a special request tonight."

"Oh, really?" She fingered her cheeks, which were getting warm.

"He'd like you to stay again."

"I don't know...I mean, do you think it's appropriate, considering you just offered me a job?"

"Hmmmm." Zane nibbled on his lower lip. "You have a point. It probably wouldn't be appropriate. You might assume I would expect this kind of thing from you all the time."

"I might."

"Which I wouldn't, of course."

"Of course."

Zane narrowed his eyes. "I only mentioned it because I got the feeling you were interested in him."

Damn, this man was sharp. Should she tell him the truth? Or shouldn't she? *Don't do it. Don't tell him about the case.* "Okay, yes, I was—am—interested. As long as there isn't any penetration."

Something flashed in Zane's eyes. Mandy couldn't quite read it. "That's what I thought. No penetration. Understood." He placed his hand lightly on the small of her back. "Over here." He set her in position, sitting on some kind of bench, facing Clark, who was still staring down at the floor. She noticed his shoulders rising ever so slightly and the color in his neck deepening as she waited for Zane to tell them what to do.

"Since you've been so good, I've brought you something." Zane circled around the back of Clark, bending to speak into his ear. His gaze, however, was fixed on Mandy's face. She wasn't exactly clear to whom he was speaking. "You may look up."

Clark's eyes lifted. His gaze drifted over her form. His breathing visibly quickened, his wide chest rising and falling with each heavy breath. "Master." He licked his lips.

"Would you like to see her tits?"

Clark nodded.

Mandy shifted on the bench, pressing her thighs together. She was feeling awkward and unsure. And turned on. Clark was looking at her like she was a great big sundae. That was a little unsettling. Zane was looking at her like she was a cute little bunny and he was a hungry wolf. That was extremely unsettling, but not necessarily in a bad way. Instantly, she recalled the last time she'd been in one of these rooms with him.

Her nerves started tingling all over.

"You know what you must do, then."

"Yes, master." Clark bent over and flicked his tongue over his own dick. Then he opened his mouth and sucked about a third of it in.

Mandy had never thought such a thing was possible. The man was sucking his own cock.

She watched, mesmerized, as a hunched-over Clark sucked himself to near orgasm. He started trembling all over, his skin glistening with sweat. His skin tinted a deep red. He stopped, jerking his head up. His eyes snapped to her chest, which was still clothed.

"Very good." Zane smiled. "Did you enjoy that?" he asked Mandy.

"I ... yes. I've never seen anything like it."

"Then you'll give him his reward."

Mandy's gaze jumped back and forth from Clark's eager expression to Zane's dark hunger and back to Clark. He was like a puppy dog, waiting for his master to throw him a bone. She almost pitied him.

Feeling a little weird, she tugged her top up until the material was bunched above her breasts. Like last weekend, she was wearing no bra. Her nipples, she noticed, were hard. That wasn't the only part of her anatomy that was reacting to this bizarre scenario.

Standing behind Clark, Zane demanded, "Take it off. All the way."

She pulled it off, folded it, and set it on the floor beside the bench.

Clark's gaze locked onto her boobs.

Zane's meandered up and down her entire body. "What would you like him to do next?" Zane asked her.

"Well, gosh, I don't know. What could possibly top a man giving himself a blow job? That was impressive."

Zane went to the closet, returning with a dildo. He pulled over a bench and had Clark kneel at one end and rest his body over the seat, his profile turned to Mandy so she could watch from the side. "You'll take my cock. All the way. My cock in your ass."

"Yes, master. All the way. Thank you." Clark accepted a bottle of lube from Zane, squirted some of the liquid onto his fingers, and spread it between his ass cheeks. Then he parted them for Zane.

Zane inspected his ass. "Good." He handed the dildo to Clark. "Take my cock slowly. One fraction of an inch at a time. I want you to feel it go in, filling you, stretching you."

Yessss. Mandy could imagine a thick, hard cock filling her pussy, slowly inching inside until she was deliciously full. Breathing heavily now, too, she watched Clark tremble as he gradually inserted the toy until there was only a small part remaining visible.

"Now I'll fuck you. But I'm going to take my time building my pleasure. You like it that way, don't you? My cock gliding in and out slowly."

She sure did. "Yessss," she said, realizing after she'd spoke that she'd said it aloud, rather than thinking it in her head. She sank her teeth into her lower lip and squeezed her thighs together. Her pussy was hot now, a pleasant pulsing sensation throbbing through her tissues. She clamped her inner walls around the tingling emptiness, wishing Zane would give her a big dildo to fuck herself with.

"Now, faster. My need is building," Zane said, his voice changing. He sounded tense and breathless, as if he truly were fucking Clark's ass. "Damn, you're tight. So hot. So wet."

Mandy swallowed a moan. He was looking at her like he was genuinely fucking her, and he sounded like he was, too. She could practically feel his cock gliding in and out of her clenching tissues, stretching them, stroking that magical spot inside.

"Faster, harder. Dammit, I want you. I want to hear you scream. But not yet." Zane raked his fingernails down Clark's back, and Clark trembled visibly, arching his spine, thrusting his ass up.

"Yes, master. Please more, master." Clark was jamming that toy in and out of his ass now, the muscles of his shoulders and arms rippling as they tensed. The muscles of his ass bunched as they knotted. "Please, may I come?"

"Not yet," Zane snapped. He licked a path down Clark's back, from his nape to the top of his ass. He hooked his fingers again and dragged his nails down Clark's back, leaving red welted stripes on his skin.

Mandy's gaze lurched from Clark's shaking body to Zane's. What parts of him that were visible were strained with tension. Arms. Face. Neck. His lips parted. His teeth flashed bright against his dark skin. For a brief moment, they almost looked bigger than normal. Must have been the way the light struck them.

"Please, master."

"You may not take your pleasure yet. No. Not until I give you permission."

"Yes, master." Clark slowed the pace of his thrusts slightly.

"No, I'll fuck you as hard and as fast as I want. I won't slow down." Zane's eyes dropped to her pussy. His tongue swept across her lower lip, and she remembered how incredible that same tongue had felt flicking over her clit.

Clark picked up the pace again. It was plain to Mandy's eyes that he was on the verge of coming. Droplets of precum glistened at the tip of his ruddy cock. The flared head had widened, the color deepened. His testicles had risen, nestling up against his pelvis.

Zane bent over Clark, his head tipping down to nibble his neck or ear. Clark went still for the briefest second and then screamed. A jet of cum spurted from his cock. Another. More. He tossed his head back and thrust his hips back and forth until his orgasm had eased and he was sated.

Zane stood. Smiled. "Yes, very good. Now you'll have your reward." He went to the cabinet again. Produced another wrapped dildo. But instead of handing it to Clark, Zane scooped up the lube and handed it and the dildo to Mandy. "Amanda. He'll take his reward now."

7

Mandy looked down at the toy, then up at Zane.

Helping Clark up, Zane gave her a sharp look. "You watched him. Now he will watch you."

They wanted her to masturbate in front of them? She shook her head. "But I—"

"You said 'no penetration.' My slave is not penetrating you."

Clark was sitting quietly on the bench, waiting, his cock hard again.

"True. But—"

Zane silenced her argument by taking one of her nipples between his finger and thumb and giving it a little pinch. The pleasure-pain zinged through her body.

She jumped a little. Her pussy spasmed a lot. Maybe there was something to that whole pain-is-pleasure thing, when it came to sex.

"Are you going to try to convince yourself you don't want to? Why?"

Now that was a question she didn't know how to answer.

Did she want to masturbate in front of these two gorgeous men? Her pussy sure wanted her to. What would be the harm in it? "I'm going to touch myself? You won't touch me? And Clark won't either?"

"We won't. Unless, of course, you want us to."

"O-okay."

"You'll enjoy it. I'm going to fuck you with my cock until you beg me for release." He pointed at the dildo, making it clear that was the cock he was referring to. "And my submissive is going to watch." Zane helped Mandy lean back on the slanted backrest. She lifted her hips and slipped her panties off, leaving her skirt on. When she parted her legs, the skirt bunched up, revealing her legs and her throbbing center.

"Before I push my cock inside, I want to touch your clit. Lightly at first."

This was kinda like phone sex...not that she'd ever called one of those sex lines.

Assuming Zane meant for her to touch herself, Mandy squirted some lube on her fingertip and started drawing slow circles over her clit. Round and round. With each stroke, her body warmed a little more. Her pussy became wetter. Ached a little worse.

"Yes, that is one pretty little pussy. I love to stroke it."

This was crazy.

And insanely sexy.

She increased the pressure on her clit a tiny bit. Ah, yes. Better. A wave of heat washed through her body.

"Open your legs wider." His voice was a low rumble. "Now, I want to feel how tight your cunt is. I want to fuck you with a finger while I stroke your clit."

She stretched her legs wider apart and, while still circling her clit, pushed the index finger of her other hand into her wet pussy. She contracted her inner muscles, tightening her slick heat around her finger.

"Damn, you're wet. And tight. I can't wait to thrust my cock into that heat. You're going to take me deep inside soon. But first I want to tease you, bring you to the verge of release."

Zane was one cruel son of a bitch, but she'd already figured that out. She shuddered as another wave of carnal need buzzed through her body. She kept her eyes closed as she stroked herself to the edge of release. Two fingers fucked her pussy while the others tormented her aching clit. Hotter she became. Her body tightened. A slight sheen of sweat slickened her skin. A tingle started at the base of her clit....

"Stop. Now," Zane ordered.

Breathless, and one stroke away from an orgasm, she threw her hands up over her head. She dragged in one, two gulps of air, then slowly exhaled.

"Damn," Clark murmured. "I want that pussy."

"She's not yours," Zane said, his voice sharp. "She's mine."

His? Since when?

A quiver raced up her spine.

His?

She blinked open her eyes, and her gaze was instantly captured by his. His expression was intense. A glimmer of something feral, carnal, flickered in his eyes.

"Mine," he repeated. Then, shifting his position ever so slightly, he ordered, "I am going to eat your pussy now. I'm going to taste your honey, fuck your cunt with my tongue, and lick away your cream."

Was he? Or did he want her to imagine it again?

Hands trembling, she nodded.

He moved like a panther, every motion graceful and smooth. His gaze never left hers as he stalked across the room. He loomed over her for a handful of heartbeats. She swallowed a lump.

This was really going to happen.

"Mine," he repeated as he sank to his knees. His fingers

curled around her ankles. He pulled them wider apart, opening her heated center to him. His nostrils flared as he inhaled. "You smell so fucking good." His tongue swept across his bottom lip. A current of electricity buzzed through her system.

She'd never seen a hotter fuck-me look, not ever. Not even in the movies or in a music video. Just his expression alone was making her pussy clench and unclench. Sticky cream was trickling down her ass cheeks.

Did this man know how to stir a girl's anticipation!

"Slave. Come hold her legs," Zane said. "Hold them up high and out."

Clark walked around behind the slanted bench back, caught her ankles in his fists, and lifted them high up in the air. He spread his arms to their fullest reach, creating a wide vee with her straight legs.

Shifting forward, Zane nipped the supersensitive back of her thigh, now exposed by her position. He licked and nibbled the other one. He alternated back and forth, from one leg to another, teasing, tormenting, until she was trembling from head to toe. Finally, he spread her labia, exposing her throbbing clit, and gave it a couple of light flicks with his tongue.

Her back arched. Her heart jerked in her chest.

She was about to explode.

He stopped. "Not yet. You can't come yet."

Was he freaking crazy? Or just unbelievably mean?

"Please," she whispered.

"I just started." Gently, he applied pressure on her stomach, coaxing her to flatten her back against the bench's back.

"I know, but..." She didn't finish her sentence. She couldn't remember what the hell she was about to say.

He swirled his tongue round and round her clit, the movement slow, the pressure absolutely perfect.

"Oooohhhhhh," she heard herself say as Zane ate her pussy

like no man had ever done before. He was a master of the art, knowing exactly how to stroke, where and how fast and how hard, and ohmygod she was going to come…

He stopped. "No!"

She whimpered. Her muscles were pulled so tight she felt like she was tied in one big knot. She was so hot, she thought she might spontaneously combust. And she was so desperate for release that she was willing to do just about anything to have an orgasm.

"When you come, you're going to scream my name," he said, sliding the tip of his index finger between her lips. He tasted salty, good. She flicked her tongue over it, swirled it round, simulating oral sex. His jaw clenched. "My name." He withdrew his finger, traced a meandering line down her chin, the side of her neck, the center of her chest. It took a turn to the right, moving over the swell of a breast to take a few turns around a nipple. Her sensitive flesh responded, pulling into a tight little tip. Tiny currents of pleasure zipped through her.

She looked at him, framed by her spread legs. The man was her vision of a wet dream, in every sense of the word. His face as impossibly gorgeous as any model or actor. His body a work of art. But it was his eyes that made her melt. She saw something in them. Not just raw, primal need. Something more.

He shifted forward again, this time using his fingers to open her cunt lips wide. His tongue plunged in and out of her, the shallow thrusts more of a tease than a relief. On the verge of tears now, she curled her fingers into his hair, fisting the silken strands, and held him to her swollen, throbbing center.

"Please."

He grabbed her wrists, jerking her hands away from his head. "Now you're ready for my cock." Not giving her any reason to suspect he meant the real thing, he unwrapped the dildo. His face was gleaming with her cream as his lips curled into a wicked smile. He placed the head of the dildo at her entrance. She strained, waiting, breathless, desperate for that first blissful thrust.

"Tell me what I have been waiting to hear," he said.

What was he waiting to hear? Confused, she looked at him, her eyes searching his. What?

"Tell me this pussy is mine."

"It's yours," she whispered.

The dildo plunged inside, pushing through her swollen tissues to fill her perfectly. She moaned with the pleasure, grateful she wasn't empty any longer.

"Yes, please fuck your pussy," she murmured, throwing her hands up over her head to curl her fingers over the top of the backrest. As the toy slammed in and out of her, stroking her intimately, she clenched her pussy, heightening her pleasure. In and out it thrust, each gliding movement bringing with it a flurry of glorious sensation. The pleasure of each intimate stroke. The scent of her own desire in the air. The sound of her little moans and groans.

Zane tongued her clit as he rammed that thick toy into her, adding another level of bliss to what was quickly becoming overwhelming.

"Please? Now?" she asked, quaking with the need to come. "Now?" She was ready. Right there. Just a little more. Would he let her this time? "Oh, please."

"Yes. Now. Come now."

Her pussy spasmed around his cock as a tidal wave of carnal heat crashed over her. She was swept away into a world of sensation for a handful of glorious seconds. Gradually, the climax ended, leaving her feeling satisfied and giddy and tingly all over.

Her legs were gently lowered, but she didn't pull her knees together to hide herself. She wanted him to see every little twitch.

Zane angled his body over hers, fisted her hair on either side of her face, and kissed her furiously, his groin grinding against her still-sensitive flesh. "Damn you, Amanda," he muttered into their joined mouths. "Damn you for making me want you so badly." He broke the kiss.

More than a little dizzy, Mandy slowly lifted her heavy eyelids. Clark was pulling on his clothes. He was talking to Zane in a hushed voice. Zane responded.

Trying to make out what they were saying, Mandy sat upright, turning her head toward them.

Not a word.

Clark left while Zane watched him go.

Zane didn't turn around to face her right away, leaving her to study his body language. One arm rested against the door frame. The other was bent in front of him. His head was lowered.

Was he upset? Why?

Feeling a little uncomfortable, Mandy stood, tugging her skirt back down where it belonged. She grabbed her shirt and yanked it over her head. "I guess I should be going," she mumbled, tottering toward the door. She'd have to walk past him to leave. She had a feeling it was going to be awkward for some reason.

Sure enough, as she shuffled by him, he grabbed her arm. There'd be no quick escape.

His gaze snapped to hers. She couldn't read his expression.

"You forgot something."

She did?

Oh! "Camera."

He pulled it from his pocket and placed it in her upturned palm. His fingertips grazed her skin. That tiny touch sent a wave of electricity buzzing through her whole body.

"Thanks for not breaking it this time," she said.

"You were almost caught. You don't want that to happen."

"I hear you."

His gaze intensified. "Whatever the client is paying, it isn't worth it."

"I'm not at liberty to discuss my case." She shoved the faux lighter into her pocket. "Speaking of cases, I'm sorry but I can't accept your generous job offer."

He didn't look surprised. His mouth tensed ever so slightly. "Very well."

"I appreciate the offer."

"Sure."

Now she felt really, really uncomfortable. She pulled her arm. Thankfully, he released it. "I guess I'll see you around." Feeling some sense of relief, she passed through the doorway.

Maybe he was right. Maybe she needed to find another way to catch Clark in the act. Clearly, this was getting her nowhere fast. At least, no closer to collecting another paycheck.

He stopped her again, this time by looping an arm around her waist and hauling her back against him. His body was hard and hot. A very pronounced rigid lump was pressing into her spine. He gathered her hair and brushed it over one shoulder. She stood there, immobile, and just about melted.

"I don't know what it is about you."

"I don't know either," she mumbled, letting her head fall back.

Holding her tight, he tongued her earlobe. "I can't stop thinking about you."

She had to admit, but only to herself, she'd been thinking about him, too. More than she wanted to. "I...I don't know what to say."

He loosened his hold, but only to coax her around to face him. His eyes were dark as he stared down at her, full of emotions. Before she figured out what he was feeling, he kissed her. While his mouth claimed hers, he backed her into the wall. She was trapped. She was at his mercy. And, ohmygod, she wasn't about to try to escape.

She'd kissed her share of men in her life, but none had kissed like Zane. He made kissing an art. With soft lips, agile tongue, and occasionally teeth, he drove her into a state of desperation. She tried to fling her arms up over his shoulders, but grabbed her wrists and held them at her sides, flat against the wall. He wedged a knee between her legs, and her hips started slowly rocking back and forth. Her center ached for his touch. Her whole body did.

He mumbled into her mouth, "I want my pussy."

His pussy wanted him, too.

Next thing she knew, she was being walked back into his room. The door slammed shut. Her clothes were removed, one piece at a time, while he tasted and licked and nibbled on just about every inch of her exposed skin.

This was really going to happen. She was going to let this man have her, fuck her, if that's what he wanted.

Abruptly he stopped, looked at her. His expression was... troubled?

"Is something wrong?" she asked, struggling to inflate her lungs. She fingered her kiss-swollen lips with one hand while making a half-assed attempt at covering herself with the other. "You seem conflicted."

"I don't fuck my submissives."

He didn't? Her pussy clenched. Did that mean he wouldn't fuck her? Right now, that was kind of disappointing to hear. "I see."

"I don't kiss them either."

What was he trying to say?

"I'm sorry. I don't understand."

He shoved his fingers through his hair and audibly sighed. "You're going to make me say it, aren't you?"

"Say what?" Her skin was cooling off. She was actually starting to feel a little chilled.

He removed his jacket and wrapped it around her. It was a

sweet gesture, gentlemanly. She waited for him to find whatever words he felt he needed to say. A heated minute passed, a second. "I've never felt this way about a woman before."

"Are you trying to say you...like me?"

"No."

"No?"

"*Like* isn't the right word." He caught a tendril of her hair between his fingertips and gave it a soft kiss. "I am captivated by you."

Captivated. That was some word. This gorgeous man was "captivated" by her? What a boost to the ego.

What a terrifying, thrilling, overwhelming prospect.

"Come to my party this weekend." He tucked the hair behind her ear. "Attend as my personal guest." He chewed on his lower lip.

"Just to clarify, you want me there not as an employee." Smelling his scent on the jacket's collar, she pulled the garment tighter around her nude body.

"I don't want you to work for me. I want you there with me."

"Okay. I'll be there, then."

"Good." His eyes glittered as he bent to give her another kiss, this one sweeter, more patient. "Don't think you can sneak a camera onto my property."

"Warning heeded."

"If I have to, I'll strip-search you." His lips curled into a devious grin.

"You might anyway, I'm guessing."

"You're right." He kissed her again and didn't stop until her toes curled and her heart was thumping against her breastbone. Against her mouth, he murmured, "I might."

8

Mandy had been in some hellholes, but this dump had them beat. The neon sign outside glowed red, LIVE NUDE GIRLS! FANTASY BOOTHS. She would've thought there'd be no need for these dens of filth anymore, with so much porn readily available on the Net. Evidently, at least in this neighborhood, Internet porn hadn't taken such a big bite out of the adult entertainment industry.

Lucky her, because that meant she got to follow her mark into this dump. It was so nasty inside, she realized immediately, that she wished she could've worn a full-body condom over her clothes.

She tried to ignore the guy at the counter. His leer was creepy enough to make any girl feel dirty. But, because Clark wasn't in the main lobby/store area, she had to assume he'd taken residence, with his stripper friend, in one of the private booths.

Which meant she needed to get into the back, hopefully without parting with any of her hard-earned cash. "I'm looking for someone," she said to the guy at the counter.

The guy took a glance around. "Nobody's here."

"Yeah. I can see that. I think he headed into one of the booths."

The guy shrugged.

Assuming he was paid little more than minimum wage, Mandy shoved her hand into her pocket and withdrew her small wad of cash. "How much?"

"For a booth? Thirty-five for five minutes."

"That's insane."

The guy shrugged. "You want to get back there, you gotta pay. Unless..." His icky gaze crept up and down her body before pausing at chest level.

Understanding exactly what he was trying to suggest, she slapped the cash onto the counter. "I'll pay."

The creep sneered as he handed her a key. "That's too bad. We could use some fresh...faces...."

"Not in this lifetime." Fisting the key, she waited for him to let her into the narrow back hall. The door slammed behind her. She took a hesitant step forward, grimacing. It was claustrophobic back here. Small and dirty. Lit only by strings of red-colored Christmas lights stapled to the paneled wall. The hallway ended only about ten feet ahead. A metal door led out to the alley that snaked behind the crumbling building. There were only five doors lining the left wall. None on the right. Each door had a letter spray-painted on it. *A* through *E*. Clark and his friend had to be in one of them. Booth B was empty. She was holding the key for that door.

She was here now and had very little time if Clark was as cheap as she was. How would she catch him in the act?

Feeling a little brave, she tried the doors of the other four booths. All locked. She pressed her ear to each door. She heard people, voices, moaning, in only two of them. Booths A and D. Which one was Clark in?

A. Or D. It was a fifty-fifty shot.

Fifty-fifty was better than she'd had so far.

She thought about the stack of overdue bills sitting on her desk, collecting dust.

She thought about Sarah, who'd given her a little nudge this morning about the raise she'd promised...three months ago.

And she thought about her empty refrigerator. She'd been living on ramen noodles and rice; she'd almost forgotten what real food tasted like.

This was it, the best chance she'd had so far to get her proof, collect the much-needed bonus, and put this case behind her at last. She fished her maxed-out JCPenney credit card out of her wallet, hoping to jimmy the lock, eanie-meanie'd the two doors, picked Booth D, and with her camera ready, she slid the card between the door and the jamb. The door swung open, she rushed in, and without checking to see who was in the booth, snapped a picture and dove back out, racing to her booth and locking herself in.

"What the fuck?!" a man's angry voice boomed.

There was a sound of slamming doors, pounding feet, angry shouts. Mandy crouched in the darkest corner of the booth, trying not to think about what was probably spattered all over the wall behind her, and flipped the camera to view mode to check the shot.

Oh, yes, it was a money shot. She'd gotten him *in flagrante delicto*, pounding into some young woman.

Unfortunately, *he* wasn't Clark.

"Dammit," she whispered, listening for signs that the angry subject of her photograph had left. She didn't hear anything, so she inched open the door and peered out into the hall.

The door to Booth A swung open, and Clark and his friend—looking freshly fucked, her hair askew, her clothes mussed—stepped out. Mandy pulled her door shut as they walked by, then followed them out into the alley. They ducked into a car parked in the alley and sped away.

She stood there, cussing.

Just her luck, it wasn't just raining; it was pouring. A flash of lightning startled her as she dodged the biggest puddles on her way around the west side of the building, where she'd parked her car. Her gaze locked on her destination, she scurried to her car. Rain dripping from her hair, she unlocked the door and dove into the seat, but just as she pulled the door closed, a fist pounded on her window.

Uh-oh!

She hit the locks.

The fist hit the window again.

Something hard slammed into the side of the door.

She shoved the key into the ignition and jerked it.

"You bitch! You were the one who took the picture!"

Oh, shit!

She shoved the gearshift into drive and hit the gas. Tires screeched on the wet pavement. Two seconds later, the car zoomed forward. She probably hit a new record for acceleration of a 1998 Focus as she careened down the street, took the first corner at an insane speed, and rocketed toward the freeway. She didn't breathe easier until she was well outside of the city limits.

She'd said it before, but this time she meant it. It was time for a career change.

Her cell phone rang. Hands still a little shaky, she checked the number, then answered.

"I've got her!" Sarah yelled into her ear.

"Got who?" Mandy asked as she checked the right lane. Her exit was a mile up ahead. The lane was packed, bumper to bumper. This was going to be fun. She flipped on her turn signal and zoomed past a few cars, looking for a gap.

"Your missing old lady, the one with the clown hair."

"Ah, that 'her.'"

"Who else would I be talking about?" Sarah asked.

"I don't know. I'm a little distracted." Making her third attempt at a lane change, Mandy positioned her car in front of a semi. The gap between the truck and the pickup in front of it was on the small side, but with only a quarter of a mile left before her exit, it was do or die.

"Distracted with what?"

"Hang on." She set her phone in her lap, wincing as her car drifted into the lane. Her Ford was small. That truck was huge. In an accident, she'd be the clear loser.

Fortunately for her, there was no accident. The truck driver, anticipating her move, slowed down slightly. But he wasn't happy to have done that. The semi's headlights flashed in her rearview mirror. Huffing a sigh of relief, she gave the truck driver an I'm-sorry wave over her shoulder as she maneuvered into the exit lane to her right.

She scooped up her phone and tucked it between her shoulder and ear. "I'm back. Are you still there?"

"Yes. Anyway, where are you?"

"Why?"

"Because Ruby Belton's plane leaves in two hours. I figure she's probably already at the airport."

"Plane?"

"Yeah. She's headed to Vegas. And she's not alone. She bought two-round trip seats. First class."

"Cool. I'm only fifteen minutes away from the airport." Currently on the freeway service drive, Mandy changed lanes, preparing to get back on the highway. "What airline is she flying?"

"US Airways."

"Got it. Thanks!"

Fifteen minutes later, she was pulling into the short-term parking lot. After squeezing her car into the only parking spot she could find, she jog-walked the mile-long trek to the terminal. She made a beeline for the line at the US Airways check-in counter, her eyes skimming the travelers, looking for her target.

Too young, too young, family with kids, male, male, male,

another woman who was too young. Where was Grandma Belton?

The door behind her swished open, and out of reflex, she stole a glance over her shoulder.

Yes! Ruby Belton. And who was that? Her companion was, maybe, in his early forties. Many, many, many years younger than her. And he wasn't hard on the eyes either.

Grandma Belton gave his ass a pat.

You little cougar!

Mandy met them at the end of the check-in line. "Excuse me, Mrs. Ruby Belton?"

"Excuse you." Ruby Belton gave her a squinty stare. "Do I know you?"

"Not exactly."

"Then how do you know my name?" Ruby turned to her companion, thumbing over her shoulder. "This lady knows my name."

"I see that," he said, giving Mandy a what's-up look.

"Her family hired me," Mandy explained.

"Oh, hell!" Ruby shouted. "They just can't leave me alone. I'm not going back there." She wagged an arthritic finger at Mandy. "You can't make me."

Mandy lifted her hands in the universal sign of surrender. "I'm not trying to make you do anything. They just hired me to find you."

"Good." Ruby tried to push Mandy aside. She couldn't. At five feet nothing, she couldn't weigh more than eighty pounds. Mandy figured she had to outweigh her by at least forty pounds. "You found me. Now, get outta my way. Me and Bob have a plane to catch."

"Yes, I won't make you late for your flight." Mandy pulled out her phone and handed it to Ruby. "As soon as you call your daughter and let her know you're safe, I'll leave."

Ruby's lips thinned. Considering her lips weren't more than

pink slashes, that was saying something. "I don't want to. She'll try to stop me."

"Babe," Bob said, taking the phone from Mandy. "I think it's a good idea. If you don't call her, she may try to report you as kidnapped. I don't want to spend my honeymoon in jail. She's going to know where to find us."

Honeymoon? These two were married? This was going to be interesting.

Ruby's sigh was highly exaggerated. "I see your point." She accepted the phone from Bob, poked the number pad with an index finger, waited a few seconds, barked, "I'm fine, now leave me the hell alone," and cut off the call. She shoved the phone back at Mandy. "There. I made the call. Now let me go."

Swallowing back a chuckle, Mandy stepped aside. "Have a wonderful honeymoon."

Ruby's smile was 100 percent naughty. "You know I will." She gave Bob's ass another crack, then hurried to catch up with the end of the line. Bob followed, dragging three suitcases behind him.

That was the end of that.

Feeling some sense of accomplishment, Mandy headed outside, into yet another downpour. She was soaked to the skin by the time she reached her car. Her hair was wet. Her clothes were saturated, glued to her skin. By some miracle, however, her cell phone, which had been in her jeans pocket, wasn't ruined. It rang shortly after she'd flung her soggy self into the driver's seat. Blinking at the rain droplets dribbling off her eyelashes, she answered the call.

"Hey!"

"Did you get the old lady?" Sarah asked.

"I did. Get this—she's going on her honeymoon."

"Go, Grandma!"

"There's more."

"What?"

"Grandma's new husband is probably at least forty years younger than her. And he wasn't hard on the eyes at all. In fact, he was a pretty decent-looking man."

"Why would a guy like that marry an old woman, you think?"

"I would've guessed her money, but after seeing them together, I think he married her for the sex. I think Grandma Belton's into some kink."

"That's wrong, on so many levels."

Starting her car, Mandy wedged the phone between her shoulder and ear. One of these days, she was going to have to get around to replacing the Bluetooth headset she'd killed. "Hey, who are you to judge, Mistress Sarah?"

"Touché."

Mandy navigated the car out of the parking spot. "So, did you call me just to ask me about Grandma Belton, or did you need to talk to me about something else?"

"Oh, yeah, all this crazy talk about kinky Grandma made me forget. A guy came in here looking for you about an hour ago."

"Did he leave a name?"

"Yeah. I put his card on your desk."

"Okay." Driving toward the freeway, Mandy checked the clock. It was almost ten. Sarah was normally gone by six. "Which class is it this time? English Composition?"

"No, psychology." Sarah was attending classes at the local community college a couple of nights a week. She didn't own a computer, so she would periodically stay late and use her work computer to do her homework. "I have a paper due tomorrow night."

"Good luck."

"Thanks. It's almost done. Thank God for the Net. I don't know what I'd do without it."

"I hear that. I'll call that man tomorrow. I was caught in a downpour not once, not twice, but three times tonight. I'm cold, I'm wet, and I'm tired. So I'm going to head home, dry off, and chill out on the couch."

"Sounds pretty good to me. See you tomorrow."

"Yeah."

She clicked off, dropped the phone on the passenger seat, and drove home, feeling pretty good about how things worked out today. She still didn't have any photographic evidence on Clark, but she'd wrapped up one case and hopefully tomorrow she'd be collecting a retainer for a new one.

When she arrived home, she was greeted by a delivery tag on her door. The UPS guy had left a package with her favorite neighbor, Mrs. Wentworth. Funny, she wasn't expecting any packages. She hadn't ordered anything online in months. And she never received packages from anyone else. Curious, she pressed an ear against Mrs. Wentworth's door. She heard voices but didn't know if they were from the television, which Mrs. Wentworth left on day and night, or from real, live people. Knowing Mrs. Wentworth was prone to insomnia, Mandy knocked lightly on the door. A minute or two later, the door swung open.

Sporting a ratty robe, slippers, socks, and a head full of little pink foam rollers, Mrs. Wentworth grunted, hobbled over to her coffee table, and pointed. "This damn thing's heavy. I'll let you come in and get it."

"Thank you." Mandy hurried in, lifted the box, which was large but not particularly heavy, off the table and shuffled back out into the hallway. She started to say something to her cranky neighbor, but the door slammed shut before she got a word out. "Oh, well, I tried."

Mandy read the label on her mystery package as she scurried back to her apartment. Shock of the century, it was from Zane. What the heck was he sending her? The carton was pretty big. If he'd thought to replace the two cameras he'd crushed, he wouldn't have needed to send them in something so huge. She wasted no time tearing into the package.

Inside were two smaller boxes, one pretty big, the other shoebox-sized. Both were gift wrapped, with silver paper and pretty gold ribbons. There was no card.

She opened the small one first, of course, because everyone knows good things come in small packages.

Once again, that cliché had proven to be true. The box, which identified the brand, was plain brown. Inside, the shoes were far from plain. Or brown. Black, with a jewel-encrusted platform and spike heel, they were the most insanely sexy shoes Mandy had ever seen. She didn't even want to think about how much they might have cost. Fortunately, there was no price anywhere on the box.

Undecided whether she dared accept the gifts, Mandy opened the other box. Inside was a black dress. It was simple, elegant, and one shouldered, with soft pleating sewn into the bodice. She carefully put the dress back into the box and stripped out of her sodden clothes, afraid the water might stain it. After hanging them up in the bathroom to dry, donning some fresh undies, and drying her hair, she slipped into the dress. The soft material cascaded down her body and swirled around her legs as she walked. She dug out the shoes, slid her feet into them, and, feeling like she was wearing a million bucks, floated to the full-length mirror hanging on the bathroom door.

Wow.

How had he known that dress would fit her so well?

After taking a look from every angle possible, Mandy forced herself to take the shoes and dress off. She hung the gown in her closet and made the shoes cozy in their box. Her phone rang as she was carrying the box back to her bedroom.

She checked the number. It was local, but she didn't recognize it. She answered the call. "Hello?"

"What do you think of your gift?" Zane asked. His voice sounded husky, breathy. She liked it when it sounded like that.

"They're beautiful. I've never owned a dress that magnificent. And those shoes. I mean...wow! But, Zane, they're so expensive. I really shouldn't—"

"Don't. Do they fit?"

"Yes. Perfectly."

"Good. Wear them this weekend."

"Sure."

"What are you doing now?"

Mandy looked down at the shoebox. Her bare boobs. Her black cotton panties. "I'm putting away the shoes."

"What are you wearing?"

Her face warmed. She thought about lying and telling him she was lounging around in big, ugly sweats. But something made her say, "Panties and a smile."

"Mmmmm. I like that."

She liked the way his voice had rumbled when he'd mmmm'd. Feeling a little naughty, she flopped onto the bed. She set the shoebox on the floor. "And here I thought you didn't care much for a girl wearing panties." Rolling onto her back, she stared up at the ceiling.

"It depends upon the girl. And the panties."

All this talk about panties was making hers wet. "Then would you like me to wear some this weekend?"

"Only if that's all you'd be wearing."

"I guess that'll have to wait for another time, then. I'd hate to miss out on a chance to wear the beautiful dress you bought me."

"I'd be fine either way."

Typical male. Of course he would.

Her hand, the one not holding the phone, skimmed down her body, coming to rest over her warm mound. "I'm sure you would."

"You sound a little tense. What are you doing now, Amanda? Are you lying on your couch, touching yourself?"

"No. I'm on the bed."

"Mmmmm."

For a moment, Mandy could swear she might come at just hearing that sound.

"Take off your panties."

Mandy had never had phone sex. She'd always thought it was kind of silly. At the moment, however, it wasn't sounding silly at all. With that melt-your-bones-hot voice, Zane could have a second, very successful, career in the phone-porn industry. She tugged off her panties and laid back down.

"Spread your legs," he said, his voice as commanding as it had ever been in the bondage dungeon.

She bent her knees and inched them apart.

"Wider," he said, as if he could actually see her. She slid her feet a few more inches apart. "Are you wet for me already?"

She ran her flattened hand over her slick folds. "Yes, I am."

"Good. Do you have some lube? A vibe or a dildo?"

"I can get them."

"Do it."

She pulled her favorite toy and some lube out of her nightstand drawer and set them within reach, then returned to her position on the bed. The vibrator was a slender hot-pink number. Simple and small, with a nicely rounded tip. It was all she'd ever needed. She was tight. The little toy fit her perfectly.

"Have you ever been fucked in the ass?" he asked.

"No." She shuddered, but not because the notion was scary or unpleasant. Quite the opposite. She'd been wanting to try anal for quite some time, but she hadn't known how to go about it. "Only with a finger."

"What kind of toy do you have?"

"It's a vibrator. A smallish one."

"Perfect. Close your eyes. Imagine I'm there with you and your ankles are bound, your knees bent, your legs spread wide apart." She took the position as he narrated. "I have to taste you first. My tongue flicks over your little pearl. How does that feel, Amanda?"

She simulated the sensation using a fingertip. A pleasantly warm wave rippled through her body. "Good."

"Yes, you like having me eat you while you're restrained. You can't move. That makes you hot, doesn't it?"

"Yes." She slid one finger inside her vagina. The slick walls clamped tightly around it. Her fingertip grazed her G-spot, and she quivered all over.

"I can't wait to fuck you, Amanda. Just the thought makes my cock hard."

His voice was still warm and mellow, but there was a slight tension to it now. Amanda could imagine him kneeling there beside her, his hand slowly stroking his thick cock. She finger-fucked her pussy, that image burning in her mind.

"You aren't ready for me yet."

He was so wrong about that. But how could he know? Holding the phone between her shoulder and ear, she used two hands now. One index finger drew slow, lazy circles around her sensitive clit. The other glided in and out of her hot channel.

"Lube your ass."

She spread some cool gel on her anus, then inserted her middle finger into her hole while fucking her pussy with her index finger. In the digits went and out. With each small movement, she grew closer to orgasm, hotter, tighter, and more breathless.

"That's it, I want to see you fuck that little ass of yours. Get the toy. Do it now. I can't wait much longer."

Her pussy quivered around her invading finger. She snatched up the toy, added some lube, and placed the tapered end at her tight hole.

"Ease it in, baby. Relax."

Trembling now with need, she drew her knees farther apart and concentrated on relaxing the ring of muscles.

"I need to see that toy buried in your ass."

She increased the pressure, pushing against her body's resistance. The skin burned. But the pleasure-pain only added to what was quickly becoming an overwhelming blaze burning through her body. Her anus opened and the tip of the toy slid inside. She groaned as it slid in farther, until a couple of inches remained outside. Leaving it where it was, she pushed two fingers into her pussy. "Oh, God." A surge of carnal heat blasted through her body.

He groaned in her ear. "Come for me."

"Yes." Fucking her pussy harder, she increased the pressure to her clit, fingering the hard nub until the heat gathered in her center. It churned there for one, two, three blissful seconds and then exploded through her body. "Ahhhhh," she said as her pussy and ass convulsed, and pulses of pleasure raced up and down her body. Zane growled like a beast, and Mandy imagined him throwing his head back as he found his own release. The scene playing out in her head prolonged the pleasure, sparking a second orgasm. When she was finally able to catch her breath, she murmured, "Wow."

"We're going to play out that scene sometime," Zane promised, sounding like he was still fighting to catch his breath. "But instead of that damn toy, it'll be my cock filling your ass."

Mandy had some doubts about being ready for that, but she didn't voice them just then. Instead, she said, in a weak voice, "I want that."

"I'll make sure you're ready. It'll feel better than you ever dreamed." Then, without so much as a good-bye, he ended the call.

Mandy slid beneath the sheets and let dreams of one hot dom carry her away.

9

"That is some smile on your face this morning." Sarah, main-lining a mocha-chino at her desk, gave Mandy an eyebrow waggle. "Who did you sleep with last night?"

"I slept with myself."

Sarah's waggle stopped. "How is that possible? You have the look of a woman who's been well fucked."

"Phone sex?" Mandy shrugged, heading to her office.

"Phone sex?" Sarah scurried after her. "Really? With who?"

"Zane."

"Ohmygod! Seriously?" Sarah gave her a look of pure awe. You'd have thought she'd just witnessed the reincarnation of Marilyn Monroe, her ultimate dream girl.

"Seriously."

"I guess I don't need to ask how it was."

"No, you don't." Mandy felt her cheeks warming. She and Sarah had shared some intimate conversations in the past, about all sorts of things. Why she was feeling a little embarrassed now puzzled her.

"You go, girl." Sarah smacked her on the back. "My baby's

growing up." Faking a teary-eyed snuffle, she dabbed at her heavily mascaraed eyes. "I'm so proud of you."

Mandy plopped into her chair and took a quick survey of her cluttered desktop. "Okay, that's enough. I need to get to work. Where's that message you told me about last night?"

"Here." Sarah pulled it from the middle of a stack of pink *While You Were Out* notes. She smacked it on the desktop and poked at the top line. "He said he'd be available to talk anytime today."

"Okay." Mandy dialed the number. "Thanks."

Sarah threw her a wave over her shoulder as she bounced out of Mandy's office. Clearly, the caffeine had kicked in.

Mandy skimmed the notes on the other pink slips as she waited for Jim Marcum to answer his phone. After the fourth ring, the call clicked to voice mail.

"Hello, you've reached the Schrader home," said a woman's voice. "We can't come to the phone right now. Please leave a message after the tone—"

Schrader? Mandy hung up. Had she dialed the number wrong? She tried it again. The line rang, then clicked over to voice mail once more and the now-familiar female voice greeted her. Mandy ended the call and stepped out of her office to find Sarah playing FarmVille. "I tried calling this Jim Marcum guy. But I'm getting some other family's home voice mail. Is it possible you took down the number wrong?"

Sarah shrugged. "I suppose it's possible. I thought I had it right."

Mandy set the paper on Sarah's desk. "See if you can find another number for this guy. Maybe he's listed in the phonebook."

"I'll do my best," Sarah said, clicking on her little farm plots and planting eggplants.

Mandy went back to her office to see if any of the other messages looked promising.

Nope.

One was from Ruby Belton's granddaughter, asking for a return call. She didn't sound particularly happy. Mandy had a feeling she knew how that conversation would go. No doubt she'd expected Mandy to drag her mother home. Problem was, she had no authority to do that.

The other messages were all from bill collectors.

A girl of action, Mandy decided she needed to get her ass out there and take care of business. Her first stop would be the Clark residence. If she had to tail that little weasel all day, she was going to catch him in the act of fornicating with another person or she was going to die trying.

Stopping at Sarah's desk on her way out, Mandy asked, "Anything on Jim Marcum?"

"Um, not yet. I ran a Social Security inquiry, and the only Jim Marcum I'm getting lives in Washington State."

"Maybe he's here on business?"

"Yeah. But this Jim Marcum is only two and a half years old."

That meant this Jim Marcum either didn't have a social, was not a U.S. resident, or was using a false identity. She wondered which it was.

Deciding it wasn't worth worrying about, Mandy looped her purse over her shoulder and headed for the door. "If he calls back, get some more info on him."

"Do you want me to give him your cell number?"

"No. Not until we know who he is."

"Okay." Sarah went back to her planting.

Mandy headed out to her car.

The drive to the Clark residence was uneventful. Conveniently, Mandy saw a Starbucks coffee shop a half mile from her destination. She splurged on a Double Chocolaty Chip Frappuccino and a double-iced cinnamon roll. The cost was a little steep, but consuming that many calories in one sitting meant she could skip lunch.

Ten minutes later, parked outside Clark's home, she slurped and nibbled in her car while waiting for the weasel to make his morning getaway. At ten to ten, roughly a half hour after Mandy had parked, his sleek black Maserati rolled out of the attached garage.

Cautiously, Mandy checked to make sure he was the driver as the car rolled by. It was him. She tailed him to a nearby gym. Watched him haul a duffel bag up to the building. He was dressed in a pair of sweats and a T-shirt. She saw no reason to follow him inside. An hour and a half later, he came out wearing a pair of black slacks and a sweater. She followed him to his office and parked outside, hoping he'd sneak out for a special lunch at noon. Sure enough, he came strolling out at exactly twelve o'clock. Staying several car lengths behind him, she followed him to a Red Roof Inn.

Finally, she had him!

She waited as he checked in, then drove around the side of the building. Not wanting to take the chance of him recognizing her car, she grabbed her gear—lock-picks, cameras, and cell phone—and headed after him on foot. She caught him just as he entered the first-floor room. Like every Red Roof Inn she'd ever seen, the rooms opened directly to the outside. There were no interior hallways.

How convenient.

Cautiously, she approached the window, hoping the drapes would gape enough to get a peek inside. No such luck.

She heard voices. Male and female. Laughter. It sounded like things were getting rolling. She checked out the door. It was a standard key entry, thank God. No card key. She could risk picking the lock, hoping the room's occupants would be too involved in whatever they were doing to realize the door was slightly ajar. It had worked for her in the past.

She had the lock disengaged within seconds. Slowly, she

twisted the knob, holding her breath. All she needed was an inch. Just enough space to get her scope and camera inside.

Using her toe to hold the door open, she inserted the scope, putting the eyepiece to her eye.

Bingo! She had him! He was on his knees, doing it doggy style with a blonde with fake boobs.

She replaced the scope with the camera and hit the RECORD button, leaving the camera running for several minutes. Then, as a safeguard, she snapped a few still shots with her digital camera, closed the door, and hurried back to her car. She quickly double-checked to make sure there were no problems with the cameras before driving back to her office.

"I got him!" she announced the minute she stepped into the lobby.

"You got who?" Sarah asked, staring at her computer screen.

"That sneaky weasel, Clark. He was slippery, but I finally caught him in the act." She brandished the cameras. "Got both still shots and video. He's going down."

"Great!"

"Did Jim Marcum call back?" Mandy asked as she hurried into her office. She wanted to take a good look at the footage before calling Clark's wife, make sure she had a decent enough shot to identify Clark.

"Nope."

"Huh." Mandy plopped into her chair and connected the video camera to her computer to play back the footage. It was a money shot, all right. His profile was clear as day. There'd be no denying it was him.

It was payday!

Mandy dialed Clark's wife. No answer. She left a message. She checked the clock. It was almost two. She was getting kind of hungry. Her blood sugar was crashing. And her desk was clear. What the hell? She could call it a day early for once. Considering how many hours she'd put in on the Clark case alone, she deserved some downtime.

She bid farewell to Sarah and headed out. Feeling guilty for her sugar-and-fat-laden breakfast, she stopped at a sub shop for a turkey sub—no mayo—on the way home. She parked her car in the lot and, slurping at a diet cola, scuttled up to her apartment building.

She ate her sandwich while watching the latest episode of *Dancing with the Stars*, which she'd TiVo'd. After the program ended, she channel surfed for a while before picking up her netbook to check her e-mail.

There was nothing to watch on TV.

There was nothing going on in cyberspace.

And she didn't even need to chase Clark around the dungeon.

She glanced at the clock. It wasn't even four yet. On a Thursday afternoon. Tomorrow was Zane's party. In about twenty-eight hours, she'd be at his house...as his date...doing...God only knew. A tiny jolt shot through her nerves.

She jumped to her feet and started pacing the floor. She was nervous as hell about tomorrow. There was no way she could sit around here, staring at the walls. She'd go nutty. She dug her cell phone out of her purse and called Sarah.

"What're you doing tonight?" she asked.

"I don't know. Why?"

"I'm bored."

"Hmmm. I was going to do a little shopping. You know, pick up a few things."

"Shopping! That sounds great." Mandy thought about the money she would be returning to Zane tomorrow. Would he miss a few twenties?

"I'll be there in ten."

"I'll be ready." Mandy clicked off, then dashed into the bathroom to touch up her makeup. She changed into something cute and sassy, knowing Sarah loved to window-shop at the high-end luxury mall across town for inspiration before hitting the resale shops. Exactly ten minutes later, Sarah called to let her know she was waiting out in the parking lot. Mandy, now sporting a cute skirt, heels, and a knit top that made her boobs look big and her waist tiny, *click-clacked* to her car and slid into the passenger seat.

"You look cute," Sarah said, giving her a once-over before shifting the car into gear.

"Thanks." Mandy noticed Sarah wasn't wearing her usual going-shopping look. "Didn't have time to change your clothes?"

"Didn't see any need for it. Not where we're heading."

"Where's that?"

Sarah's smile was devious. "You'll see."

Ten minutes later, Mandy saw.

They were in one of the seediest areas of town, not far from the peep show she'd followed Clark into. The buildings on the street, most of them concrete block, had probably been erected back in the sixties and seventies. All of them had seen better days. A few of them looked completely abandoned.

"You could've warned me," Mandy said as Sarah pulled her car into a weedy lot. She read the sign. "What is this place?"

"Sex-toy shop." Sarah tucked her purse under her arm. "It's still daylight. It's perfectly safe."

"Sure...maybe. But aren't there other sex-toy shops in better neighborhoods?"

"Of course there are. I've been to every single one of them. But this place has the best selection."

"Great." Mandy put on her tough PI game face, and together she and Sarah walked up to the door. A cowbell clanked overhead as they stepped inside. All it took was one sweeping glance to see that Sarah was right. This place had, it seemed, just about anything a girl could want. From fetish wear to toys to BDSM gear.

Sarah made a beeline for the BDSM stuff. Mandy, on the other hand, wandered into the toy section. Minutes later, she decided she needed to make a purchase.

10

"Girl, you look fierce!" Sarah, looking insanely hot herself, walked a little circle around Mandy. "Is that the dress?"

Mandy ran her shaking hands down the skirt. Her hair had never looked better. Her makeup was as perfect as she'd ever managed. She had primped and shaved and loofahed. She had never felt prettier. And, thanks to a certain surprise she had planned for Zane, she'd never felt sexier either. But, still, she was nervous as hell. "This is the one."

Sarah squealed. "Ohmygod, those shoes! You've got to let me borrow them sometime."

"Sure. It's not like I go out dressed like this every day."

"But since you're seeing Zane now, maybe you will."

Mandy's face must have turned ten shades of red. Maybe even twelve. "I'm not 'seeing' him."

"In my book, if a man buys you a present, he's serious."

"I can't comment yet. So far, the only time we've spent together has been at the dungeon. I don't consider that a 'serious' relationship at all. I consider a steady thing to be when you buy groceries together...puppies—serious."

"Fair enough." Sarah pulled open Mandy's door. "Ready to head out?"

Mandy took a long, deep breath. Her nerves were strung tight already. She hated to see how she'd feel by the time they got to Zane's house.

Clacking out of the building, her bondage gear packed in a chic Gucci tote—a gift from one of her subbies—Sarah said over her shoulder, "At least this time I won't have to worry about you getting kicked out."

"Yep, no need to sneak in a camera now. That case is done. Wrapped up. Thank God!"

"Did the soon-to-be-ex-Mrs.-Clark pick up the footage yet?" Sarah asked.

"No, she hasn't returned my call."

"That's strange." In the parking lot, Sarah stopped between her car and Mandy's. "Who's driving?"

"I'll drive this time." Mandy made herself comfy behind the wheel. "I thought it was weird, too. You'd think she'd be eager to get the footage to her lawyer and get the ball rolling. I'll try her again on Monday. Maybe she didn't get my message."

"Sure. That happens to me all the time."

Sarah kept Mandy's mind off what was about to happen with all her energetic jibber-jabbering. Before she realized it, they were at his house, rolling up to the entry. The parking valet, an extremely gorgeous man, opened the passenger-side door first. Sarah gave him a visible once-over as she stepped up to the porch. Mandy followed her. They exchanged grins.

"This is going to be one helluva night," Sarah said as they stepped into Zane's mansion.

Once again, Mandy found herself overwhelmed by the opulence of his house and the number of incredibly beautiful men found within. She'd never have guessed there were so many men who looked that good living in the area.

"My, oh my," Sarah said on a sigh. "This is like a chocoholic walking into a Hershey factory."

"Yeah." Mandy searched the thick crowd as they walked deeper into the house, her gaze skipping from one man to another. "Do you see Zane anywhere?" The place was packed wall to wall. How would she ever find him?

"Not yet. Knowing him, he'll be in the dungeon."

"Okay." Following Sarah, who was very adept at winding her way through crowds, Mandy kept searching. But, thanks to her petite size, which was in stark contrast to many of the party's guests, she was having a hard time. What she needed was to get up above the crowd somehow.

Sarah grabbed her hand, dragging her into the dungeon. "Sheesh, lost you for a second there. Stick with me."

"I'm trying." Mandy took a step forward. Something, or rather someone, grabbed her around the waist. Her hand slipped from Sarah's. A little startled, she twisted to look over her shoulder. A hand pinched her chin, stopping her from turning her head.

"There you are."

She knew that voice.

Her body knew that voice, too. And liked it.

"Yes," she said, very much aware of Zane's heat as he pulled her back against him. "Here I am." She thought about her surprise, and her body quivered in anticipation. Bodies, most of them male, were crowded around her, but she was focused on only one—his. The one she couldn't even see.

Using the arm circling her waist, he pulled her flush to him. The rigid thickness of his cock was pressed against her buttocks. She wondered how long he'd make her wait to touch it, to feel its silky-skinned length slide through her fingertips or past her lips.

He gently gathered her hair into his fist. His fingertips massaged her scalp, giving rise to pleasant tingles. "I've been waiting. You're late."

"Sorry. Sarah had to make a quick stop on the way."

Ever so slowly, he pulled on her hair, coaxing her head to one side. "Mmmmm," he said, his mouth barely touching her neck. Goose bumps sprang up all over the left side of her body. "Perhaps I should punish you."

She didn't know exactly what he had in mind this time. That made her both keenly aroused and slightly uncomfortable. She shifted her weight, resting most of it on one foot. "I did apologize. That counts for something, doesn't it?"

He chuckled. The sound vibrated through her whole system, making her nerve endings all twitchy. "Perhaps." He dragged his tongue down the column of her neck, and she quivered. "I can't get over how responsive you are. To my words. My touch. My . . . kiss." One of his hands slid down the front of her body. It stopped at her mound.

Her body proved exactly how responsive it could be. Her knees turned to gelatin and her bones melted. She leaned into his heat and let him support her. "Can we go somewhere private?"

"Are you sure you want to be alone with me tonight?" His teeth grazed her skin. "I can't guarantee I'll maintain control."

She could pretty much guarantee she wouldn't maintain control either. "I'm sure."

"This way, then." Gradually he released her, giving her time to steady herself. He took her hand in his. "To my suite. I think I may show you the whole space this time. I believe you'll like it."

There was something about the way he said those words that made her wonder exactly what secrets he kept hidden behind those doors. The lounge area had been nice, furnished with quality pieces and accessorized with tasteful art.

He walked her through the throng, stopping once in a while

to respond to a guest who greeted him. Without exception, every one of those people, male and female alike, gave her an appraising once-over when Zane introduced her. She wondered if she measured up to their expectations.

Once she was safely enclosed in his suite, she released a heavy sigh.

Smiling, Zane unfurled his fingers, letting her hand slip from his. "Are you nervous, Amanda?"

"I'm alone with a man I barely know. I'm in a setting that's new and strange to me. And I feel like everyone here is playing some kind of secret games. They know all the rules. I don't."

At the small bar positioned against the wall, Zane leveled his gaze to her. "You're very astute. I admire that about you." He lifted a glass decanter. "Wine?"

She wasn't sure if drinking alcohol was such a good idea. "No thank you. But I would appreciate a glass of water."

"Very good." He dropped a few cubes in two glasses, then opened a bottle of water and filled them. He handed one to Mandy, keeping the other for himself. "If you'd decided to drink tonight, that would have put a damper on my plans."

Mandy almost drained the glass. "What plans would those be?"

His eyes sparkled as he looked at her over the rim of his glass. After taking a drink, he lowered it. "You'll see. Soon."

"You are quite the tease, aren't you?"

"No. I don't tease. I intend to follow through with every single promise I make to you."

All the cells in her body appreciated that statement. She guzzled the rest of the water, then handed her glass to Zane. Her hand was shaking. "I need to talk to you about the retainer—"

"Take off your clothes, Amanda." Calmly, his every movement smooth and steady, he set the glasses down, then turned back to her.

So much for discussing business. So much for foreplay, too.

He was jumping right into things. She supposed she should be grateful he wasn't going to make her sit and struggle to make small talk when her tongue was tied in knots.

Feeling like her throat was coated with dust, she gulped. She fumbled with the back zipper of her dress, thinking how sad it was that she'd worn this beautiful dress for so little time.

"Let me help you." He eased her around with hands on her shoulders. Her spine tensed as he dragged the zipper down, down, down. A fingertip traced the same line, but from nape to the base of her spine, right above her ass. "You have the sexiest back I have ever seen."

"Thank you." She quivered.

The dress slowly slid down her body, softly caressing her as it made its journey to the floor. She didn't move, just stood there, trembling, her pussy already hot and wet.

"You smell delicious," Zane said, still standing behind her.

"Thank you. It's lavender. My favorite scent." She wanted to turn around or at least glance over her shoulder to see what he was doing. She could feel his gaze wandering over her form. It was like a laser, warming her skin. She didn't move, though. Something kept her there, frozen in position, while he stared at her.

"I'm not talking about the lotion. I'm talking about you." His hand cupped her ass, and a blade of heat sliced through her body. He was going to discover her surprise soon. Very, very soon. She had a feeling he was going to be pleased. "How wet are you for me?"

Her burning pussy clenched. Some of her juices trickled down the inside of her thigh. "Very."

"Show me."

She widened her stance and bent at the waist, bracing her hands on her knees to keep herself semisteady.

"Mmmmm." His fingers slipped between her ass cheeks. Down they traveled, toward her anus, stopping where the flared part of the butt plug remained outside her body. "What's this?"

"I thought you'd like it."

"I do. Very much." His fingers continued their journey, bypassing the butt plug to plunge into her pussy. "Yes, very, very much." He curled his fingers inside her, withdrew them to the fingernail, and then drove them back inside.

Mandy shuddered from head to toe.

"Come here, baby. You deserve a reward." Zane took her hand and led her across the room, to the door that led to what she had to assume was his actual bedroom. He opened it.

It was a bedroom, but nothing like any she'd ever seen.

For one thing, it was huge. In the center of the room was a raised platform, the bed. It was probably the size of two California-king mattresses laid side by side. The Goliath bed was piled with pillows and cushions and looked very comfortable, luxurious . . . inviting.

Various pieces of wood and leather bondage furniture lined the walls. Despite being built from common materials, the bondage furnishings were very different from any she'd ever seen. Each piece was adorned with intricate carvings—legs, supports, any vertical or horizontal piece that was visible.

"Sit here." As Zane positioned her on the bed, sitting and facing the door, Mandy saw the enormous armoire standing in the corner adjacent to the door. It, too, was heavily adorned with carvings. She couldn't make out exactly what the designs were from a distance, but it was beautiful nonetheless.

Zane gave her one lust-filled look, then strolled to the armoire. She got only a glimpse of his collection of equipment when he opened the door. He gathered a variety of wrapped items into his arms and brought them to her.

Some kind of metal stand.

A wrapped dildo.

Some lube.

Some leather cuffs.

"Up, on your knees." He unwrapped the dildo, then picked up the metal stand.

Mandy shifted into position, standing on her knees with her butt as high off the mattress as it would go.

"Legs apart."

She spread her legs slightly.

"Good."

Holding her position, she watched Zane attach the dildo to the metal stand. He set it on the bed in front of her. From the look of it, the very tip of the dildo would probably just touch her pussy if he set it under her.

"Straddle it."

So, she did have the right idea. Moving carefully, she positioned herself over the erect toy. Just as she'd thought, the very tip of the dildo barely grazed her swollen labia.

"Now it's time for your reward." Dropping to his knees before her, his legs straddling the frame as well, Zane pressed his hands to either side of her face and kissed her.

It was one hell of a kiss.

A kiss that made a million stars explode behind her closed eyelids.

A kiss that made her heart thump in her chest.

A kiss that made her blood burn through her body.

When he released her, he looked at her with dilated eyes and a flushed face. His lips were swollen from the kiss. The heated expression on his face could probably cause a weaker girl to combust. Mandy practically did.

"That was some reward," she said, her voice sounding as shaky as she felt.

"That was only the beginning. You've surprised me, Mandy. Nobody does that." He kissed her again, and she practically came when his tongue plunged into her mouth to taste and stroke and possess.

He kissed very much like he did everything else. With an intensity she found incredibly thrilling.

This time, when he broke the kiss, he reached between her legs. He plunged his fingers into her slick heat and dragged some of her juices forward, to her clit, before teasing it with light, quick strokes.

She threw her arms over his shoulders, using his body to steady herself, and closed her eyes. Her head fell back. Stars danced behind her closed eyelids. Her breathing quickened. Her heartbeat sped up. Her body temperature rose to a nearly fatal level.

Somehow, the toy raised up. The end of it slipped between her nether lips to remain inside her. But just barely.

Now, that was a tease. One of the worst she'd ever endured.

"You bastard," she mumbled, not expecting him to hear her.

"What's wrong, Amanda?" His tone was mocking. He knew exactly what was the matter.

She thought about lowering herself down and taking the entire toy's length inside. She knew, for a fact, that it would feel good. Very good. "This isn't a reward. It's pure hell."

"Patience, baby." He added some lube, increasing the pressure on her clit. Her pussy clenched but the damn toy wasn't in deep enough to give her any relief.

She slumped forward, boneless, and shook and trembled. He continued to torment her body with those deft fingers of his. Then, being beyond cruel, he started pinching her nipple, too, rolling it between his finger and thumb until it was so sensitive her jaw hurt from clenching it so hard.

This was so unfair. She'd come here tonight hoping he'd finally let himself become vulnerable, or at least take off his fucking clothes and let her suck his cock.

Burning up, she bit his neck and clawed at his shoulders and arms. The toy slipped deeper inside, penetrating her a few more inches. But once in place, it remained stationary, just like before.

She wanted a thick cock, yes. But a real one, pumping in and out of her. Attached to a real male body. This male body.

"Dammit, Zane. Why can't I just have you?" Clinging to him, she threw her head back and groaned as a powerful climax rocketed through her body. Her pussy spasmed around the dildo. Her ass clenched around the butt plug. She heaved and huffed and quaked, and in the midst of her release, Zane's arms enfolded her body, lifting it off the toy and cradling her against him.

"You will," he whispered into her hair as he stroked it. "You will have me. All of me. But not yet." He kissed her, then retrieved her dress. "We need to return to the guests. As much as we'd both like it, I can't let you keep me to yourself for the whole evening."

Feeling less than satisfied, Mandy dressed and, sliding her hand into his, followed Zane out into the hallway.

So much for his promise to make her fantasy come true. Evidently, tonight hadn't been the "sometime" he'd been thinking of.

"About the retainer," she began for the second time.

"Keep it." At the top of the steps, he waved down at a man who was looking up at them. "Consider it a gift."

"But, Zane—"

"Please." He eased down the steps, making sure she stayed close to his side.

11

"We have a problem."

Mandy had heard those words before. They were always the hallmark of disaster in her world. Particularly when they were spoken by a client. As was the case today.

Her mood plummeted.

"What's wrong?"

The soon-to-be-ex-Mrs.-Clark set the pictures on Mandy's desk, pointed a manicured fingertip at the woman in the photograph. "That's me."

"That's you?" *Shit.*

"Yes, you see, I'd been harping on Andy about our nonexistent love life for a long time. But he'd never made any effort to change things. It was quite a surprise when he left the key and the card last week, telling me to wear a disguise and meet him at the hotel." Mrs. Clark smiled. "That was one helluva afternoon."

I bet. "I guess these won't do us any good, then." Mandy shoved the pictures back into the envelope and handed them to Mrs. Clark for safekeeping. "So what's the story? Are you still going through with your plans to divorce him?"

"Absolutely! One fabulous afternoon does not a marriage make. He hasn't touched me since."

"Ooookay." Mandy was getting tired of this case. Very tired.

"Since it was sort of my fault for you wasting your time, I want to give you an extra bonus." Mrs. Clark pulled out her checkbook.

"That's not necessary."

"Yes, it is. I should've called you and let you know the blonde was me. You probably wasted at least an hour."

More like three.

"I hope this is adequate compensation for your time." She handed over the check.

Mandy glanced at the amount. Five hundred dollars. "Thank you."

"You're welcome." Flipping to a new check, she started writing again. "You haven't billed me for your hours. But I'd like to get all paid up. How much do I owe you?"

"Let me take a look..." Mandy checked the Clark log. She'd clocked over thirty hours in the last month. If she didn't know for a fact that Mrs. Clark couldn't care less how much she paid, she'd feel more than a little guilty for asking for so much money without having produced any results whatsoever. "This month, I clocked thirty-three hours."

Mrs. Clark didn't blink an eye. "You've been working hard. I appreciate it." She signed the check and handed it to Mandy. "The amount is correct, right?"

Nine hundred ninety dollars. "Yes, that's correct." Mandy stared at the check for a moment. Guilt was getting the better of her. "Look, Mrs. Clark—"

"I understand Andrew is being very cautious, and that's causing some difficulty." Mrs. Clark pulled out her checkbook again. "How much can I pay you to stay on the case?"

"It's not about the money. I feel bad enough about what

you've paid me already. I have never billed a client for so many hours. Your husband is being extraordinarily cautious. I haven't been able to get a photograph of him yet, and I've seen him in some extremely...delicate situations." She took a deep breath. "The bottom line is, I may not be able to get the proof you need." Mrs. Clark slumped into the chair, looking boneless. Her head dropped. She didn't speak for a few agonizing seconds. "I am sorry. I've done everything I could to help you. But, from the looks of things, I'm beginning to believe your husband isn't being unfaithful. At least not technically."

"What does that mean?" she asked, raising pain-filled eyes to Mandy's.

"It means...your husband is involved in some unusual activities, involving bondage and D/s, strippers and peep shows. But from what I've witnessed during those activities, he's refraining from any sexual contact."

"Great," she mumbled on a sigh. "Lucky me, I'm stuck with the jerk if I can't get him on infidelity." She turned pleading eyes toward Mandy. "Do you have any idea how horrible it is to live in a lonely, loveless marriage?"

Mandy would never have guessed the Clark marriage was loveless after witnessing that very heated exchange last week. "No, I don't. But I can guess."

"You couldn't possibly know." Mrs. Clark chewed on her lower lip. Her eyes reddened. Oh, damn. She was going to cry. Mandy never knew what to do when somebody cried in front of her. "I'm so fucking lonely...." She snuffled. She dripped. She smudged her eye makeup all over her face. "I just want somebody to love me. Is that such a bad thing?"

"Of course, it isn't." Mandy sat there, feeling awkward and not knowing what to say.

Mrs. Clark sat there shaking and sniffling, waiting for her to say something.

"I'll keep trying."

Mrs. Clark's waterworks dried up. "You will?" She blinked a few times. A fat tear dribbled down her cheek.

"Yes."

"I'll pay whatever you say. Money's no object." Mrs. Clark pulled out her checkbook again. "How about I give you another retainer? Let's say, another thousand? That should cover you for a while." She began scribbling furiously.

"No, please."

"I insist." She ripped the check out of the book and tried to hand it to Mandy.

"If I need that many hours—"

"Dammit, take the fucking money!" Mrs. Clark screeched. Her eyes were bugged so far out of her head, she looked like a pug.

Stunned by Mrs. Clark's outburst, Mandy snatched the check out of her hand.

Mrs. Clark's expression instantly changed back to mournful wife. She stood. "Thank you for your time, Miss Thompson. We'll be in touch soon, I hope."

"Yes." Still reeling from Mrs. Clark's bizarre behavior, Mandy watched her client saunter out of her office.

Two minutes later, Sarah raced in and flung herself into the chair opposite Mandy's desk. "Spill."

"I tried to do the right thing." Mandy gathered Mrs. Clark's checks into a tidy stack.

"Right thing? What the hell are you talking about?"

"I'm talking about Mrs. Clark. Isn't that what you're asking me about?"

"No." Sarah leaned forward. "But now that you're on the subject, I'd like to hear about her, too. Did I hear her actually scream at you?"

"Yes."

"Why?"

"Because I was trying to drop her case."

"*Why?*"

"Because I don't believe her husband is being unfaithful, as is defined in her prenup, and I don't feel it's right milking her for more money."

"Uhn. I see your dilemma."

"Yeah."

"So, what are you going to do?"

"I don't know. I accepted her check, but only because I was a little afraid of what she might do if I didn't."

"Gotcha. Maybe you could just tear it up and not cash it? Then you wouldn't feel obligated to her for anything."

"But what if she calls me next week for an update? Then what?"

"Then you lie."

"I can't do that. She'll believe I'm still working the case. It would give her false hope."

"You really believe he's not cheating on her?"

"Not technically."

"What about when he went to the motel with that stripper?"

"We *think* he went to a motel. We don't actually know he did."

"True, that. But what about the peep show? You know he went to one of those. And didn't you say he wasn't alone?"

"Again, I have no proof he did anything but watch."

"Really. Are you that gullible?"

Mandy wanted to tell Sarah about what had happened with him at the dungeon; she really did. But she just couldn't seem to force the words out. Instead, she mumbled, "I guess I'll keep working the case. I just won't waste a lot of time on it so that I don't have to bill her for any more hours."

"There you go. Problem solved." Sarah flung one knee over the other. "Now, tell me what happened at Zane's party."

Mandy's face sizzled.

"Oooh, girl! It was that good? I have got to hear this. And

don't you dare leave anything out. Not one measly detail. I have been waiting since Friday. Do you know how hard it was to be so patient?"

"I'm sure it was difficult."

"You have no idea."

That was the second time somebody had said that to her today.

Zane tried to shove the image of Amanda from his mind as he opened the door.

A familiar face greeted him. Lips curled up into a ghost of a smile. A flicker of need shone in dark eyes. "It's been a long time," Zane's guest said, stepping inside. "Too long."

"Are you complaining?" Still haunted by the memory of this past Friday night, those few moments he'd shared with Amanda, Zane pulled his guest to him. He curled his fingers into deep brown-black waves, pulling to force his visitor's head to one side.

"No. Never." Bruce shivered as Zane's teeth grazed down the column of his neck.

Zane inhaled deeply, drawing the scent of man and need and hunger deep into his lungs. This man needed him. More than anyone ever had. He knew that. And, for the first time, he felt guilty. It was, after all, his fault. Maybe he had made a mistake all those years ago, choosing one person to see to his most basic need.

Unfortunately, there was no going back to change things now.

In his defense, how could he have foreseen this?

A woman had bewitched him. *A woman.*

If anyone had suggested that could happen, even a few months ago, he would have laughed. When it came to submissives, gender didn't matter. He enjoyed dominating both. But when it came to lovers, he had always preferred men. That preference had been so strong, he'd never contemplated the possibility of one day falling in love with a woman.

Okay, first off, he wasn't in love. He wasn't so soft that he'd fall in love after such a short time.

But he was mesmerized. Intrigued. Bewitched. It irritated him how she'd sauntered into his mind and refused to leave. Thoughts of her haunted him. During the day. At night. In his dreams.

Zane's tongue darted out, stealing his first taste of Bruce's skin. As always, the flavor sent waves of anticipation rippling through Zane's body. He would feed soon, quenching the hunger that could never be fully satisfied.

Zane released his visitor, leading him deeper into the house. Up the stairs. To his suite, where they could be comfortable. "Drink?" He went to the stocked bar.

"Thanks."

Zane dropped a few ice cubes into a rock glass and poured some bourbon over them. He turned, handing the glass to his guest. Their gazes tangled. Bruce's fingertips grazed his as he accepted the glass.

"Thank you," Bruce said. He took a swallow. His tongue swept across his lower lip as he lowered the glass. "What's wrong?"

"Nothing." Zane poured himself a drink, even though it wouldn't ease his thirst, nor would the alcohol have any effect on his mood.

Bruce took another drink, then set down the glass. Saying nothing, he tugged his button-down shirt out of the waistband of his pants.

Zane drained his glass as his guest slowly unbuttoned his shirt, revealing a gradually widening vee of tanned, smooth skin stretched over taut muscle.

Bruce was as gorgeous, as flawless, as the first day Zane had met him all those years ago. And yet...

Damn Amanda for doing this to him. To them.

Zane refilled his glass. He tossed his head back, gulping the bourbon. How he wished it would do more than burn his damn throat.

Now shirtless, his guest approached him. He slanted his brows at Zane as he took the glass from Zane's hand. "I've never seen you like this."

"I said it's nothing. I'm fine." Driven by frustration, Zane captured Bruce's face between his hands and kissed him. Their tongues stroked and battled. His lover's hands grasped at Zane's clothes, tugging, pulling, tearing. Zane released his lover's face to torment his flat nipples with his fingertips, pinching, tugging.

Bruce's groan filled their joined mouths.

Zane broke the kiss. Their gazes met again.

His lover's lips, now swollen from their kiss, parted slightly. His chest rose and fell swiftly. His dark eyes smoldered with hard male need. "How much longer will you make me wait, dammit?"

Zane knew what he had to do.

"You know how I love to make you suffer?" He led Bruce out of his suite, unable for some reason to share his bed with him today. He took him to the guest room. His lover asked no questions.

"Undress. I want to see you."

"I've been aching to hear those words."

Zane swallowed hard. He rubbed his cock through his clothes as Bruce stripped off his shoes, socks, pants, and finally his boxer-briefs. His gaze swept up and down his lover's body, taking in all the glory of its perfection, from the broad shoulders to the nipped waist to the well-defined abs and thick, muscular thighs. Finally, it landed upon his lover's erect cock, its ruddy head already glistening with precum.

Was there any way to release this man? Zane needed to find out.

"Undress me." Knowing how much his lover enjoyed peeling away one garment at a time, Zane worked with him, moving to aid his ministrations. Bruce kissed and licked his neck, shoulders, chest, stomach, legs, and, finally, cock as they were revealed. Finally, they stood facing each other, unclothed.

"Please, you bastard." Bruce lowered himself to his knees, dragging his fingernails down Zane's unclothed body. He fisted Zane's cock and twirled his tongue round and round the swollen head until a droplet of precum finally escaped. Groaning, he opened his mouth wider, relaxing his throat to take Zane's cock to the base.

Zane fisted Bruce's hair, holding his head still so he could glide in and out of his mouth. His lover's groan of need vibrated through Zane's body, igniting the first spark of desire he'd felt since Amanda had left Friday night.

Encouraged by the heat that was finally simmering in his blood, Zane fucked Bruce's mouth harder, enjoying the way his tongue flicked along the underside when he was almost completely withdrawn. His body tightened with each in-stroke. His heartbeat quickened with each out-stroke. Until, at last, he was warm and hard and tasting his need on his lips.

Abruptly, he pulled out of Bruce's mouth. Bruce turned tormented eyes up at him.

"There. The bed."

Bruce stood, but instead of going to the bed as commanded, he pulled Zane into a desperate kiss. Surprised by his lover's aggressive move, Zane tasted himself on Bruce's lips. He fought for control as Bruce's tongue battled with his. Hands cupped Zane's balls, fondling them, squeezing them just hard enough to spike his temperature higher. Zane returned the favor, adding a moistened finger to Bruce's tight hole, preparing him for what would come next.

His lover forced him back until Zane was pinned between his hard, hot body and the wall. He was no submissive. But damn did that feel good. He rocked his hips back and forth, grinding his pelvis into Bruce's. His cock flattened against his body as he moved; the friction as it scuffed up and down against Bruce's hip made that spark flare brighter.

Zane broke the kiss and shoved Bruce back. They wrestled, battling for control. This time, Bruce found himself pinned against the wall. Zane forced his knee between Bruce's legs. And while his tongue plunged into the sweet, smoky depth of Bruce's mouth, Zane's foot kicked his lover's feet wider apart.

"I've never seen you like this, either," Zane said into their joined mouths.

"I can only take so much, you asshole."

Zane chuckled as he nipped Bruce's earlobe. He traced the whorl of his ear. "Maybe I need to make you wait like this more often."

"Fuck you." Bruce shoved him, hard, then charged him, lunging forward to tackle him to the floor. Down they went, rolling around on the pristine white carpet, wrestling like a couple of assholes who'd had too much to drink. Bruce almost had him pinned, but Zane flipped him over and nailed him to the floor. Sitting on Bruce's stomach, legs straddling his broad body, Zane took a moment to let them both catch their breath.

Bruce, being mortal, needed more time. He took advantage of that fact by angling down to torment a nipple with his tongue and teeth. "Yes, I like this very much," Zane said before pulling the hard little tip into his mouth. He suckled, drawing on the tight bud until Bruce arched his back and begged for him to stop. Then, because he wished to torture him a little longer, Zane used his teeth, biting ever so gently.

"Goddamn it."

"What's wrong?"

"You know what's wrong." Bruce grappled with Zane, trying to throw him off. But this time, Zane maintained control. "What's it going to take to get you to fuck me?"

"I don't know yet."

"Let me know when you do."

Zane closed his fist around Bruce's cock and gave it a slow pump.

Bruce groaned. His eyelids fell shut, shielding his dark, shadowed eyes from Zane. "Ohhh, yesss," he hissed. "Please, fuck me. Do it now." When Zane gave his cock another few strokes, he growled, "Goddamn it, now. Begging, dammit."

Zane angled off his desperate lover to get some lube out of the nightstand. Meanwhile, Bruce flipped over, lifting himself onto all fours. Returning to him, Zane grasped Bruce's hips, and after smoothing some lube over the man's puckered anus, guided his cock to the opening with his hand. The muscles beneath Bruce's skin rippled and flexed as he tightened in anticipation of the pleasure that was to come.

Zane wasn't feeling much in the way of anticipation, even with the man who'd once been able to make him come with barely a heated look. If it weren't for the fact that he needed Zane, both as lover and as more, he would have ended this thing and walked away for good.

But, as it turned out, he couldn't.

Clenching his jaw, Zane closed his eyes and concentrated on Bruce's pleasure. He breached him roughly, just the way Bruce liked it. He pumped in and out slowly, withdrawing almost completely before thrusting deep inside. Bruce trembled as every stroke brought him closer to orgasm. His skin warmed under Zane's hands, the heat a welcome relief to the chill that permeated his being.

"Yes, like that. Oh, yes," Bruce mumbled.

Zane raked his fingers down his lover's back, leaving red stripes from the swell of his well-formed shoulders to the base of his rounded ass. Zane struck Bruce's ass with his flattened hand, and Bruce's spine arched, changing the angle of Zane's penetration.

Oh, hell yes. Zane's body reacted at last. A charge of blinding hunger buzzed through his system. His fangs extended.

Succumbing to the hunger, Zane drove into Bruce harder, faster. Bruce rocked back and forth on hands and knees, meeting his every thrust. "That's it. You want it. Beg me."

"Please, harder. Please," Bruce hissed.

Spurred by the plea, Zane fucked him with everything he had. With every thrust, his body grew hotter, his need spiking. "Stroke your cock," he demanded.

Bruce did as he was told. His anus clamped tightly around Zane's cock, ratcheting up Zane's need to greater heights. Blind now, and swept into a thrashing current of feral hunger and need, Zane took one final thrust, seating his cock deep inside his lover's body. He caught Bruce's hair in his fist, pulling him upright. Bruce shuddered, his cum spurting from his erect cock. He extended his neck, and Zane sank his fangs in. With his cum surging from his body, Zane pulled in the first gulp of blood. His mouth filled with the salty-sweet flavor.

Bruce screamed as a second orgasm enveloped him, brought on by Zane's potent venom. Zane stroked his cock in and out, drawing out Bruce's pleasure, as he drank his fill.

Sated at last, he licked the wound clean of all blood. He withdrew his cock, taking Bruce into his arms.

Bruce cupped his cheek and smiled into his eyes. "You've made me wait so long."

Holding the man he had come to cherish but not love, Zane pressed a gentle kiss to his forehead. "I promise, I won't do that again. No matter what."

"Thank you."

Once again, the image of Amanda played through his mind.

He didn't owe her any explanations. Not yet.

So why did he feel so guilty?

12

Name: Larry Nickerson
Age: sixty-three
Height: six feet
Hair: salt and pepper
Eyes: steel gray
Tattoos: none

Mandy studied the photograph of her newest client's husband as his wife spat, "He bought her a Jaguar. A *Jaguar!* I've been driving the same Chevy for ten years. The son of a bitch has to pay. My gosh, the girl is barely out of high school."

Ah, yes, yet another sixtysomething man chasing twenty-something girls. It was no wonder Mandy had a very jaded view of marriage.

"I'm assuming he is seeing one girl in particular?" Mandy asked the fuming wife.

Her client ran her hand over her silver hair, smoothed back from her face and knotted into a tidy bun. "Yes. Her name is Brittany."

"Do you have any information about this Brittany?"

"She works for him. Not directly below him, but for his company."

How convenient. Mandy scribbled some notes. "Have you seen her? Can you describe her?"

The wife's lips thinned. "No. God help the little tramp if I do ever meet her face-to-face. I swear, I'll tear her hair out, every last strand."

Mandy flipped to a fresh piece of paper in her notebook. "Please, don't do that. Things get a lot more complicated when a client goes to jail. I know this for a fact."

The woman's shoulders slumped. "I would never do such a thing. The fact is, I'm not that type. I'm faithful. Trusting. Trustworthy. And…" She blinked. Her eyes reddened. She clapped her hands over her face. "I'm just so shocked and angry," she said between sobs. "How could he? After thirty-five years."

Always prepared for the possibility of grown women crying in her office, Mandy grabbed the box of tissues from her desk drawer and set it in front of Mrs. Nickerson. She said nothing until her client had collected herself.

Finally, as the woman dabbed her swollen eyes, Mandy promised, "I will do my very best to get the proof you need to win your court case. What you do with that proof is up to you."

"Thank you." Mrs. Nickerson placed a personal check, made out to Mandy, on the desk and stood. Looking like her world had crashed down around her shoulders, she gave Mandy an empty smile. "I'm guessing you see a lot of this kind of thing, huh?"

"More than I wish." When Mrs. Nickerson extended a hand, Mandy accepted it, giving it a shake. "I'll be in touch as soon as I have something." She watched her newest client shuffle from her office.

Another marriage destroyed.

A family decimated.

All because of lust.

Her cell phone rang. She checked.

Speaking of lust...

She hit the receive button, answering the call. Her heart did a little jump in her chest. "Hello?"

"I made reservations for tonight," Zane said. His voice was a low, sexy rumble. It made her feel warm all over.

"Oh."

He'd never said anything about seeing her again, after that incredible night at the party. Tomorrow, it would be a week to the day. She'd begun to think she wasn't going to hear from him again. She looked down at her notebook.

She *should* work.

What are you thinking? This is a no-brainer.

"Amanda," he said.

"Where?" she asked.

"The Fox and Hound."

That was one of the most exclusive restaurants in the entire tricounty area. She'd heard plenty about it but never been there. "What time?" she asked, glancing at her clock. She'd need to go home, change her clothes. She combed her fingers through her hair. Do something with her hair...

"Six. I'll pick you up at five-thirty."

She glanced at the clock. Three-thirty. "Okay. Do you need my address?"

"No. I have it."

"Yes, of course you do." She wasn't sure how she felt about that. She had gone to great lengths to make sure she wasn't listed in any directory. And she periodically checked to make sure she hadn't been added, particularly to the ones that were easily accessed by the general public. But he had sent her that package....

Sarah bounced into her office like she did at least a dozen times a day and made herself comfortable in the chair in front of Mandy's desk.

"Okay. I'll see you at five-thirty," Mandy said into the phone.

Sarah gave her a who's-that look.

"Good," Zane said.

"Good-bye," Mandy said. The line went dead. She stared at her phone's screen. "I guess he isn't much of a talker on the phone."

"He who?" Sarah asked. "Is it Zane?"

Mandy's face flushed. "Yes, it's Zane."

Sarah's eyes widened. "What did he want?"

"He asked me out to dinner." Feeling a little haughty, Mandy added, "He's taking me to Fox and Hound."

"No kidding? I've never been there." Sarah squinted at her. "It's official. I'm jealous."

"Don't be. Please. Outside of dinner—"

"Shut the hell up. Of course there's reason to be jealous. The man is clearly interested in you. *Seriously* interested. He's playing every card in his hand. First the gifts, now the fancy dinners. What's next? A—"

"Don't say it," Mandy interrupted. "I don't know where this thing is going. Frankly, because I hadn't heard from him since the party, I was beginning to think he'd grown tired of me."

"I'm guessing it's the opposite." Sarah jumped to her feet. "I'm guessing he's so overcome with desire for you that he's making himself stay away. He's intentionally trying to play it cool. I don't think he's used to feeling the way he does about you."

"How could you have any idea what he's feeling?"

Sarah shrugged. "It's just a guess."

"Based on...?"

"Intuition?"

Mandy shook her head. "You and I both know what kind of trouble your intuition gets you into." Mandy copied a few notes from her notebook onto a fresh sheet of paper. "Here, I've got something to keep you out of trouble for a little while. Can you hack into this company's computer system and access their personnel files? I need to find out who this Brittany is."

"Okay. Piece of cake." Sarah folded the paper, watching Mandy as she gathered her purse and car keys. "Where are you headed?"

Mandy hit the power button on her computer. "I'm leaving early. I need to run over to the mall and pick up something to wear. And I'd like to have some time to do my hair, maybe put on a little makeup."

"My God, they must be ice-skating in hell today. Just joking. You go get him, girl." At Mandy's office door, Sarah gave her an elbow in the rib cage. "Zane Griffin is so freaking hot. I don't know how you'll sit through dinner without ripping his clothes off."

Mandy couldn't help laughing. "Hopefully I'll manage okay. Would hate to be thrown out of the restaurant."

"Yeah. That would be a shame. You've got to at least get through the main course before that happens. Though I've heard the desserts are to die for." Out in the reception area, Sarah plopped into her chair. Her fingers began flying over the keyboard. "Brittany...," she mumbled. "Let's see what we can dig up on you."

Mandy headed out into a warm, sunny afternoon, feeling jittery and excited. She hopped into her car and motored to the closest mall. Inside, she made a beeline for the store she assumed would carry the classiest, highest quality evening wear within her limited budget. She found a black cocktail dress, knee length, that fit her perfectly. The best part about it—the price.

After paying for her purchase, she sped home (going no more than five miles an hour over the limit) to get ready. She showered, shaved, plucked, dried, curled, and spritzed herself to perfection. A knock sounded at her door as she was applying the final coat of lip gloss to her lips.

She gave herself one last up-and-down look before high-heeling it to the door to let Zane in.

His eyes widened when she opened the door. "Hello," he said, those wide eyes twinkling.

She waved him in. "I just need to grab my purse, and I'll be ready to go." After giving him a smile, she turned to snatch her purse off the sofa table. She didn't quite make it, though. A thick arm wrapped around her waist, and she was hauled backward, into Zane's embrace. He cupped her chin with his hand and lifted it until her head was tipped back. He kissed her forehead, the top of her head, her eyelids.

"Mmmm. I wish I'd made our reservation for later."

Her stomach rumbled. If he decided to forgo dinner for some alone time, she was going to collapse from low blood sugar. She wriggled a little, not sure if he'd let her go. "We'd better get going."

He audibly exhaled. "Yes, we'd better." As she turned to get her purse, this time expecting to reach it, he ran his hand down over her buttocks. "Are you wearing panties?"

"I am." Straightening upright, her clutch purse tucked under her arm, she turned to face him.

His sparkly eyes turned dark. "Take them off." His expression and the way he said those words made her feel all warm and tingly inside.

She reached under her skirt, tugged the barely-there scrap of black lace down her legs, and kicked it off. A draft caressed her pussy. Her inner muscles clenched. Suddenly, as he opened the door for her, she was aware of how floaty and loose her dress's skirt was. It almost felt like she was nude from the waist down.

With one hand pressed against her thigh to hold her skirt down, thinking a small draft might kick it up and give her neighbors a show, she followed Zane out to his car.

He was driving a black car. A sleek, low-to-the-ground model. Supersexy. She glanced at the hood.

Was it a...Lamborghini?

It is. Holy smokes, she was riding in a car that cost more than the average house.

The engine purred with a low rumble. Much like its owner.

Snug in the passenger seat, Mandy ran her hand over the supple leather seat. "This car is something else."

"Thank you. It was one of my few impulse buys."

"Well, I'm guessing if I had the money, I wouldn't be able to resist the urge to buy one of these either."

As Zane maneuvered the car down the street, it felt like it was floating on air. Made her little car feel like a bumpy, jerky carnival car.

Zane said nothing else as they drove to the restaurant. He did, however, slip his hand under her skirt, leaving it to rest on her bare thigh. The entire time, she could think of nothing but the miniscule movements of his fingertips as they lightly grazed her skin. He didn't remove it until they'd pulled up to the front of the restaurant.

A young, eager-faced valet hurried out to the car as Zane pushed open the door. He circled around the front to open her door and offer a hand as she stood. The car rolled away. They strolled up the walk to the entry.

The hostess greeted Zane by name when they entered the dimly lit, atmospheric lobby area. They were immediately escorted to a semisecluded table in a quiet corner.

Zane pulled her chair out for her. She sat, thanking him as he pushed it in for her. Then he took his own seat and turned his full attention on her. He stared. His tongue swept across his lower lip. His eyes glittered with what she read as sensual hunger.

"This is a very nice place." Feeling a little uneasy, Mandy sipped some ice-cold water from the full glass that had been poured before they'd arrived. "Have you been here before?"

"I have. You?"

"Never."

"Then you're in for a treat."

Looking at the wicked expression spreading over his face, Mandy wasn't sure if he meant the food or something else.

Their waiter rushed up before she'd had the chance to figure it out. He set a plate of hors d'oeuvres in the center of the table, then placed a clean plate in front of each of them. "Wine?" he asked.

"Please," Zane responded.

"Very well, sir."

"And we'll both take the usual," Zane added.

Nobody had ever ordered for Mandy before. She wasn't sure how she felt about it.

"Yes, sir." The waiter hurried away to place their orders and get the wine.

Zane's attention shifted back to Mandy. She realized, belatedly, that they hadn't been given any menus. He slid his hand across the table, flicking his eyes down, as if to tell her he wished her to place her hand on or under his. When she reached, he lifted his so his palm faced her. She pressed her hand to his, and they wove their fingers together. His lips curled into a small smile.

"What's 'the usual'?" she asked, staring at their joined hands.

"You'll see." He pointed at her plate, and she handed it to him. He placed a few pieces of food on it and handed it back. Then he helped himself.

"You aren't the most talkative man I've ever met," she said, waiting for him to pick up his fork.

Something glimmered in his eyes. "Does that bother you?" He nodded to her plate. "Please. Eat."

She took a taste of something salty, garlicky. It was delicious. "Maybe it makes me feel a little uncomfortable."

"Why?"

"I don't know. I guess I feel compelled to fill the silence."

"There's no need for that. Silence can be very pleasant." As if to illustrate, he stood, walked around the table to stop directly behind her. He rested his hands on her shoulders and began working the knots out of her muscles. She hadn't even realized she was so tight until he'd started rubbing.

She let her head slump forward and relished the pampering he was giving her for a few moments, until their waiter shuffled up, a bottle of wine and a pair of glasses in his hands. The waiter showed Zane the bottle, waiting for his nod before opening and pouring. He handed the first glass to Zane and let him taste before pouring a glass for Mandy. Then he disappeared again.

"Such service." She sipped the white wine. Crisp. Sweet. Delicious.

"Yes. That's one of the reasons why I like to come here. I'm never disappointed." After taking a drink, he lifted his glass. "What do you think?"

"It's very good. The perfect complement to the appetizer."

"I agree." He took a few swallows.

She didn't point out the fact that he hadn't yet taken a bite of the appetizers. After eating a few more bites, Mandy asked, "What do you do for a living?"

"I handle a few investments for some close friends. And I own some property."

Translation: he didn't work.

She was so out of her league here. She was a working girl, like just about everyone she knew. Zane was...insanely wealthy and probably hadn't worked a day in his life. With those differences in mind, it was no wonder they had a hard time finding something to talk about.

Where could this thing between them possibly go? They lived in two different worlds. Her heart sank a little.

"I see." After swallowing some more wine, she added, "You already know what I do."

"Yes, I do."

She finished her appetizer in silence. Zane ate very little, if anything. The main course was brought just as Mandy was swallowing the last bite. She stared at the plate as the waiter set it before her. It looked like a lamb chop with some green beans and red potatoes. "Looks delicious. Thank you."

The waiter swapped out the white wine for a red dinner wine.

Salivating, Mandy cut a piece of the butter-soft meat and delivered it to her mouth. It practically melted on her tongue. "Oh, this is heavenly." Shoving aside her concerns about their differences, she enjoyed the meal. There was no sense in letting all this wonderful food go to waste.

Zane set his fork and knife down. "Something is bothering you."

"No," she lied. Of course, he was right; something was bothering her. But how could she explain it? How could she make him understand? After all, she didn't have any idea where he thought this thing between them was going—outside of the dungeon. It seemed he'd be content to continue to explore that part of their relationship. And their differences in lifestyle wouldn't get in the way once they were in the dungeon.

The waiter returned with dessert, took their plates, and hurried away.

She gave herself license to devour the decadent chocolate

confection. It was sinful. By the time she'd taken the last bite, she was feeling a little better about things.

And a little bolder.

"Why did you invite me out to dinner tonight?" she asked.

Zane didn't answer right away. He looked at her, nibbling on his lower lip for several agonizing moments. "I wanted to spend time with you."

"Why? It's pretty clear to me you don't care to talk. When you take a woman out to dinner, you kind of have to talk."

"Hmmmm." He nodded.

That was it? Hmmmm? "Is this how you are every time you take a woman out?"

"I don't take women 'out.'"

"What are you saying?"

"I'm saying I don't take women out."

"You don't date? You just play in dungeons?"

"Yes."

"Why?"

He shrugged. "That's all I've ever wanted from women."

"Okay. But what about the women? Didn't any of them ever want more from you?"

He shrugged again. "No one has complained."

"I feel sorry for you."

Instantly, his expression changed. His eyes became cold. "Don't."

"Shoot. I didn't mean to insult you. That was the wrong thing to say. What I meant to say is I feel a little sad for you, that you haven't experienced true intimacy with anyone."

"I didn't say that."

"Then you have been intimate with someone?"

"Yes." He stood, walked around the table, and pulled her chair out.

More than a little aware of his nearness, Mandy stood. She turned to look at him. "I'm sorry—"

He placed his index finger on her lips, cutting off her apology. "It takes me a long time to open up. I hope you'll be patient." He kissed her, gently, his lips brushing back and forth across her mouth until she was a little dizzy.

"I'll try."

"Thank you." He took her hand and led her out into what had become a cool, still night. The air smelled fragrant, of warm concrete and freshly mown grass. Mandy gathered her bearings as she waited at Zane's side for his car. A true gentleman, he opened her door for her, closed it, and then went around to his seat.

Off they roared, into the night.

13

Twenty minutes later, they were parked in Mandy's apartment lot. Zane's Lamborghini rumbled like a sleeping bear. He cut off the engine but stared straight ahead.

Something was wrong. Not forgive-me-and-be-patient wrong. Much wronger than that.

Oh, shit.

Mandy twisted the handle of her purse, wrapping it around her wrist. "Um, thanks for the dinner. It was very nice."

"You're welcome." His voice was stiff. His expression was stiff, too. He finally looked at her. He opened his mouth as if to say something. No words came out.

Was he so out of his element that he really didn't know what to say? How to act? Or was he trying to say something he knew she wouldn't want to hear?

She blurted, "Would you—"

At the same time, he said, "I think—" He motioned to her. "Go ahead."

Instantly, she second-guessed what she had been about to say. "I'd rather you go first."

"Very well." He gnawed on his lip. It was such a nice lip. She could think of much better things to do to it. She wondered if she'd be given the chance. "I think I made a mistake tonight."

"What mistake?"

He jammed his fingers through his hair. "Shit, this is so complicated."

"It is?" Mandy had some notion where this was heading. The truth was, she'd had some notion from the moment they'd stepped into the restaurant. Zane had been so different tonight, nothing like himself.

"I like...I was hoping. But there's no way..." He sighed yet again. "I think it would be best if we stopped..."

She finished for him. "If we didn't see each other anymore?"

"Yes, that."

Damn. Her heart felt a little yucky. It was a blow, but not such a horrible one she wouldn't recover. "Okay." She opened her purse, took the envelope full of money he'd given her—minus a few twenties—and set it on the dashboard. "In that case, I insist on giving this back."

"No." He tried to force her to take it. "Please."

"Absolutely not." She made it impossible for him to force it on her, closing her purse and tucking her hands under her legs. He set the envelope on her lap, but she quickly shoved it into the glove box and yanked open the passenger side door. She scrambled out, ducking down so she could see him. "I don't know why you insist on giving me money—guilt, maybe?—but there's no way in hell I'll take it." His expression was unreadable. "Thank you anyway. For the thought. The dinner. Everything." Turning, she slammed the door.

Giving herself a pat on the back for handling that situation with grace, she hiked up her chin and walked into her apartment.

She made it inside before the first tear fell.

Damn you for falling for yet another man who's afraid of intimacy.

* * *

Feeling like she needed to earn the retainer Andrew Clark's desperate wife had paid, not to mention, desperate for any distraction that would keep her from thinking about that not-so-great date with Zane, Mandy decided to stake out the Clark residence.

She'd heard nothing from Zane since that night. Not a word. And although she supposed she should be glad for that small measure of kindness, she wasn't. She found herself jumping every time her phone rang, hoping it was him.

Four days had passed now. Four long, dull days. Empty, blah days.

How could she possibly miss him so much? She barely knew the guy.

Afraid she might go nuts sitting in a car for hours by herself tonight, she dragged Sarah along as her backup.

Some backup.

"How much longer do we have to sit here?" Sarah asked for the third time.

"We've only been at it for a half hour."

"Are you sure about that? It seems like it's been a lot longer than that. At least three hours. Maybe four."

Mandy pointed at the clock. "See? It's only ten. We got here at nine twenty-eight."

"I think your clock is broken." Sarah shoved her hand into her purse. "I'll check my phone." A second later, she grumbled, "Damn."

"I thought you wanted to be a PI."

"I thought I wanted to, too. I'm starting to think it isn't all glamorous and exciting, like what you see on TV and in the movies."

"I told you that."

"I thought you were lying."

"Why would I lie?"

"To discourage me so I wouldn't quit being your reception-ist."

"I'm not that selfish."

"Uhn." Sarah grimaced. "I think I'm hungry. Do you have any snacks in the trunk?"

"No."

"Why not? If I were a PI, and I had to sit in my car staring at someone's house night after night, I'd keep a well-stocked trunk. I'd have plenty of Doritos. Those are my favorite. And some cheese balls. And, of course, chocolate."

"Chocolate melts in the summer."

"Not a problem. I'd have a cooler back there, too. You know, for drinks. I could sure use a nice cold diet cola right now."

"If you drink, you have to pee. That's a bad thing when you're on a stakeout."

"Ah, I didn't think of that. Good point."

Mandy swallowed a chuckle. Sarah's ramblings sure beat sit-ting there alone. But she did wonder how long it would be be-fore Sarah bailed on her. It was going to happen. The only question was when.

Sarah started punching buttons on her nifty Android phone. The thing had more bells and whistles than a cruise liner. "Holy shit. I've got no coverage here? Just my luck." She heaved a heavy sigh. "I was going to play a little Pac-Man. That would kill the time."

"You're supposed to be watching the Clark house with me. Remember?"

Scowling, Sarah poked at her phone's keyboard some more. "Yeah. But there's nothing going on. I think they're in for the night." Evidently giving up, she dropped her useless phone back into her bag. "I have an idea. How about we go check?"

"Go check?"

Sarah didn't wait to explain; she just scrambled out of the car, leaving Mandy with no choice but to chase after her. Mandy hadn't realized how fast Sarah could run. Evidently, Sarah's time on her treadmill had been well spent.

Before Mandy could catch up with her, Sarah dashed around one side of the house, disappearing into inky shadows. By the time Mandy had rounded the corner, Sarah was hunched down in front of a window. From Mandy's angle, she could tell the window looked into a dark, empty dining room.

"We need to go around to the back. I can tell there are lights on."

"We don't need to spy on a married couple, Sarah. We just need to catch Mr. Clark sneaking out to meet with his mistress, if he has one, which I'm still doubting."

Sarah crept along the side of the house, staying in the shadows. "Well, at least this isn't so boring. Who knows, maybe you'll learn something useful."

"Like what? What kind of television shows they like to watch?"

Sarah shrugged and kept moving. She didn't stop until they'd reached a four-foot wooden fence. She shook it.

"What are you doing?"

"It isn't so high. And it feels pretty solid. I can climb this."

"You could. But you're not going to."

"Why not?"

"Because we don't need to get into the Clarks' backyard. You're just playing around. It's time to leave, before Andrew catches us. Or we trip an alarm or something. People have alarms in these nice neighborhoods, you know."

"I know. But I don't see any floodlights or motion detectors." Sarah pointed up, at the roofline. "I already checked."

She pushed into a patch of shrubs planted in the corner where the house's brown brick exterior met the wood fence. "Perfect. There's a big green electrical box thingy back here." A dull metallic thunk followed, and Sarah's head popped up, above the shrubs. She swung a foot over the wood fence's pointed planks, found her footing on a horizontal support, then followed up with the other foot. A second later, she was grinning at Mandy from the other side of the fence. "Easy peasy. Come on."

This was the last time Mandy would bring Sarah on a stakeout.

Mandy shoved through the wall of shrubs, finding the humming green box. Getting poked from all angles by the evergreens' branches, she stood, carefully climbed onto the wood cross board, and jumped to the ground. She stayed somewhat hunkered down as she scuttled toward Sarah.

"They're getting snacks," Sarah pointed out. "I'm hungry. Oh, look at that. They're having sandwiches. I could handle a toasted ham and cheese right now."

"If you agree to leave right now, we can head to your favorite Coney Island restaurant for a gyro."

"Mmmm. That sounds good. Tempting." Sarah smacked her lips. "But I'm kind of liking this PI thing now."

"We're not accomplishing anything. Let's go."

"Shhhhh." Sarah pointed at the window. "Looks like Mrs. Clark is heading upstairs with her snack. But Mr. Clark isn't. Maybe he'll make his move?"

"If he leaves through the *front door,* we'll miss him."

"What man would be stupid enough to sneak out through the front door?"

They watched for a moment.

Andrew Clark looked back, in the direction his wife had gone. He disappeared into a room that branched off from the main kitchen/family room, returned a minute later, and headed straight toward the French doors leading out to the backyard.

Sarah inched back against the house. "See? He's sneaking out. We can follow him."

Holy shit, was she right?

Clark opened the door very slowly, as if he didn't want anyone hearing it. He stepped outside, closed it. Looked left. Looked right. Thank God for the lattice privacy wall they'd nailed along one side of the wood deck, or they would've been caught.

He started moving in their direction.

Mandy ducked lower, inching back until her spine was pressed against the cool brick. Her shoe landed in something squishy, and just as the scent of dog shit reached her nose, a little rumbling growl cut through the dark shadows under the deck.

"Holy hell, they have a dog," Mandy said.

The dog said, "Yap, yap, yap!"

Sarah screamed like a girl.

The dog attached its teeth to Mandy's ankle. Mandy bit back a howl, kicked her leg like a crazy woman, and made a run for it.

Clark was on their tails. "Who's there? Shit! Rambo! Here, boy!"

Rambo finally let go of Mandy's ankle, after being kicked and dragged to the fence. He let them know, in no uncertain terms, what he thought of their little impromptu visit while they scrambled over the fence.

Sarah didn't stop laughing until they'd run at least three blocks, in the opposite direction from their car. Not the least bit winded, she plunked down on the curb. "Ohmygod, that was so funny!"

"Glad." Gasp. "You." Gasp. "Think." Gasp. "So." Gasp. Grimacing, Mandy lifted her pant leg to see if she had any flesh left on her ankle. The light sucked, but from what she could see, it was more intact than she'd expected. "I am so not into animal cruelty, but damn, that hurt."

"You kicked that little pip-squeak into tomorrow."

"He was tearing my leg apart."

"Let me see." Sarah grabbed her ankle. Mandy yelped. "Hmmm. Looks like he barely scratched you."

"I think it's worse than that."

Sarah stood. "What do you think, should we head back?"

"No. I'm guessing any plans Clark had for sneaking out have been summarily abandoned. And I'm not convinced he was sneaking out anyway. He was probably going out to find their little beast of a dog."

"Can you be so sure?" Sarah started walking. "To me, he reacted a little weird when he heard Fido going nuts. Like he didn't expect the little guy to be outside."

"Where are you getting that?"

"He said 'shit.' Would you say that if your dog was attacking an intruder?"

"No, I wouldn't. He said 'shit'? Are you sure?"

"Positive."

"I didn't hear him say that."

"Well, if I'd had a furry piranha chewing my ankle, I might have been a little distracted, too." Sarah sniffed. "Speaking of shit..."

Mandy grimaced. "Yeah, I stepped in some." She half walked, half limped back toward the Clark house. Looked pretty quiet.

"I say we go around back again."

"I say we go to the nearest emergency room. I think I need a tetanus shot. Maybe a rabies shot, too."

"Drama queen."

"How about gyros? My treat?" Mandy offered. Anything to ensure she wouldn't be climbing back over that freaking fence tonight.

"Okay, fine. But only if you buy dessert, too." Sarah sniffed again. "But I'm not going anywhere with you until you do something about that shit on your shoe."

"Fair enough. I keep a spare pair in the trunk." Mandy hobbled toward the car.

"Well, at least you have something useful in there."

14

Approximately twenty hours later, Sarah asked, "Where are we headed tonight?" She bounded from her chair. Literally bounded. Mandy didn't have that kind of energy tonight. She wished she did.

She checked the time. Four forty-eight. "Where are *we* headed? Looks like you're ready to hit the gym."

Sarah had changed from her usual work clothes—cute skirt, knit top, and Jimmy Choos—to a pair of snug black pants, a black hoodie, and black Nike Shox tennis shoes. "The gym? No, these are my new PI clothes. They're so much more practical than what you wear, don't you think?"

Mandy looked her goofy friend up and down. "I gotta say, they do look pretty practical—if you're going on a stakeout. Which you're *not.*"

Sarah's mouth pursed into a pout. "Why won't you take me?"

"I have my reasons." She pointed at her ankle, which was still throbbing—one of the primary reasons why she was feeling so tired and cranky. She shoved the other reason out of her mind.

"I promise I won't complain about being bored." Sarah grabbed a backpack she'd evidently been hiding behind her desk. "Look, I brought my own stuff." She shoved her hand into the bag and pulled out a bag of Fritos. "Snacks." She dropped the chips onto her desktop and dug into the backpack for something else. "Entertainment." She slapped a paperback novel onto her desk. "And..." She dug into the bag for yet another item. "Pepper spray, in case we run into another ankle-biter."

"You're definitely well prepared."

"So, will you take me?"

"I don't know." Mandy glanced at her phone a second time. It was almost five. She needed to get a move on if she was going to make it over to Nickerson's building before he left. "I'm following Nickerson tonight. You're going to stand out like a sore thumb in that getup where I'm headed. You look like you're ready to rob a bank."

"I do not. I look cute. And hot. And don't these pants make my butt look great?" She turned sideways and ran her hand down her flat ass.

"Yes, they do."

Sarah beamed. "Let me go. Pretty pleeeease?"

Mandy sighed. She hated it when Sarah begged and made those sad puppy eyes. "Okay, fine. I'll bring you along. But only on one condition—you will do what I say, or this will be the last time. Got it?"

"Got it." Sarah hauled her backpack over her shoulder. Something metallic clanked as it smacked against her body.

Holding the door for Sarah, Mandy scrutinized Sarah's big, heavy-looking backpack. "What else do you have in there?"

Sarah's face pinched. "Nothing." She scurried to Mandy's car.

Mandy set the building's alarm and locked up.

Over the car's roof a few seconds later, Mandy said, "Hmmm. Tell me that 'nothing' isn't going to get me arrested if we get pulled over."

"It won't." Sarah settled into the passenger seat. "But I would suggest you avoid getting pulled over anyway, just in case."

Mandy slid into the driver's seat and plugged the key into the ignition. "In case of *what?*" Mandy twisted the key to start the car.

"It's nothing suspicious. I'm just saying..." A very guilty-looking Sarah shrugged. "You just got your driving record cleaned up a few months ago. Your insurance rates have finally gone down. You wouldn't want to have to pay those higher rates again, would you?"

"This isn't about insurance."

Sarah stared out the window.

Twenty minutes later, as Mandy parked the car in front of Nickerson's company's five-story steel-and-glass office building, Mandy asked, "Don't you have anything better to do tonight than sit in a car with me?"

"Um. No." Sarah unzipped her backpack and started rummaging through its contents.

"But it's Tuesday night. Don't you usually—"

"We broke up."

"Oh. Ohhhhh." Now Mandy understood why Sarah had become such a pest.

"Last week." Sarah's voice cracked.

"I'm sorry, hon."

"It was awful. I caught him in bed with another woman."

"Oh." Mandy realized she'd been saying that word a lot. But Sarah's romantic relationships were...complicated...and Mandy tended to be speechless whenever Sarah talked about the ups and downs of her love life. For instance, this last boyfriend was bisexual. And Sarah had made it clear a long time ago that she was okay with him having sex with other men. In fact, she'd joined in the fun sometimes, having sex with Eric and his gay lover, Christopher. She (wrongfully) assumed Sarah was okay with sharing.

Evidently, she didn't care to share Eric with other women, only with men.

"The bastard didn't even stop what he was doing. Just kept on fucking the bitch like I wasn't even there." Sarah sobbed. She sniffled and snorted.

Damn, Mandy didn't have a box of tissues in her car. She twisted to console her friend, gathering the blubbering mess of a girl into her arms and stroking her back gently while Sarah unloaded an ocean of tears onto her shoulder. Sarah stopped rather abruptly.

"There's your man," Sarah said between snuffles.

"Huh?"

Sarah pushed out of Mandy's arms and pointed over her shoulder. "He's with Brittany."

"Oh, shit." Mandy whirled around, catching them talking as they walked toward the parking lot. She motioned to her bag, sitting on the floor next to Sarah's. "Camera."

"Got it." Sarah rummaged around in her bag. "See? Isn't it a good thing you brought me along?"

"Hurry."

Sarah grunted. "It's so fucking small. Why do you have to carry such a puny camera? Aha. There it is." She slapped the camera into Mandy's outstretched hand.

Mandy snapped a few shots of the couple as they entered his Mercedes, then handed the camera back to Sarah. "Okay, here we go. Don't put that camera away. Hopefully we'll need it again very soon." Mandy started her car and shifted into gear. She followed him carefully, making sure to keep a vehicle or two between them so he wouldn't realize he was being tailed. They stopped at a cozy little restaurant a few miles away.

Mandy parked in the lot, as close to the building as she could get, where she'd have a clear view of the restaurant's entrance, the target's car, and the only exit out of the parking lot.

"Now what? Are we going inside?" Sarah asked.

"No."

Five minutes later, Sarah said, "I have an idea. How about I go inside? With the camera? You can stay out here and...be ready, in case they make a hasty exit."

"How about you stay here with me?"

Sarah huffed a sigh.

Another five minutes later, Sarah, crunching on Fritos, said, "I need to use the bathroom."

"You're kidding."

She waved an empty water bottle. "I was thirsty."

Argh.

"While I'm in there, I'll try to snap a picture or two with your super-duper spy camera. Don't worry, nobody will see me."

Mandy had genuine doubts about that.

Especially ten minutes later.

Sarah hadn't returned yet.

And a blue police car rolled up to the front of the building.

"Dammit, Sarah, what did you do now?"

Cussing under her breath, Mandy exited the car. She slammed the door a little harder than normal, but, hey, who wouldn't? She stomped up to the restaurant's entry. Inside, she looked left. She looked right.

The hostess bounced up. "How many?"

"I'm not here to eat. I'm looking for my friend. She came in here about ten minutes ago. Dressed in black workout clothes."

"Oh. Sure." The hostess pointed toward a narrow corridor

she hadn't noticed as she'd entered. "I think she's back there, talking to the officer."

"Thank you."

Mandy turned the corner. Sure enough, Sarah was standing with her back to the wall, a huge patrol officer looming over her.

Sarah batted her eyelashes.

He angled forward, bracing one arm on the wall.

Things seemed to be under control.

Mandy headed back outside, taking a seat on the metal bench positioned next to the entry for guests when the wait was long. Another ten minutes later, a very flush-faced Sarah came trotting out.

"Oh, there you are." Sarah fiddled with her hair, which was a little on the messy side.

"Yes. Here I am. What happened?"

"Oh, nothing," Sarah said, making good time back to the car.

"Was there a problem?"

"No. No problem."

"Why were the police called?"

"Well..." Sarah got into the car.

Mandy hurried around to the driver's seat. Sat. Waited. "Yes...?"

"I wouldn't call it a problem."

"Tell me."

"I have good news." Sarah beamed.

"What's that?"

"You can get paid now. Maybe."

"What's that mean? Did you get something on the camera?"

"Um, yes. And no."

"Huh?"

"I did. But then Nickerson called the police and they confiscated the camera. Or rather, they asked me to voluntarily give them the camera. In return, the meanie promised not to press charges." Sarah grinned. "But it doesn't matter."

"Why do you say that?"

"Because Nickerson and Brittany aren't having an affair. She's *his daughter.*"

"And you know this *how?*"

"Because that's what he told the police."

Head smack.

"Hon..." Mandy swallowed a sigh. "Did you honestly expect Nickerson to tell the officer he was having dinner with his *girlfriend*... who just happens to be half his age? Of course he said she was his daughter."

Sarah's expression dimmed. "Oh." Her lip quivered. "I'm sorry. I'll buy you another camera."

"It isn't necessary. Just please tell me you didn't say who you worked for?"

"I didn't. At least, I don't think I did. That officer. I mean, if you'd seen him, you'd see why I got a little distracted." She glanced out the window. "Oh! There he is now." She pointed.

"I see him. Please don't call him over here."

"Too late. He saw me." Sarah tugged on her top, pulling it down a little to expose more boobage. She donned a saucy smile and rolled down the window as he came strolling up to the car. "Hello again, Officer. Is there anything else you needed?"

"Sure." Standing as straight as a marine, he stopped a few feet from the vehicle. "If you'd please get out of the car, miss."

"Sure." Sarah broke records getting out. One second she was there, in the seat; the next she wasn't.

Mandy watched as the two stepped aside to talk. The policeman put his bulky body in her line of vision, blocking not only her view of Sarah but also the restaurant's door. Not good. On either count.

She shifted positions, focusing on Nickerson's car.

Oh, shit, they were in it.

Mandy looked at the police officer's back.

Hurry!

She looked at Nickerson's car again. It was rolling out of the parking spot.

Dammit.

She opened her window. Cleared her throat. The officer didn't respond. Neither did Sarah.

Nickerson's car zoomed to the driveway and sped out into traffic.

So much for tonight.

Mandy's teeth gritted.

Five minutes later, a bouncy Sarah plopped into the passenger seat and waved out the window. A pair of handcuffs were clamped around one wrist.

"What's that?" Mandy asked, pointing.

Sarah's eyebrows waggled. "Handcuffs."

Mandy swallowed a curse word. She swallowed at least a dozen more. "Tell me you weren't flirting with that police officer while I watched Nickerson and his little friend speed away."

"Uh." Sarah blinked. "Um. Okay, I won't tell you."

Mandy jerked the key into the ignition.

"Where are we going now?"

She shifted the vehicle into reverse. "I'm going home. After I drop you off at the office."

"We're done doing stakeouts?" Sarah asked, spinning the metal cuff around her wrist.

"Yes, we're done." Mandy maneuvered the car out of the parking spot, shifted it into drive, and the car roared toward the street.

Sarah pointed at the clock. "But it's not even late."

Mandy stomped on the brake, glaring at the line of cars rolling down the road, blocking her exit. "I'm tired."

"We could go back to the Clarks'."

"No."

"Why not?"

"Because...I don't have a camera. The only one I brought with me is in your new friend's patrol car." Catching a break in the traffic, Mandy hit the gas. The car lurched onto the road.

"You know what I think? I think Clark-Old-Boy is sneaking into the pool house and doing the nasty with someone in there."

"That would be asinine. His wife could go down there at any time and catch him."

"See? Maybe he figures she won't because she'd think that would be stupid, fucking another woman right under her nose."

"Just out of curiosity, where'd you catch Eric and his bimbo?"

"In the pool house."

Oh, God. A thought passed through Mandy's head, but she wasn't heartless enough to say what she was thinking aloud.

Sarah's handcuffs rattled. "It's worth another look. I brought pepper spray. That little beast won't get you again. I promise."

Mandy glanced down at her still-achy ankle. "But we don't even have a camera. If you're right, then what?" She looked at her friend's eager face.

Was there anything to her theory?

She supposed it was possible.

"If we're right, we can come back armed with everything we need to get the job done. I've got my cell phone as a backup camera." Sarah produced said item and hit a button. A flash blinded Mandy. "It has a flash."

Blinking to try to clear her vision, Mandy grumbled, "Okay. We'll take a quick trip to the Clarks'."

"Yeah!" Sarah pumped her fists. The handcuffs rattled again. "Isn't Mr. Policeman going to miss those?"

Sarah shrugged. "He said he had another set in his car. He'll be picking them up at the end of his shift."

That made Mandy smile.

If Sarah's new friend kept her busy, Sarah wouldn't want to go on any more stakeouts. That would be a very good thing.

"I don't suppose you could convince him to give back my camera? I've lost too many to count lately, thanks to Zane."

Sarah's smile was devious. "I don't think that'll be a problem."

Sarah sang along to the radio as they drove to the other side of town. It wasn't quite dark enough yet, so Mandy opted to make a stop at the Chicken Shack for some fried chicken and broasted potatoes. They both used the bathroom, too. And with a little help from a squirt of liquid soap, Sarah was handcuff-free when they returned to the car. By the time they'd pulled onto the Clarks' street, the sky was dark to the east and streaked with salmon to the west. It was another half hour before it was dark enough to risk sneaking into the Clarks' backyard.

This time, Mandy was prepared. She had a pocketful of chicken for the beast.

They tiptoed around the house, listening for any signs of Clark or his ankle-mangling best friend. Mandy volunteered to climb the fence first. Sarah followed. Side by side, they crept toward the house first, peering in through the French doors, looking for husband and wife.

The little beast was lying on a plaid dog bed next to the door. Mrs. Clark was lounging on the couch. Mr. Clark was nowhere to be seen.

Mandy motioned toward the pool house.

Sarah nodded.

They dashed across the lawn, tiptoeing up to the building. Mandy pressed a finger to her lips. Although there didn't seem to be any lights on inside, or suspicious sounds, she didn't want to risk being caught.

She peered into the window next to the door.

Empty.

So much for that thought. Mandy motioned toward the front. *Time to call it a night.* Sarah nodded. Mandy started across the lawn. She got to the fence before she realized Sarah wasn't behind her.

What now?

She whirled around.

A shadow, a large one—too big to be Sarah's—traveled across the far end of the yard. It was headed toward the pool house. Squinting, Mandy made out Sarah's smaller form, scurrying through the building's door.

Oh, shit!

Mandy waited a few minutes to see if anyone else was headed out to the pool house. Sure enough, a smaller shadow bounced over the fence adjoining a neighbor's yard. That person was also going to the pool house.

Now what?

Mandy risked a dash back to the pool house. No lights. She peered in the window, spying two forms, one male the other female, in an embrace.

Yes! At last, she had this guy.

But dammit, she had no way to nail him. She stuffed her hands into her pockets, wishing she had a camera.

She visually searched the pool house's open space for Sarah. No Sarah. She guessed she might be hiding in a bathroom somewhere. With no other choice, she took a position along the darkest side of the building, where she could watch for Sarah when she snuck out.

Twenty minutes later, she was still waiting.

Ten minutes after that, a muffled scream cut through the silence.

Thirty seconds later, Sarah put those running shoes of hers to the test, making record time in the hundred-yard dash. Clark came stumbling after her, his pants down around his knees. She vaulted the fence in a single bound and disappeared from sight. Clark hauled his pants up and followed, but Sarah had a solid head start on him. There was no chance he'd catch her. Mandy didn't move, knowing Clark's lover was somewhere close by. She held her breath and watched, eyes sharp, heart pounding. Finally, the woman scampered back in the direction from which she'd come, hopping the fence. This time, Mandy paid attention to where she went.

Into the house next door.

Aha. She could now find out a name.

Ironically, thanks to Sarah, she was going to earn that retainer Clark's soon-to-be-rich ex-wife had paid her.

She headed back to her car, figuring Sarah would eventually meet her there. Five minutes later, Sarah was giving Mandy a blow-by-blow description of what had happened inside the pool house. Looking oh so proud, Sarah waved her phone. "And I've got proof! That bastard's busted."

"I can't believe you pulled it off. I've got to hand it to you, Sarah. You've got nerve."

"Thank you. Coming from you, that means a lot. So, does that mean I get the promotion?"

"I'll have to think about that. What time is your cop off the clock?" Mandy asked, driving them back to the office. She was anxious to take a good look at the pictures on Sarah's phone, see if she'd managed to take any quality shots.

"Midnight. Want to go have a drink?" Sarah asked as they pulled into the office parking lot. She tipped her head at the restaurant a few doors down.

"I don't know…"

"I'm buying. Come on. I'm in the mood to celebrate."

"What're you celebrating?"

"The bonus you're going to give me when we close the Clark case." Sarah gave Mandy a big Cheshire-cat grin and bounded out of the car.

15

Mandy groaned.

Mandy sighed.

Mandy shook her head.

If it wasn't for the two beers she'd had, she might actually be disappointed. Mandy handed Sarah back her phone. "There isn't a single useful shot here."

Sarah's brows furrowed in confusion. "Are you sure?" she slurred. Sarah'd had a lot more than two beers. "I thought I had at least one good one."

"I'm sure. Take a look." Mandy leaned to the right to allow Sarah to look over her shoulder at her laptop's screen. A cloud of alcohol-laced air wafted over her.

"Oh. I guess I wasn't holding my hand very still." Sarah straightened. "But in my defense, it isn't easy holding your hand perfectly still when you're running. And it isn't easy aiming for a target in the dark either. I was shooting blind, as they say." Sarah waved her hand. "Doesn't matter. We can go back tomorrow."

"I have a feeling they won't be going for any more midnight swims after tonight."

"Damn." Sarah plunked down on her butt. "That's okay. We'll get 'em." She flung one knee over the other. "What time is it?"

Mandy checked the clock on her computer. "A quarter after twelve."

"Shit. I'm late." Sarah staggered to her feet. "Where'd I leave my purse?"

"Hold up." Since Mandy'd had only two beers, versus Sarah's two beers *and* three shots of tequila, she beat Sarah to the keys. "You're in no condition to drive anywhere."

"But I'm supposed to meet...um...Whatshisname at midnight."

"You'll have to make plans for another night."

"No, I won't. You can drive me home. I'll call him." Listing to the left, Sarah dug a slip of paper out of her purse, then poked at the numbers on her cell phone. "Hello? Hello? Is this the sexy police officer I met at Buca's? I have your handcuffs. Wanna play?" Sarah's face wrinkled up. "What do you mean I have the wrong number?" She poked a button, cutting off the call. "That bastard! He pretended he didn't know who I was."

"It's probably for the better." Mandy threw an arm over her drunk friend's shoulder. "I think there's a reason why you got tanked tonight, and it doesn't have anything to do with celebrating the bonus I'm paying you."

"So, you are still paying me the bonus?" Her friend turned watery, bloodshot eyes her way. "Even though the pictures sucked?" Sarah threw her arms around Mandy's neck. "You are the best boss in the world. I love you." She started sobbing on Mandy's shoulder.

"I love you, too, hon." Mandy patted her blubbering friend on the back.

Several minutes later, after she'd stopped crying, Sarah said, "You're right. I got drunk because I was scared."

"I kind of figured that out."

"I haven't been with another man in four years. I mean, I haven't had actual intercourse without Eric being there with me. I don't know if I can do it. I don't know if I can start over with someone else. Someone new." She dragged the back of her hand across her tear-smudged face.

"You need to give yourself some time." Mandy steered Sarah toward the door, figuring it was past time to get her home. Better to do it now, while Sarah was upright and moving. Once she crashed, it would be impossible to get her anywhere. Especially since Sarah outweighed her by at least thirty pounds.

Sarah wobbled outside with Mandy, using her for support. They made it to Mandy's car. Mandy held Sarah upright with one hand while opening the car door with the other. After she had Sarah inside, she rounded the car and slid into the driver's seat.

"Love sucks. Yeah, yeah," Sarah sang.

"I think it's 'Love Stinks,'" Mandy corrected, starting the car.

"That it does." Sarah's head flopped back. "Whatever you do, don't ever fall in love. Men are good for only one thing—and it sure the hell isn't commitment."

"Thanks for the advice."

"What happened to the fancy restaurants? This place is beyond creepy," Sarah grumbled the next evening as she trotted across the trash-strewn parking lot toward the dilapidated building. Granted, after Sarah had made such a mess of things last night, Mandy had sworn that she'd never take Sarah along again. But when it had come time to head out tonight, Mandy couldn't stomach the thought of going alone.

The truth was, whenever she was by herself, especially in a quiet place, she still kept thinking about Zane. Even now, after almost a week, she couldn't stop wondering what had happened. His non-excuse had been confusing, frustrating. But because they'd been no more than casual lovers, she hadn't felt like she could demand a better explanation.

With the exception of last night—she'd crashed the minute her head had hit the pillow—she'd had a horrible time falling asleep.

"Hey, you know this job isn't all five-star restaurants," Mandy said, stepping over a used condom lying in a puddle.

Sarah shook her hands like a little girl seeing her first earthworm. "Ew! I think we might catch something just by walking into the place."

Highly amused by Sarah's squeamishness, Mandy pointed out, "You wanted to be a PI...."

"Yeah."

"You know what kinds of places I've had to go into before."

"Sure, but it's different now." Sarah tiptoed around an overturned cup.

"How's that?"

"Because now I'm going into these places, too."

"Would you rather go back to answering the phones?"

Sarah stopped walking. "Can you give me a few minutes to think about it?"

"No. Let's go. Whether you like it or not, you're with me now. We're going in." Realizing Sarah had fallen behind, Mandy waved over her shoulder. "Come on, this place isn't so bad."

"This place is worse than bad. I mean, look at it." Sarah swept an arm in a wide arc.

Mandy could agree it was probably the most disgusting dump she'd ever laid eyes on. But this was her job. This was what had to be done.

"Why would a guy like Nickerson bring a girl here? He has money. And he's already proven he doesn't mind spending it."

"Maybe his wife tightened the purse strings."

"She'd have to pull them so tight he couldn't squeeze more than a handful of pennies. Shit, it would probably be better to just go park somewhere and have sex in his car."

"Maybe she's been checking his car, too."

"The poor bastard." Sarah shook her head. "Having to resort to *this?*"

Mandy halted midstep. "Tell me you're not feeling sorry for him."

"Well..."

"Sarah. What did I tell you was the number-one rule?" She continued up to the building's front entrance.

Behind her, Sarah recited, " 'Just do the job. Don't take sides. Don't get emotionally involved.' But I'm not getting emotionally involved. I'm just...disturbed."

"Get undisturbed." Mandy covered her hand with her sleeve, grasped the motel office's door handle, and pulled, holding it open for Sarah. "Ladies first."

Sarah shuffled inside, hanging back by the door.

Mandy strolled up to the counter, smiling at the dark-complexioned man behind the safety glass. *Please tell me he speaks English.* "Good afternoon, sir."

"You and girlfriend want room?" he asked in broken English.

"Oh, no—"

"She not girlfriend?"

"No. We're here—"

The clerk's eyes narrowed. "Friend want date?"

"No. I'm sure she doesn't 'want date.' "

"Too bad." The man frowned. "What you want?"

"We're looking for someone who just checked in."

"Sorry. Don't know him." The man backed away from the counter.

"Wait. You haven't even seen a picture yet."

"No matter," the guy sneered. "But maybe I remember if friend go on date. With me."

"Are you kidding me?" Sarah spat.

"Not happening," Mandy said, shoving a ten-dollar bill through the opening in the smudged barrier between her and the disgusting, horny clerk. "How about a date with Hamilton?"

"No, thanks." The clerk took the money.

"Do you like threesomes? How about two more Hamiltons to sweeten the deal?" This time Mandy just waved the bills in front of the man's face.

The man's lips pinched.

Mandy shoved the bills back in her wallet. "Your loss. You could've had a threesome...." She looped her elbow through Sarah's and walked her outside.

"That got us nowhere," Sarah said, grimacing.

"It rarely does. But that doesn't stop me from trying." Mandy led Sarah back to the car. They took their respective places, she behind the steering wheel, Sarah in the passenger's seat.

"What now?" Sarah asked.

"We'll drive around back, find Nickerson's car, and do things the hard way."

A cluster of young, threatening men walked by. Pants hanging off their asses. Hats backward. They leered. Sarah scowled. "Are you sure this is safe?"

"It isn't. But I have my gun."

"That's fine and dandy for you. I don't have a gun."

"And you won't carry one until you learn to use one safely."

"What are you trying to say? It wasn't my fault I shot that

guy in the ass last year. He stepped in the way *after* I pulled the trigger."

"You shouldn't have been pulling the trigger at all. Not in *a store.*"

Sarah smacked her arms across her chest. "Yeah, well, he shouldn't have had ammunition in the gun, either. Who keeps a loaded gun in a shop? Isn't that like the first rule of gun sales?"

"That, I will agree with. It shouldn't have been loaded. But still, the first thing you learn about gun safety is never to point a gun at anyone unless you're prepared to shoot."

"Consider that lesson learned."

They cruised around the dumpy single-story, U-shaped building until they located Nickerson's car, parked behind a line of overflowing Dumpsters at the far end of the lot.

"I'm guessing he's in one of these back units." Glad each motel room had its own entry outside, exactly like the Red Roof Inn, Mandy parked around the corner from the south-facing wing of the building. She grabbed a camera and shoved her gun into the waist of her pants before getting out of the car. "Stay close to me. God only knows what we'll run into back here." Trying not to be too obvious, Mandy strolled along the front of the west-facing units, peering through gaping curtains. She saw a lot more than she would have cared to, on more than one occasion, but she didn't see Nickerson.

When she reached the south end of the building, she glanced over her shoulder, looking for Sarah, who had stopped a few units back. She was gaping like a landed fish.

"Pssst!" Mandy waved a hand.

Sarah turned widened eyes toward Mandy.

"Come on." Mandy motioned with a hand. "You need to stay with me."

Sarah jogged over to her, whispering. "Did you see what I did?"

"I did."

"That's...disturbing." Sarah wasn't exaggerating. There'd been a dog in that room. A big Doberman. And from what Mandy had seen, it wasn't there for security purposes. "I need to disinfect my eyes—and my brain—after seeing that. Isn't that animal cruelty?"

"From the looks of the man who was being serviced by the dog, maybe."

Sarah gagged.

Mandy practically gagged, too. "We don't have time to worry about any potential animal abuse right now. We need to catch Nickerson in the act. Help me check these rooms."

Peering in a hazy window, Sarah asked, "Are we going to bust the door down when we find them?"

"Not if we can avoid it."

They made it to the end of the south-facing wing of the motel without seeing any more bestiality. That was a good thing. But they didn't find Nickerson either.

"That is his car. He's here somewhere." Sighing, Mandy headed toward the corner. "You'd think he'd take one of those units in the back, where he'd be less likely to be found."

"Unless he doesn't care, or doesn't expect to be found."

Mandy halted.

Sarah bumped into her from behind.

Mandy did a one-eighty, pushing Sarah back around the corner.

"What's wrong?" Sarah asked, stumbling.

"Those guys we saw earlier are huddled in front of one of the units. And I think I saw a gun."

"Where?" Sarah poked her head around the corner.

Mandy yanked on her arm.

Sarah didn't budge.

Mandy took a peek, too.

One of the guys gave a signal, then kicked in the door. Suddenly, the air filled with the *pop, pop, pop* of gunfire.

Frozen in place, Mandy watched as the three men dashed back out of the room. The ringleader looked right at her, shoved his gun into the back of his pants, then strolled away as if nothing had happened.

"Ohmygod," Sarah mumbled.

"One of them saw us," Mandy said.

"What should we do?" Sarah was wringing shaking hands. Her face was the color of milk.

"We saw what happened. We need to call the police." Mandy wobbled on shaky legs back around the south end of the motel, making a beeline for her car.

"But what if those guys find out who we are?"

"Chances are they won't. How would they?"

"I don't know." Sarah counted off the possibilities with her fingers. "First, they could find our car. Look up our license plate..."

"Do you really think they'd go to that much trouble? Or have access to that kind of information?"

"Probably not. At least, not on the latter."

Back at the car, Mandy plopped into the driver's seat, grabbed her cell phone, and dialed 911. The line rang fifteen times. She was about to hang up and redial when the line clicked and an operator said, "Nine-one-one, what's your emergency?"

Mandy blurted the basics and followed up with a few details. The operator told her a unit had been dispatched and thanked her and ended the call.

Mandy stared at her phone. "Well, I guess that's that."

Sarah, sitting beside her and looking anxiously out the window, still hadn't regained much of her color. "Do we need to wait?"

"I think we should."

"What if the men come back? What if they see us? What if they decide to shoot us before we get a chance to give our report?"

"Hmmm." Mandy started the car. She wasn't a big fan of being shot. And she didn't want to risk being seen in her car by a felon with a loaded gun. A license plate might offer them some way to track her down, if they were so inclined. And yet, she wanted to do the right thing. "What if we drove to the police station? We could give our statements there. Chance are, the shooters aren't hanging around outside the city administration buildings."

"Good point. O-okay. I guess that would be all right." Sarah strapped on her seat belt.

Mandy shifted the vehicle into gear, and it rolled toward the road. "Would you rather I take you home first?"

"Yes, I'd rather you take me home first. But if I go home and let you report the crime, that would make me a spineless chickenshit. And, even as scared as I am, I don't want to be that."

"Okay. So we'll go file a report?"

"Yes."

Mandy punched the local police department into her GPS and followed the computer-generated voice to the police station. Inside, it was mayhem. People everywhere. Babies crying. Mandy had second thoughts. She had third thoughts, too. But she still figured it was safer to give the information at the station than to hang around a crime scene, risking the guilty parties' return.

After waiting in line for forty-five minutes, she trudged up to the counter and told the officer, "I witnessed a shooting."

"Yeah?"

"Yeah," she said.

"Where at?" he asked, sounding bored.

"At the Greenwich Motel."

"Can I see your ID?"

Mandy dug her driver's license out of her wallet and handed it to the officer. He wrote it down on a piece of paper, then clipped it to a board and handed it to her. "Write what you saw." He glanced at Sarah.

"Me too," she said.

He did the same with her.

Ten minutes later, they handed back their clipboards, their statements completed. The officer gave them a quick, "Thank you."

"That's it?" Mandy asked.

The officer nodded, calling, "Next."

Mandy and Sarah exchanged looks.

Outside the station, Sarah said, "I'm hungry. I think I'm in the mood for chicken. Then maybe we could go scope out the Clark place again. What do you think?"

Mandy stared at the clock. It was early, too early to go home. Much too early. "What the hell. Why not?"

16

_____

"My God, don't these people ever pick up their little beast's shit?" Sarah grumped, dragging her foot in the grass.

Once again, they were in the Clark's backyard. Hoping, beyond reason, that Clark would be stupid enough to meet his neighbor in the pool house. Yes, Mandy would admit she was probably being a fool for thinking Clark would be so dumb. But she wasn't ready to call it a night yet. Creeping around the Clark's backyard beat lying in her bed, staring up at the ceiling and wondering why she was alone.

As she picked her way through the bushes next to the fence, she put up a silent prayer for things to go her way tonight. Lately, it seemed Lady Luck had abandoned her. Either that, or she'd lost her edge.

With Sarah at her heels, she dashed across the lawn, heading to the back of the lot. She found a cozy spot in the deepest shadows and hunkered down. Best to try to get comfortable, if that was at all possible. They could be waiting there for hours. And yet, she couldn't get too comfortable, in case they needed to make a quick getaway.

"Maybe I should hide in the pool house with the camera?" Sarah whispered. "You can watch out here and if you see them coming, signal me."

"Hmmmm. I guess that makes sense. Just do me a favor—don't take any unnecessary risks. Please. I don't want to have to bail you out of jail."

Sarah's eyes widened. Mandy could clearly see them, even in the semidarkness. "Why would we go to jail? Don't we have the wife's permission to be out here?"

"Yes, we do. But Clark doesn't know that. And if she isn't home and he calls the police, we could end up spending the night in jail, waiting for Mrs. Clark to back up our story." Indeed, Mrs. Clark did give them permission to sneak onto her property, after Mandy had informed her about their last impromptu visit to the house. She'd taken some risk by giving Clark's wife as much information as she had. If the woman wasn't able to keep what she knew to herself and decided instead to confront her husband, the whole case could be blown apart. Clark might break it off with his neighbor, and she'd be back to square one. "And that's if he calls the police. What if he decides instead to take matters into his own hands . . . ?" Mandy let the sentence trail off, knowing Sarah would fill in the blanks. She had an active imagination.

"I see where you're going with that. I'll be careful."

They exchanged a nod. Sarah ducked into the building. Mandy leaned against the wood exterior wall, facing the neighbor's backyard.

Three hours later, Mandy's thighs were on fire. She'd shifted positions at least a hundred times, but being half sitting, half squatting for so long had worked every muscle of her legs to fatigue. She needed to sit down.

Time to call it a night.

Her thighs trembling, and not for a pleasant reason, Mandy started curling around the front of the pool house, keeping to the shadows. As she approached the door, she caught sight of a shadowy figure creeping out of the building. Cool, Sarah must have been reading her mind.

She waved at Sarah and started toward the fence.

Sarah followed.

She climbed over.

Sarah followed.

She strolled out to the street, cutting right to return to the car. She heard Sarah's footsteps following behind her. She ducked into the car and pushed the key into the ignition.

A knock on her window made her jump.

She turned her head.

Her car door swung open.

She registered a woman's face, not Sarah's. Before she could react, a fist made contact with her jaw. Stars exploded behind her eyelids. She felt the world swoop.

Next thing Mandy knew, she had one hell of a headache. Her jaw was killing her. And her wrists were handcuffed to the steering wheel. Her car keys were gone.

What happened? Where's Sarah?

Her head throbbed as she twisted to check the backseat.

Sure enough, there she was. Hog-tied and gagged. Her eyes were open.

Panic setting in, Mandy glanced around before asking, "Sarah, are you okay?"

Sarah nodded and said something Mandy couldn't understand.

"My hands are cuffed to the steering wheel." Mandy tried curling her hand to make it as narrow as possible and wiggled it, trying to work it out of the cuff. No luck. She looked back at Sarah again. "Do you know why they tied us up in the car?"

Sarah nodded.

"Did they call the police?"

Sarah nodded a third time.

That was both good and bad. Mandy let her head slump forward until her forehead struck the steering wheel. She'd never been arrested before. She'd never been caught tailing anyone either.

She *was* losing her edge. She was taking more risks, stupid ones, getting sloppy. And it was something to be concerned about. This was one hell of a wake-up call.

Never again.

Mandy watched the clock, waiting to see how long it took the police to respond here in this nice little burb. She guessed it might be fifteen minutes. She was wrong. Ten minutes after she'd woken up from her little nap, two black-and-whites pulled up behind her car, and one swooped around in front of it. Four armed officers approached the car with guns drawn. One of them demanded, "Put your hands up!"

Hoping they'd hear, she shouted, "I'm handcuffed. I can't." A tense few minutes passed while the police decided whether it was some kind of trap or if she was telling the truth. Finally, one of them, with his gun pointed at her head, pulled open the driver's door.

It was Sarah's new friend, Officer Whatshisname. Mandy wondered how this would play out. Could be good. Could be bad.

"You. Again?" he said, his eyes snapping to her secured wrists.

"I'm a private investigator. I've been hired by the lady who lives in this house to follow her husband." Mandy checked his name badge. Valdez.

Valdez turned to wave off his fellow officers, pointing at one. "O'Neil, why don't you get statements from the guy who called?" He glanced in the backseat. "Is that Sarah?"

"Yeah."

"Anyone hurt?" he asked, yanking open the back door.

"Sarah indicated she's okay. Clark's neighbor, with whom he's having an affair, decided to go vigilante on my face."

"Neighbor?" Valdez looked at Clark's house. "Which one?"

"The one on the west side."

Sarah tried to say something. Of course, nobody could understand her.

Valdez untied the gag.

"I am so sorry about the other night," Sarah blurted, her words sounding a little strange, like she had a wool sock in her mouth. "Ugh. Tongue feels a little swollen. Probably from the stupid gag."

"Are you hurt?" Valdez asked, pulling at the rope binding Sarah's wrists.

"No, I'm fine. Thank you." Sarah gave Mandy a little grin in the rearview mirror.

"Is what your friend said true?" Valdez asked.

"Of course it is," Sarah said.

"You know, this is twice you two have been made. Maybe it's time to consider a career change?" Returning to Mandy, Valdez pulled a handcuff key off his utility belt.

"If I had any marketable skills, I'd seriously consider it," Mandy told him as he unlocked the cuffs. She rubbed at her sore wrists, then her even sorer jaw. "That woman clocked me good. I'm pretty sure she knocked me out. What kind of girl punches like that?"

He scowled, the first time his military-cool mien had cracked a little, displaying a bit of the humanity hidden beneath. "I can call for medical."

"No, that's okay. I'll be fine." Mandy gingerly tested her jaw to make sure nothing was broken. "But if Sarah needs to get checked out—"

"I told you, I'm fine. Clark didn't hit me. He just surprised me in the pool house." Leaning forward, Sarah whispered in

Mandy's ear, "I think I peed my pants he scared me so bad. I need to go home and change."

"How long after you went inside did he get you?" Mandy asked, groping around the floor for her missing keys.

"Right away. He jumped me the minute I stepped inside."

"Shit. He was waiting for us."

"You think?" Sarah said sarcastically.

Mandy patted around the floor, checked the passenger seat, the console. "Someone took my keys."

"We can try asking Clark if he has them," Valdez offered. "Maybe he's holding on to them so you couldn't drive away."

Mandy figured there was basically no chance he'd give them back if he had taken them. But she said, "What the hell, it's worth a shot."

Valdez stepped back and spoke into the radio clipped to his uniform.

Having been bent over while looking for the keys, Mandy sat upright. Her head pounded and her stomach twisted. "Ohhh. I'm feeling a little woozy."

"Maybe you'd better go to the hospital, to be safe," Sarah said, sounding worried.

"I hate hospitals."

"Don't we all?"

"It was only a punch."

"A punch to the face. And it was hard enough to knock you out. You could have brain damage."

"Bad news." Valdez ducked down to peer in the window. "Clark says he doesn't have your keys."

Mandy smacked the steering wheel. This was turning out to be the night from hell. "I bet that he-she who punched me took them."

"If you're talking about the neighbor, she says she doesn't have them either," Valdez said.

Mandy shoved open the door. "One of them is lying, of course." She lurched out of the car and staggered around, searching the street for her key ring. "With any luck, she threw them where we can find them."

Sarah joined the search.

"Clark wants to press charges," Valdez informed them while they walked around in the dark, dragging their feet in the grass. At least he shined his superpowerful flashlight on the ground to help.

"Yeah, no surprise there," Mandy said, digging her shoes into the grass intentionally.

"Invasion of privacy and trespassing," Valdez informed her.

Mandy dug her heels in deeper. She was ready to dig a fricking ditch she was so angry. "Has anyone called his wife yet?"

"Not sure. I'll find out." Valdez handed her the Maglite and stepped out of earshot.

"Do you think she'll back us up?" Sarah asked, taking a break from the search.

"I hope so! If not, we're screwed."

A minute later, Valdez returned. Mandy and Sarah were still searching for the keys. "We've heard from the wife. She's backing your story. You're lucky. This time. Clark doesn't have a case on either count." Valdez extended a hand, wordlessly asking for the return of his flashlight. "Clark isn't happy. He knows what you look like, what kind of car you drive. I suggest you drop this case and move on to something else."

"I'm sure Clark would be very happy if we did that. Then he could run around with his mistress all he wants and his wife couldn't do a damn thing about it." Mandy plopped her ass onto the curb. "I feel like crap. And we're not going to find my keys in the fucking dark."

Sarah sat beside her and gave her some sad eyes. "Do you have an extra set at home?"

"Somewhere. But I can't remember where I put them. Maybe in my dresser drawer...?" Mandy rubbed her sore jaw. "Shit, that hurts."

"How about I take you to the hospital to get checked out? And Sarah and I will go to your place to look for the extra set of keys?" Valdez offered.

"Can you do that?" Sarah asked him. "Don't you have to go back to work?"

"Nope. I'm off the clock in ten." He motioned them toward his car.

Sarah beamed. "That's very nice. Thank you."

Mandy was a little less enthusiastic but no less grateful for his help. She slid into the backseat with Sarah and concentrated on not throwing up during the ride to the hospital.

17

Mandy was reading over her discharge papers when she heard footsteps approaching. Hoping it was Sarah, coming to take her home, she glanced up.

Zane?

Ohmygod, what's he *doing here?*

His jaw was clenched.

His eyes were dark.

"Hi," she said, not bothering to hide her surprise.

"Sarah called me."

"Oh?"

He moved closer, stopping next to her bed. "She asked me to take you home, said she wasn't able to locate your extra set of keys."

"She could've had her friend Valdez drive her over to the office. She left her car there."

Zane shrugged. "Maybe she was busy. Maybe they both were." He leaned in, brushing his mouth over hers. "You're hurt."

"I'm okay. Just a little bruised and sore." Mandy fingered

her jaw. "I was punched in the face. By a woman. The doctors think I might have a slight concussion."

"Hmmm. If that's the case, you shouldn't be alone tonight." His eyes twinkled, the dark shadows fading slightly.

"Are you volunteering to stay with me?"

"I might be." He glanced around. "Are you finished?"

"I think so. They gave me my discharge instructions." She waved the papers.

"Good." He offered her a hand. "Let's get out of here."

Cautiously, she slid to her feet. Zane wrapped an arm around her waist, giving her plenty of support as she walked out to the lobby. He left her waiting outside, in a wheelchair, while he dashed out to his parked car. A few minutes later, she was safe and sound in his sleek sports car as it prowled the streets.

At Main Street, Zane made a wrong turn. Had he forgotten where she lived?

"Um, you needed to take a left," she said.

"I'm not taking you to your house. You're staying at mine."

This was one of those moments when she wasn't so sure she liked that dominant, take-charge air he carried. She was exhausted. She was sore. She felt sick to her stomach. In summary, she had been looking forward to falling into her own bed, wearing her own pajamas...though she was over-the-moon thrilled to see Zane again. The problem was, she was in no condition to deal with all the emotions his presence stirred up. "I'll be okay. You can take me home."

"You'll stay with me."

Sarah, why'd you call Zane instead of coming up and getting me yourself?

Feeling conflicted, Mandy crossed her arms over her chest and stared out the window. The landscape changed as the car carried her farther from her home. The retail stores lining both sides of the street grew bigger and bigger, finally disappearing as the landscape turned rural. And when he turned onto the street taking them deeper into his neighborhood, the houses grew larger and larger, the wooded lots getting deeper and deeper until you couldn't see the houses from the road anymore.

Zane's car turned onto the long winding drive curving up to his house. He parked directly in front of the door, strode around the vehicle to open her door, and offered a supporting arm as she climbed out.

She'd been here before. But that had been during parties. The house had been packed with other people. Noisy. And full of life and laughter and music. Tonight when they stepped inside, the building was unsettlingly silent and empty and dark.

For the first time, she wondered what it might feel like for Zane to live in such an enormous place by himself. Did the echoing *click, click, click* of his heels on the stone floor make him feel cold and lonely? Did the dark rooms, empty, abandoned, leave him feeling abandoned and empty, too?

He escorted her up the stairs. But to her surprise, he bypassed his bedroom, taking her to the room next to it. Inside, he led her to a large, comfortable-looking bed, piled high with pillows. After she sat, he asked, "What do you normally sleep in?"

"Something comfy—a pair of shorts and a T-shirt."

"I'll see what I can find." He strolled across the room, opening a door positioned on the wall that adjoined his suite. "You have your own private bathroom. I have brand-new toothbrushes, toothpaste, and other personal items in the linen closet. I keep a supply for party guests who wish to stay overnight."

"Thanks." Mandy headed toward the bathroom, very aware of how close to Zane she was walking when she neared the door.

He caught her arm as she brushed past him, pulling her into

a tight embrace. He cradled her head gently. Silently screaming with glee, she flattened it against his chest and slid her arms around his waist. He was warm and strong, and yet he seemed, for the first time, to be visibly shaken.

Was he upset about her injury? Had he been missing her as much as she'd been missing him? How much did he care for her?

If only he knew how to express himself.

She closed her eyes and relaxed. This felt so good, so right.

He was the one to release her. Stepping backward, into the bathroom, she gazed into his eyes. They were full of dark shadows again, like always.

"I'll be back." He strode out of the room.

Very confused now, Mandy watched him leave before going into the bathroom to take care of her bedtime routine.

That was Zane. Broody. Silent. Powerful. Controlling. And yet she'd clearly seen a vulnerability tonight. That little chink in the armor made her want to reach out to him, comfort him. It stirred instincts she didn't know she had.

Remember, the last time you saw him, he told you he didn't want to see you anymore. You've got to keep things under control.

Easier said than done...

She turned her mind to her case as she brushed her teeth and washed her face.

Clark had known they would be back. He'd been waiting for them. She'd have to pull back now. Dammit. This had never happened to her before.

She said to her reflection in the mirror, "I've failed."

Zane knocked on the bathroom door.

She pulled it open.

He handed her a piled stack of clothing. "This is the best I could find."

"I'm sure they'll be good enough. Thanks. It's not like I'm

going anywhere." Her fingertips brushed against Zane's as she accepted the clothing from him. A sizzle of erotic heat crackled through her body.

He backed away. "I'll wait out here. I want to talk to you."

"Okay." He wanted to talk to her! She closed the door and set the clothes on the counter. Plain black T-shirt. Size XL Tall. Men's athletic shorts. Also size XL. Playing at least a dozen possible scenarios through her mind, she removed her clothes, leaving only her panties, and pulled the shirt on. The bottom hem reached the middle of her thighs. It made a perfect night-gown. The shorts, however, didn't work. She pulled them on. They slid right back off. No biggie. The shirt was plenty long enough.

Not that he hasn't seen it all before.

Her face flushed. The pink color was flattering, she realized as she did one final check in the mirror. She was ready. To hear whatever he needed to say. Out of the bathroom she went.

He was sitting at the end of the bed, waiting for her.

She sat next to him, leaving a little space between his warm body and hers. She locked her knees together. "What did you want to talk about?"

"I want you to come work for me."

Damn, that wasn't what she'd hoped to hear. "We talked about this. I don't think it's a good idea."

Staring straight ahead, he jammed his fingers through his hair. Clearly, he was not accustomed to having people refuse him. "I'm more than capable of behaving in a professional man-ner."

"That's never been in question. This is more an issue of making a wise choice. Everyone knows you shouldn't work for friends." *Or ex-lovers.*

"Your job is dangerous."

"It's all I have."

Silence.

"Would you quit if you had another option?" he asked.

She saw where this was headed. Zane was going to ask his friends for job leads. He'd probably find her a position somewhere, doing something boring, safe. But why go to all that trouble for someone he'd fucked a few times? "Possibly. It depends upon that option. How much it paid, what the job was, what the long-range opportunities were. What the environment was like. I haven't worked for a boss in years. I haven't punched a clock or had a manager standing over my shoulder, telling me what to do every minute of the day. I can't work like that."

"Understood. You need some autonomy." He flattened his hands on the mattress, curling his fingers over the edge. His elbow brushed against hers. A little flutter flitted in her belly.

"Yes. Autonomy. And challenge. I'll get bored within hours if I'm hired to file papers or answer phones."

He nodded.

"I'm—more or less—happy with my current job. Lately, though, things have gone a little crazy with the Clark case. I've gotten a little sloppy there. That's why he caught us. It won't happen again."

Zane's gaze snapped to hers. "No, it *will.* And what happens if you're shot instead of punched? You can't tell me for certain you won't be caught again because you can't know that."

Again, she had to wonder why this mattered to him. He'd made it crystal clear he didn't want to see her. He hadn't called since their last date. Not once. "True. But I plan on being much more careful in the future. I've been playing a little loose and easy because I'd always believed I was tracking cheating husbands who weren't violent. I didn't take cases if there was a history of spousal abuse or criminal activity. I minimized the risk."

"But you didn't eliminate it."

"No."

A tense moment passed.

Zane stood. He stared down at her for a moment, then cupped her cheeks in his hands. He bent to brush his mouth over hers. "Get some sleep."

"Good night," she said as he straightened up. She waited until he'd left the room before cutting off the light and settling in.

There was no way in hell she'd sleep tonight.

She woke to the smell of cooking bacon and brewing coffee. Her stomach rumbled as she climbed out of bed. It rumbled a second time as she barefooted it to the bathroom. She took a quick shower, then, smelling like vanilla and cherry blossoms, wrapped herself in one of the gigantic bath sheets she found folded in the cabinet.

Back in the bedroom, she found her clothes—everything but what she'd been wearing while she slept—folded neatly on the chair in the corner. From the smell, she guessed they'd been washed.

Nice. Zane sure knew how to treat a houseguest.

Opting to go commando since her panties were dirty, she put her clothes on and strolled downstairs. She expected she'd be greeted by a broody, intense Zane in the kitchen.

He looked intense all right.

But broody . . . not quite.

It was the apron. Not even Zane could pull off broody wearing a red apron that said REAL MEN DON'T USE RECIPES.

"Good morning," Mandy said as she shuffled up to the raised breakfast bar. "Smells good."

Zane gave her a half smile. "Coffee?"

"Thanks."

He poured her a cup. "Cream? Sugar?"

"Both. Thanks."

He produced a carton of half-and-half from the refrigerator, then went for the sugar bowl. She thanked him as he set them on the counter, next to her cup.

She poured some cream. "That's some apron."

"It was a gift."

"It's...unique. I would never have imagined you wearing something like that."

He shrugged as he tossed the eggs that were sizzling in a skillet. "There's a lot you don't know about me."

There was a lot she'd like to know about him. But she was afraid to say that. He might shut down again, become the guarded, standoffish man she'd seen all too many times. "I like surprises."

"Good." He dumped the eggs onto a plate, added some buttered toast and a few pieces of bacon, and set it in front of her.

"Wow, this is...very nice."

"What's wrong?"

"Nothing. It all looks delicious." She tasted the eggs. Yep, *delicious* was the correct adjective. And *scrumptious* would work, too. She watched Zane clean up as she ate. "Aren't you hungry?"

"I ate earlier."

She crunched on a piece of perfectly cooked bacon. It had been ages since she'd had bacon. And even longer since she'd had bacon cooked just right—crunchy but not burned. "You're a great cook."

"Thank you."

She was about halfway through eating when he sat on the bar stool next to her.

His eyes were twinkly.

His expression was downright cheery.

Something was going on.

"I found a job for you."

So, that was the *something*. "What kind of job?"

"I have an associate who's an attorney. Has his own firm.

Family law. He needs someone to do some research. It isn't a big departure from what you've been doing. But instead of doing the dirty work, you'd be hiring someone else to do it for you."

"Hmmm."

"There's more to it than that, but I don't know the details. I figured he could give you the rundown when you go for the interview."

"I don't know about this. Research? Sounds dull."

"Would it hurt to check it out?"

"Did you tell your associate I would definitely take the job?"

"No, I just told her you might be interested."

Her. Mandy felt her hackles rising. "I may not be qualified."

"I believe you are."

"But you said you don't know all the details."

"I know you." He had the nerve to poke her nose with his index finger. "I know how tenacious you are. You're intelligent and determined."

"I suppose you told her all those things?"

"I did. And more."

"Great, she'll be expecting a superstar."

"She'll be expecting you, Amanda."

God, how I love the way he says my name. "Why are you doing this?"

"Because...I like to help my friends."

"Is that what we are, Zane? Are we 'friends'?"

"I'd like us to be."

I'd like us to be a helluva lot more than that, dammit. "Friends?" she echoed.

He nodded.

Well, fuck. "Okay, I'll call her later today and set up an interview."

"The interview is this afternoon."

Her spine stiffened. This whole thing was making her uneasy. He was practically shoving her into the job. She wondered if his "associate" felt the same way she did.

Ready to tell him off for setting up the interview before talking to her, she sent him some squinty eyes.

He returned her warning glare with a big grin. She'd have thought he'd just told her he'd bought her a winning lottery ticket. More and more, she could see he was the hard-core, controlling type of man who tended to rub her the wrong way. It was probably for the best that he'd decided they should just be friends.

If only he wasn't so freaking cute. And generous. And sexy. And sweet.

"Two o'clock." He pulled a card from his pocket and set it on the snack bar's granite countertop. "I'll drive you."

"I can drive myself. After I find my keys. I'll need a ride home."

"Later."

"Now. Unless you want me to miss the interview *you* set up."

"I tell you what—if you stay here one more hour with me, I'll make sure your car is in your driveway by the time I take you home. That way all you have to do is get dressed and go."

"Zane, I don't need you to solve all my problems for me. I'm an adult. I can handle things."

"I know. I'm not trying to treat you like a child. I'm being selfish." He dragged her stool toward him. His eyes sparkled with erotic hunger. That was hardly a let's-be-friends sparkle. His lips curled into a devious smile. That wasn't a let's-be-friends grin either. Her blood warmed. A few other parts of her body warmed, too. "You'll forgive my selfishness, won't you?"

For some reason, it was easy forgiving Zane.

Especially when he looked at her like *that*. She guessed he was looking for more of a friends-with-benefits type of relationship than a strictly platonic friendship.

I can live with that.

He leaned in and nuzzled her neck. "Do you know how hard it was not to tear off that T-shirt last night?" He nibbled on her earlobe. "I wanted you. I want you now even more."

Earlobe nibbles were her kryptonite. And Zane knew that. She shivered. She sighed. When his tongue swept along the whorl of her ear, she tipped her head to give him better access. "I thought we were friends."

"Friends nibble on each others' earlobes sometimes." He supported her head with his hands, shifting it slightly to allow him to tease and torment her ear, her mouth, and her neck at will. "And they bind them, tease them, make them beg for release, too. Say the words," he whispered between nips.

"Hmmm," was her response. Her eyelids fell closed, shutting her into darkness. Now she was completely tuned in to her other senses. The taste of his lips lingering on hers. The tingles buzzing up and down her spine each time he kissed or licked her. The scent of man and food and desire hanging in the air. And the sound of her little gasps as he drove her absolutely insane with need within a few seconds.

That man knew how to use that tongue—oh, yes, he did.

"Say it. Say what I've been waiting to hear," he murmured.

She sighed. "Take me, Zane. Make love to me."

18

Hell yes, he'd take her. He'd take her every way he could imagine. She was his. Only his.

Fuck. What was he thinking?

What was he doing?

He didn't deserve a goddamn thing. Not a taste of her succulent skin. Not a sniff of her fragrant scent. Certainly not the pleasure of her slick heat wrapped around his cock.

She wasn't just asking to play with him. She'd said, "Make love to me." Those were words he never wanted to hear. So why couldn't he cut things off? Why couldn't he walk away? He'd done it before with other women. More than once.

He kissed her.

That didn't make things better. Hell no.

Now his cock was straining against his pants. His heartbeat, normally so sluggish it could barely be picked up by a doctor, was now pounding heavily in his chest.

She sighed into their joined mouths. "Oh, yes, Zane. Make me beg."

The flame in his body flared hotter.

Her tongue found his, stroking shyly. Her hands slipped beneath his shirt, her fingertips tracing tingly lines up and down his stomach.

His fingers curled, closing around two fists full of silky hair. Struggling to cling to the final threads of his self-control, he tugged. Her head fell back.

He could hear her heart beating.

He could see her pulse pounding against the thin skin.

He could practically taste her blood spilling over his tongue.

His tongue stabbed into her mouth now, fiercely, wildly. She didn't fight against his possession, didn't shy away from it. Her little fingers curled. She dragged her nails down his chest. The sting only stirred his need.

He didn't want her anymore; he needed her. All of her. Forever. Always. Desperately. With every cell of his being.

He broke the kiss. Dragged his tongue down the column of her neck, feeling the blood course through the vein lying just below the surface of her skin.

His fangs pierced through his gums.

He could bite her. Feed from her. Take her essence into him.

Don't do this to her.

"Please, Zane."

Dammit.

His need was like a steel blade, piercing clean through his heart. He jerked her against him. Her breath puffed out of her chest as her body molded to his.

She doesn't know what kind of monster you are.

"Zane, I need you."

He clenched his jaw. His blood burned in his veins. The pain was excruciating.

She wants this. Listen. Look. Feel.

"No." He pushed her back onto her stool and staggered to his feet.

"What's wrong?" she asked, looking confused, hurt.

"Nothing. Just...give me a minute."

She nodded. Wide, guileless eyes lifted to his. He looked away. "My suite. Go there. Wait for me. I'll come in a minute." He needed time to collect himself. When she hesitated, he said, "It's a surprise."

"O-okay."

He watched her walk away on visibly shaky legs.

If only she realized how shaky his legs were, too, how torn and conflicted and confused she made him feel.

She couldn't know that. Somehow he had to muscle his way out of this strange pit he'd flung himself into. She was a submissive. Just like all the others. That was all.

He took a deep breath.

Be a dom. Only a dom. And a friend. Nothing more. She can't be yours. Not ever.

Maybe it was time to find her another dom. A mortal dom. Perhaps that would be best. For them both.

Mandy stepped into Zane's silent, empty suite. Now what?

He was acting strangely, as if he was fighting some kind of need or impulse. What was the problem? Was it their so-called friendship he was struggling with? Or was it something else?

Couldn't be his definition of friends. He seemed quite comfortable with that.

Sarah had warned her about Zane's reputation. He was known to be a hard-core dom, the kind who pushed a submissive's limits unmercifully. So far, she'd seen nothing to back up such rumors. But she was wondering if he'd been forcing himself to take it easy on her, and now he was finding it difficult to hold back for some reason.

Maybe that's why he said he couldn't see me anymore.

Could she handle a tougher dom?

She didn't know yet. She wondered if she might find out soon.

She sat on the couch and waited. She wasn't kept waiting long. Zane strolled in within a few minutes, looking strong, dominant, and in complete control.

He walked up to her, took her hand. "This way." To her surprise, he led her out of the room, down the stairs, and into the dungeon she'd originally met him in. That had seemed such a long time ago. He released her hand when she reached the center of the room. "I think we need to clarify some things before we begin."

"What things?" Her heart jumped.

"We've talked about this. You know we must remain dom and submissive—"

"And friends."

"And friends. There cannot be anything more. No commitment. No monogamy. You understand, don't you?"

A little lightbulb blinked on in her head. "Oh, I understand now. It was what I said. I...I didn't mean to use that expression *make love*. I was swept up in the moment."

"I know you were. But I still can't continue if there's any chance you might have some kind of expectation for the future, might be feeling something..."

She was. God help her, she was feeling all kinds of somethings for him. And she had more than a niggling suspicion he was feeling a something or two for her, too. That was why she'd said what she did. And not just because she'd been caught up in the moment. Dammit, why was he being this way? "You're saying there's absolutely no chance we might someday decide to take this relationship to the next level?"

"No chance." His expression reaffirmed his words, though there was something in his eyes that suggested he was perhaps feeling slightly conflicted. "Not with you. Not with anyone."

Was there someone else?

"Are you married?" she asked.

"No. I've never been married. I'll never be married."

"I just wondered if that might be why you are so dead set against building a relationship with someone."

"It's not. I have my reasons."

"Will you tell me?"

"Why?"

"So I can understand. Don't you think I deserve that much? When we scene, you expect me to trust you. And I do. Without a second thought. Won't you trust me a little?"

"It's not a question of trusting you."

"If that's not it , then what … ?"

"This is why I thought it might be better if we didn't scene anymore." He shook his head. He turned from her. Stretched a thick arm, bracing it against the door frame. His head bent down.

"No. Zane. If that's why you've stayed away, I'm glad we're having this talk now. I'm okay with this. I want you to be my master. My friend. It's enough. I don't need any more than that. I don't want more. I like being independent. I like making my own choices in life." Mandy waited, breathless. How she longed to stomp over there, yank him away from that wall, and force him to face her. But she knew if she did that, he'd shut down completely. At this point, despite the fact that he had his back to her, he still seemed somewhat emotionally open to her. "Hell, I don't even like working for someone else."

If only he would show her just a tiny peek of what lay below that thick armor he always wore.

"It's no wonder you're a PI," he said. "You don't give up."

"They call me Bulldog for a reason."

"Yeah. I'm starting to understand that now."

"You should've *understood* it a long time ago, when you kept catching me sneaking cameras into your parties."

He turned to face her again. Hallelujah. "I like your stubborn perseverance. It's … charming."

The tension was easing. He was relaxing a little. *Keep it*

light. She turned on her charm, donning her best teasing come-hither look. "But is that a trait you'd look for in a submissive?"

"Perhaps."

"Really? That surprises me."

"I've trained more than my share of obedient submissives. Submissives who pretend to be disobedient."

"I don't pretend."

"That's what makes you so"—he took a step toward her— "much..." He took another. His eyes glimmered. His lips curled into a sexy half smile. "Fun." He kissed her again. And, oh, what a kiss it was. Now they were getting somewhere. The trick with Zane was to avoid being too direct. Better to dance around the issues a little, touching upon them here and there without pushing too hard.

She'd get her answer. Like she always did. It was just a matter of time.

Zane's tongue traced the seam of her mouth, and she opened to him, welcoming his decadent flavor inside. He tasted so good. He smelled even better. Like she had before, she let her hands slide under his shirt, mapping the lines cutting across his glorious abdomen. He was lean. Strong. Thickly muscled. One hundred percent hard, alpha dom. Her dom, she hoped, for a very, very long time.

She let him decide when to break the kiss. As a reward, she received more nibbles on her neck. More nips on her earlobe. And one bone-melting male growl in her ear.

If that didn't make a submissive girl fall to her knees, nothing would.

He stepped away. His expression hardened. Now he was the cool, controlled dom who made her melt. "Take off those clothes. I want to see you."

She did a slow striptease for him, watching the fire in his eyes blaze hotter with every garment she removed. By the time she was standing nude before him, her thighs were damp with her juices, her pussy was warm and clenching and aching to be filled, and her nipples were hard points. His jaw was clenched, his face the most charming shade of red.

"I am going to punish you for that," he grumbled.

She was almost certain she was going to enjoy this. All worries about him losing control and snapping evaporated from her mind. This was Zane. He didn't lose control. He would never hurt her. Not giving even a halfhearted attempt at looking remorseful, she said, "I'm sorry."

He motioned to a kneeler. This one had an angled padded platform to support the upper body. "There. On your knees." He helped position her on her knees, her body bent at the waist. Her ass was in the air, knees spread. He wrapped cuffs around her wrists, then fastened the cuffs to loops on the vertical supports. She couldn't move her arms. Not more than an inch. Not even to scratch her nose. She'd never felt so physically vulnerable. She'd never been so erotically energized.

"I'm going to turn this bulldog into a pussycat."

She had no doubt he could. But she decided it would be more fun if she didn't make it so easy. "We'll see about that. Bulldogs are notoriously stubborn."

"I know how to handle stubbornness." He went to the cupboard.

What was he going to do? Mandy's body tensed while she waited. Her pussy kept clenching. A throbbing heat pounded between her legs. Shivers swept up and down her spine. She was nervous. Excited. Giddy.

Ironically, the Clark case might not have done a whole lot for her career, but it had done a great deal for her sex life. If she hadn't been tailing Clark, she wondered how long it would have taken before she'd ventured into a bondage club.

If she hadn't been tailing Clark, she wondered how long it would have taken for her to meet Zane. Maybe she wouldn't have met him at all.

He was back. She sensed him behind her. She heard wrappers crackling. She heard other sounds, too. Sounds she couldn't identify. Her spine stiffened.

"Some doms might see that stubborn streak of yours as a fault. I don't."

"Glad to hear that."

"But that doesn't mean I don't expect you to be obedient and submissive when the time calls for it."

"Like...?"

"Like when we are in the dungeon."

"Understood." Something dragged down her back, from her nape to her ass. Tails from a flogger, she guessed. Would he strike her? She'd never been whipped before. How painful would it be?

Goose bumps erupted over her shoulders, down her back. She shivered, hot and cold at the same time.

"For a woman, sexual arousal is as much mental as it is physical. Wouldn't you agree?" He dragged the flogger down her back again.

She trembled. "I can't argue with that statement."

"So, when you're being fucked, what do you imagine?"

"I imagine..." Her face flushed. Was she really going to admit something so silly? "I saw this movie once. It was about a woman who was in a foreign country, in the Middle East somewhere. She went to jail and somehow ended up in a king's harem."

"Ah, then you'd like to be kidnapped?"

"Not in real life, no. But in my imagination, it's scary and sexy."

She felt something hard, not the flogger, touch her labia. She flinched, then relaxed. Being in this position, so helpless, unable to see what he was about to do, was so exciting. The thing nudged at her wet slit. Whatever it was, she wanted it inside her.

"Tell me more," Zane said.

Growing breathless, Mandy continued. "The woman was forced to become his wife. She was prepared for him."

"Prepared?"

"Bathed by his other wives."

"Touched by them?"

"Yes."

The toy, a dildo, inched inside her cunt. Only the tip. It wasn't deep enough.

"What else?"

"They dressed her in a beautiful gown, translucent, sexy. The whole preparation was so exciting."

"Yes, building up the tension. That's what turns you on, doesn't it, baby?" He pushed the toy deeper inside.

Still, it wasn't deep enough. Not even close.

"More."

"She went to the king. She was scared. She didn't know if he'd be cruel or gentle."

"Like me."

"Yes," she admitted in a soft voice.

"I'm your king." He pushed the toy a little deeper.

A wave of erotic heat rippled through her body.

She gulped in a deep breath. Her inner muscles clenched around the toy, holding it inside. Trying to draw it deeper. "Yes."

"What happens next?"

"He tells her to undress. She's terrified but at the same time, he's a handsome man. His clothes don't hide the fact that his body is beautifully formed. His eyes are assessing as he looks at her."

"She likes it."

"Yes."

Zane pushed the toy deeper still. It was almost there. Not quite deep enough.

"What happens next?"

"He touches her for the first time."

"And . . . ?"

"Her body reacts."

He pushed the toy all the way in, and Mandy shuddered. A charge of sensual energy buzzed up to her scalp and down to her toes.

"Like that?" he asked.

"Yes."

He touched her anus. "Hold my cock in your pussy. Hold it tight."

"Yessss." Her inner walls clamped tight, and another wave of pleasure buzzed through her body.

"Damn, your cunt is so tight. So pretty." His fingertip circled her labia, brushing lightly over her clit.

Instinctively, she rocked her hips forward, trying to press her clit against his hand.

"Oh, no. I'm the one in control now. The story isn't over yet. I can't let you come until it is." That wicked finger traveled back, toward her anus. It stopped there, and the ring of muscles clenched. Her pussy tightened, too. Another wave, this one bigger, hotter, washed through her body. "What happens next?"

She could barely think, let alone keep track of a story line. A big toy was planted deep inside her throbbing pussy. And Zane's lubed finger was now circling her anus. She knew what was coming next in this scene. But in the story . . . ?

"Think, Amanda."

A growl of frustration slipped between her lips. "You're not making this easy."

"I know." He pushed a fingertip into her ass.

Instantly, her body gripped it. Her pussy clasped the toy. A huge, almost overpowering surge of erotic need blazed through her body.

"Oh, God."

"Finish the story, Amanda."

She fought to remember. "He takes her to the bed and makes her lie down."

"You like to be on your back when you fuck? Submissive? Powerless. Open."

"Yessss."

"Mmmm. You look pretty lying on your back, your legs spread for me."

God, just the way he'd said that almost made her come. "Please?"

"Please what?" He added some more lube to his finger before pushing it deeper into her ass.

She bit back a whimper. "Please fuck me. Like that."

"The story isn't over yet."

"The king fucked his new bride," she snapped. "The end."

"Nice try."

He pushed his finger deeper into her ass. The man was far crueler than she'd ever imagined.

"Tell me what happens next or I'll take out the toy and that will be 'the end' for you, too."

"Bastard."

He chuckled. It was an evil-sounding laugh. Not scary-evil. Sexy-evil.

Her hips started rocking back and forth to the thumping pulses of heat rushing through her body. "He parts her pussy lips with one hand and slowly pushes two fingers inside."

"Mmmm." Zane withdrew his finger, but only to add a second. The tips of the fingers slipped past the tight ring of muscles, sliding deep inside.

Mandy cried out from the pleasure. "Oh, God, Zane."

"Tell me the rest."

"I c-can't."

"You must."

She quivered. Her legs were shaking. Her body was coiling

into a hard, tight knot. She could feel her orgasm building, the heat rumbling through her body like distant thunder. "He takes her. On a dais. In front of everyone. Claims her. Makes her his, with everyone watching."

"Now, that is some story."

Zane withdrew the toy, but just as Mandy whimpered, he thrust it back in. In and out, the dildo glided. Harder, faster. It was easy for Mandy to close her eyes and imagine it was Zane's cock stroking her into oblivion while a room full of people watched.

"I am your king," Zane murmured. "And I claim you, Amanda. You are mine. Let them all watch, witness, as I make you mine."

As he said that last word, Mandy tumbled over the edge, falling into a powerful orgasm. She quaked and spasmed, breath-stealing electrical charges blasting through her body, zooming up and down her spine. All thoughts vanished as sensation overtook her. Tastes. Smells. Sounds. She licked her lips, drawing in the flavor of Zane's kiss. She pulled in a gasp, swallowing the scent of her own need, heavy in the air. She heard Zane's distant voice, murmuring soothing words as she slowly drifted out of the churning, wild mire of sensation.

"Oh, God," she mumbled when she could finally speak again.

"I'm going to make your fantasy come true. Every single detail of it," Zane whispered breathlessly as he unfastened the cuffs holding her wrists.

"Including . . . ?"

"Yes, including that. I'm going to fuck you so slowly, so sweetly you'll beg for release." He helped her sit up. Sitting on the floor, he pulled her onto his lap. He brushed her hair out of her face. "Friday night. I'll tell you when and where later, after all the details are arranged."

She kissed him. "I'm looking forward to it." Pulling out of

his arms, she rose up onto her knees. Her legs were still shaky. Arms, too.

"Where are you going?"

"I have a job interview. Remember?"

"Oh. Damn. I forgot."

She checked the clock hanging on the wall. "No worries. I can still make it."

He wrapped a thick arm around her waist, pulling her back down. "Do you want to make it?"

He nibbled on her shoulder, and a fresh coat of goose bumps prickled her skin.

"Sure." She didn't sound so sure, even to her own ears.

"You owe me nothing. If you don't want the job, you don't have to take it."

"In that case, I'd rather stay here a little longer."

Falling onto his back, he pulled her down with him, until she was lying on top of him. He tucked her hair behind her ears. "That's probably a good idea. With that head injury, you could use some bed rest. You're looking a little pale yet." Logrolling, he flipped her over onto her back, wedging his hips between her thighs. "Let's see if we can bring a little color back to that beautiful face of yours." His hand slid between her thighs, and sure enough, she felt her face pinking up nicely.

19

The following Friday night, Mandy stood nude, her body tense, while lavender-and-vanilla-scented steam wafted over her body. At exactly seven, a limo had picked her up, transporting her to a building—what seemed to be a private residence—built to resemble a medieval castle. At the moment, she was standing in a large room, stone tiles gleaming. The flickering light of dozens of candles reflected off the still, clear water in the built-in swimming pool. Off to one side, a hot tub was overflowing with white, fragrant frothy foam. It was quite a setting.

But that wasn't the least of it. Three women, all of them stunningly beautiful, surrounded her. They were nude as well, with the exception of beaded chains hanging from their nipple rings, draping gracefully across their toned bodies. A third chain joined them at the center, hanging down the middle of flat, tanned stomachs, the other end disappearing into labial folds.

One of them, the tallest, motioned to the hot tub. "My queen," she said, extending a hand to Mandy.

Mandy accepted her hand as she stepped down into the water. One step, two, three and she was waist-deep in hot but not scalding water. The women, all three of them, filed in after her. Slightly uncertain about the idea of living out this particular part of her fantasy, Mandy moved to the back of the tub to give them room. She'd never touched another woman intimately. Hell, she'd never been in the same room with another nude woman. If it wasn't for the fact that her pussy was thrumming, she might have thought this was a very bad idea.

Recalling what she'd said had happened next, her tingling pussy clamped tighter.

They were going to touch her. Everywhere.

Still standing, arms crossed over her body, Mandy pressed her thighs together.

"His Majesty's instructions were very specific," the tall one said, moving toward Mandy.

"They were?" Mandy forced her gaze down, to the point where the woman's suntanned skin disappeared into the thick blanket of white foam. "What are your names?" Mandy asked.

"Jennifer," the tallest one said as she circled around Mandy, stopping directly behind her. "The blonde is Rachel. And the brunette Lindsay."

"Thanks."

Jennifer gathered Mandy's hair in her hands, gently coiling it onto the top of her head. Rachel and Lindsay each took one of Mandy's hands in theirs and massaged her palms.

This was nice.

Up, Rachel and Lindsay worked, massaging, washing her wrists, her arms. Meanwhile, Jennifer kneaded the tension out of Mandy's neck and shoulders. Oh, yes, this was very nice. She closed her eyes. It was easy to forget those were women's hands lightly caressing her arms, rubbing away the day's aches from her upper back.

Until Rachel and Lindsay reached the top of her arms and

their fingertips drew small circles along her collarbones. Then her eyelids fluttered open and she became painfully aware of the fact that those soft touches were coming from women. Sexy women. Sexy women standing extremely close to her.

A little shiver of unease buzzed through her body.

"We are here to give you pleasure," Jennifer said, her voice rich and smooth, satiny. "And to prepare you for our king."

A fingertip skimmed down the cleft between Mandy's breasts. She shuddered and squeezed her eyelids closed. Easier to relax if she didn't think about who was ... Ohmygod, one of them was lifting a breast.

Mandy jerked, and her boob slipped out of the woman's hand. Her ass brushed against Jennifer, standing behind her. That sent another current of electricity humming through her body. The sensation was part good, part bad. She wasn't sure if she liked it or not.

Once again, a soft hand cupped under her breast. Mandy's body tightened as it lifted her breast, weighing it. Fingers pinched her nipple, tugging it slightly, sending little stabbing blades of pleasure-pain along her sizzling nerves.

"Relax," Jennifer said, her hands gliding down Mandy's back. "Remember, this was at the request of your king." Those hands, which up to this point hadn't strayed from safe territory, moved south, over the globes of her ass. They tightened. Fingertips pulled them apart. Mandy's spine straightened. "We must clean you."

She'd done a fine job of that for years, thank you very much.

A hand slid between her ass cheeks, dragging sudsy bubbles up and down the crevice. A fingertip circled her anus. Of course, she clenched it. More hands worked down her front, over her stomach, lower, to her mound.

Oh, God, they were touching her pussy.

Slick fingers slid between her labia. Someone pulled her back, easing her down onto a seat. Mandy let her head fall back, closing her eyes, eagerly letting a world of swirling colors take her away from the embarrassment, the discomfort. Someone lifted her hips until her body floated on top of the water, legs dangling at the knees in the warm water.

More touches on her pussy, parting her labia. More touches to her breasts, kneading them, pinching her nipples, rolling them until they were aching points.

Slowly, gradually, all those touches started to feel good. Then they started to feel really good. Her blood warmed. Her nerves tingled. Her pussy pulsed. Her body became hot and tight and trembly. Those touches explored deeper, invading her most intimate places, her clenching pussy, her anus. They slid in and out, in and out, until she was on the verge of orgasm. Breathless. Dizzy. Caught up in decadent pleasure.

A pair of soft lips brushed over hers. A tongue traced the seam of Mandy's mouth, and without a second thought, she parted her lips. The kiss deepened. Tongues stroked, shyly at first, growing bolder with every thumping heartbeat.

It seemed like she was being touched everywhere, that there wasn't a part of her body that wasn't being stroked or kissed or fondled. And, ohmygod, she was going to come so hard.

Her spine arched. A waft of cool air gusted over her nipples. She sucked in a gasp, rocked her hips against the hand cupped over her mound, and surrendered.

Her pussy spasmed. Her anus contracted. It was one of the strongest orgasms of her life.

Shocking.

The hands left her.

She sank back onto the seat and fought to catch her breath. When she opened her eyes, she discovered Jennifer, Rachel, and Lindsay were standing next to the tub. A huge swath of fluffy cotton terry cloth stretched between two of them.

She stood and they wrapped her up.

"This way." Jennifer indicated the hallway. Mandy followed. Rachel and Lindsay trailed behind her.

They entered a gorgeous bedroom. The bed was huge. A canopy of luxurious silk hung from an ornately carved frame overhead. The bed itself was dressed in shimmering, rich fabrics. This place was unbelievable, like out of some kind of fairy tale. Mandy had never imagined such a place existed so close to where she lived.

Immediately, the ladies went to work. They smoothed fragrant oils onto Mandy's skin until she was tingly and warm. Then they helped her into a long, frothy gown of gold. Then, while she sat on a padded stool, Jennifer curled her hair while Rachel and Lindsay painted intricate, swirling designs on her hands and feet with henna.

By the time the henna paste had dried, Mandy had been pampered from head to toe. She felt so smooth and soft and. Jennifer escorted her to a full-length mirror. . . . Was that really her?

"Oh, w-wow," Mandy stammered as her gaze swept up and down her reflection.

It was amazing what a little bit of pampering, by some talented people, could do for a girl's looks. She was sexier, more beautiful, than she'd ever looked.

She couldn't stop staring.

The gown fit her perfectly, emphasizing all the bits she liked while gracefully flowing over the ones she wasn't so proud of. Her hair was a tumble of silky curls. It was sexy and gorgeous. "Can you ladies dress me every day?" Mandy joked.

"Sure," Jennifer said, smiling. She combed her fingers through Mandy's hair, pulling the curls forward so they cascaded down the front of her chest. "You like what we've done?"

"It hardly looks like me. And it isn't like I don't normally do my hair and makeup."

Mandy turned to the side, noticing how her mysteriously

bronzed skin shimmered. The darker shade looked fabulous with the gold gown. "Look at me, I'm suntanned. I take it you used some kind of self-tanner?"

"We thought it would complement the gown."

"It does. Perfectly." She turned to her miracle workers. "Thank you."

"You're welcome." Jennifer extended a hand. "It's time now."

Mandy took her hand and let herself be led out of the room. Down the hall they went, down a sweeping flight of stairs. Below, she could hear the distant echo of music.

The four of them stopped outside a pair of double doors.

"He waits," Jennifer said.

Mandy's sex clenched.

Already, this had been the most unsettling and erotic experience of her life. And it was about to get even more erotic. Probably unsettling, too.

Zane was finally going to fuck her. He'd promised. She'd waited so long for this moment. Just that alone made her breathing and heart rate speed up.

Not only was he finally going to fuck her, but also he was going to fuck her in public.

She curled her fingers into fists, then unfurled them, shaking them out to release the tension. In her mind's eye, she saw Zane sitting at the head of the room, on an ornate throne. He was wearing a pair of tight-fitting pants, no shirt. His hair was hanging around his face in sexy waves. The image did nothing to relieve her overwound nerves.

"Are you ready?" Jennifer asked.

After one final deep breath, Mandy nodded. "Yes. I'm ready now."

Rachel pushed open the door, stepping inside to make room for Mandy to pass through the doorway. Mandy froze. The room went silent. The candlelit space was packed full of people. Strangers. Probably a hundred of them. Men and women. All the women were wearing embroidered and jewel-encrusted sarees. Everyone was looking at her expectantly. Mandy's gaze lurched from one face to another. Male assessing eyes. Female assessing eyes. She felt naked, exposed. Alone.

Something moved up ahead. At the far end of the room.

Mandy's gaze jumped.

Zane.

He was standing on a raised platform. A wooden trellis stood behind him. It was swathed in translucent fabric, and flowers and vines had been wound around the vertical supports.

He stepped forward and extended a hand.

The crowd between them parted.

Mandy walked to him, the polished wooden floor cold beneath her bare feet. Zane's expression darkened slightly as she stepped up to him. It wasn't an expression of displeasure but of hard male hunger. "I have been waiting for this moment."

"So have I."

He helped her up the steps to the raised platform, which was completely cushioned, like one huge pillow-top mattress. It was covered in silky cotton and piled with silk-covered pillows. "Are you ready for me?" he murmured. Still holding her hand as they stood side by side on the dais, he brushed his free hand down her body, letting his palm skim over her breasts, her stomach. It cupped her mound. "Mmmm. Warm." Not bothering to move the thin material aside, he fingered her slick labia. "Wet."

She could hardly believe she was standing here, in front of all these people, letting Zane finger her. But she was. And, ohmygod, she was melting.

Feeling like her face might blister, she stared straight ahead, avoiding making eye contact with anyone. She was afraid to meet a stranger's eyes while Zane explored her body like this. It would be too intimate.

"I'm going to fuck you, Amanda," he whispered in her ear. "In front of all these people."

Her heart literally skipped a beat. "Now?"

"Soon." He was one cruel son of a bitch. "This is your fantasy. I wouldn't want to cheat you out of one single minute of it." He pointed out, indicating the crowd of people who were standing silent, watching every move they made. "Those are your people. You are about to become my queen. See how they wait? They want to see you surrender to me." He grazed the side of her neck with his teeth. She shivered. Her entire body became covered with goose bumps. He pushed a finger inside her pussy. The whisper-thin material of her gown rasped against her burning tissues as it was pushed deep inside her body.

"You've... gone to a great deal of trouble. The house. It looks so castlelike. The people. With their costumes. I didn't expect so much. It feels so... real."

"Good." He cupped one of her breasts, lifting it. He teased a nipple through the fabric.

Her gaze swept across the room. Everyone was transfixed, focused on her. A man in the second row licked his lips. His expression was pure, unrestrained carnal hunger. Mandy shuddered against Zane.

Zane released her. He took a step back. "Remove your dress."

Her sex clenched again. Her face burned. She started to turn around, but Zane stopped her with a firm, "No."

She swallowed. Her throat was desert dry. With clumsy fingers, she unfastened the row of tiny buttons on the front of her gown. The material shimmied down her body and landed in a gold puddle at her feet. Knowing Zane would not appreciate her covering herself, she forced her arms to remain at her sides. A gush of juices pulsed from her pussy.

"The gift," Zane said aloud.

Jennifer broke through the crowd. She was wearing a deep burgundy saree now. An ornate jeweled headdress dripped beads over her center-parted hair. In her hands she held a small gift-wrapped box. She climbed the stairs, knelt before Mandy, and, before Mandy had a chance to reach for the box, lifted the lid.

Jewelry. But what was it? A necklace?

When Jennifer lifted the piece, which glittered blue and silver, she knew the answer to that question. She stood, looked askance, and when Mandy nodded, affixed one looped end around one nipple, then moved to do the same with the other. As she pulled the loops tight around the hard tips, a sharp little biting sting zapped through Mandy's body. She sucked in a gasp of surprise but didn't move. Jennifer returned to her knees.

She glanced down at the beautiful chain of blue stones hanging between her breasts. It was gorgeous.

The onlookers all started applauding.

Mandy's face burned hotter.

"You may now show your gratitude for my gift," Zane said behind her.

She turned to discover he was standing with his legs in a wide stance. The drop-flap opening of his pants had been opened, and his thick cock was now standing hard and proud, awaiting her attention.

Grateful to be doing something besides standing on display, Mandy hurried to him, lowering to her knees. She gripped his cock in her hand, letting her thumb run over the silver ball on the underside of his glans. Her index finger curled around his thickness, just behind the matching ball on top, positioned farther back, just before the flared ridge. She'd never had sex with a man who had a piercing before. It was sexy to look at.

She opened her mouth, taking him inside. Her tongue flicked over the ball before flattening to allow him to slide deeper. Her upper lip skimmed over the top ball, then clasped closed. She used her hand like an extension of her mouth, stroking back and forth.

She rested her other hand on his thigh. His muscles tightened under the satiny-smooth skin as he slowly thrust his hips forward and back, forward and back. Someone came up the stairs. She heard soft footsteps, but she was too busy to care. Zane's breathing deepened.

"Mmm, so good," he said.

Spurred on by his encouragement, Mandy lapped at him as if he were a lollipop. With the piercing, there was no way she could take him in her throat, so she had to get creative. She flicked her tongue over him, concentrating on the glans. Meanwhile, she stroked him, head to base with her hand.

Fingernails dragged down her back and her spine straightened. A fresh coat of goose bumps puckered over her skin. A flare of heat pulsed out from her center.

"Spread your legs," Zane said.

Mandy obeyed, sliding her legs apart.

Something wet slipped between her ass cheeks. Instinct had her freezing in place. It was her turn to start breathing heavily as the thing found her anus and started prodding at the tight ring of muscles.

"Bend over, Amanda."

She lowered her upper body, supporting herself on outstretched hands. She started to glance over her shoulder, but Zane stopped her with another sharp, "No." Understanding he was doing what he believed would give her pleasure, she let her head fall forward instead and relaxed her ass. A toy slid inside, filling her.

"Now, on your back."

It felt strange moving with that toy wedged deep in her ass, but she maneuvered into the position Zane indicated. Rachel and Lindsay had joined them on the dais. They knelt on either side of her, hands resting on their laps, heads lowered.

Zane rolled on a rubber then, while Rachel applied some lube to Mandy's burning tissues. He knelt at her feet. "Her legs."

Rachel and Lindsay each took one of Mandy's legs in their hands and lifted, forcing them back toward her chest and out. Her pussy was open wide now, and on full display. She was breathless, on the verge of orgasm, and anxious to finally feel Zane's cock filling her.

He curled his hand around his thick rod. Angled over her, he kissed her until she was delirious. She flung her arms around his neck and pulled him down. How she longed to feel his weight upon her. How she longed to feel his thick cock plunging inside. Desperate now, her body aflame, she tried to wrap her legs around his hips and grind away the ache pulsing in her core. She couldn't.

She whimpered into his mouth.

He broke the kiss and looked down upon her with lust-filled eyes. Enthralled, she cupped his gorgeous face and gently brushed her mouth over his.

"Take me, please," she whispered.

"I am your king." The tip of his cock nudged at her slick opening, and a wave of erotic need rippled through her body.

"Yes, Zane. Always." She held her breath, waiting.

His hips swung up, and Mandy thought for the briefest moment that he wouldn't fuck her. A groan bubbled up from her chest, but before it made it all the way up her throat, his hips surged down, his cock slammed deep inside, and all the air left her lungs in a long hiss.

"Ohhhhh," she said. She gripped his arms, using them for leverage as she pushed her hips forward to meet his thrusts.

He fucked her hard, his body possessing hers, staking its claim, leaving its mark and she was so, so grateful. This was what she'd waited for, longed for, dreamed of.

Someone grabbed her wrists, pulling them up, binding them over her head. Now she was even more powerless. Completely at his mercy.

His thrusts were long and sure and smooth. Each one caused a chain reaction inside her body. Small sparks exploded here and there, those sparks igniting mini-blazes that grew into wild, out-of-control infernos. Before she knew it, she was shaking all over and begging him to let her come.

Changing his angle of penetration, he sat back on his knees and rubbed his thumb over her swollen clit.

"Come now," he demanded.

Her body obeyed.

A whole-body spasm overtook her, and great big waves of carnal heat crashed over her. She quaked while her pussy milked his cock, and her ass squeezed the toy still buried deep inside. So lost was she in the intense orgasm that she barely heard him cry out as he found his release.

Moments later, his body settled over hers. His arm slid under her head, cushioning it. His semiflaccid cock slipped out of her body.

When she was finally able to breathe, she opened her eyes.

He was staring at her. His expression was unreadable.

She wanted to tell him she was falling in love with him, but she was afraid to. It was frustrating, feeling what she did for Zane and not being able to simply tell him.

He kissed her hair and she closed her eyes. She could feel a smile of contentment spread across her face. Maybe they didn't need words. Maybe it was enough to have him holding her like this, having him take her in such a public way, when he was known not to fuck his submissives. Surely this whole thing meant more than merely a fantasy come to life.

Remember, he said there'd never be a commitment between us. You told him this was enough. You can't renege already.

20

Mandy's heart was pounding so loudly, she could hear it.

It had been a week since that glorious, amazing, unbelievable experience with Zane. She'd dreamed about him every night. She thought about him practically every minute of the day. And she'd looked forward to tonight with the exuberance of a kid anticipating Christmas morning.

All week long, while she'd run around in circles, chasing Clark and Nickerson around town, she'd wondered if that unbelievable experience she'd shared with Zane would change their relationship, stabilize it, add a new, deeper intimacy. God, she hoped so.

She was about to find out.

"Are you okay?" Sarah asked, keying into Mandy's jittery nerves.

"I'm fine. Nervous."

"Honey, if he doesn't fall to his knees and tell you he loves you, he doesn't deserve you."

Mandy didn't respond. Sarah could be right. He might love her. But she would probably never hear him say the words.

They'd agreed there would be no expectations, no commitment. They would be friends. Lovers. But never monogamous partners. Never husband and wife.

"He's obviously crazy about you. He's never done anything even remotely close to what he did for you last weekend. He loves you, even if he isn't able to say the words. Trust me."

Mandy wanted to trust Sarah.

"They said he's in here, in his suite." Sarah motioned toward the closed door. "Go ahead."

Mandy didn't reach for the knob. "But the door's shut. It's usually open."

"I'm sure it's no big deal. Especially with you. I've been to every party the man has hosted this year. He has always had an open-door policy, with the understanding that if you go inside, you'll be expected to join in the scene."

Mandy reached but before she touched the knob, she pulled her hand back. "I don't know."

"You've scened with him before. You know he doesn't get intimate with his submissives...."

Except for her.

Maybe there are others, too. What if I'm not the only one he fucks?

Sarah pointed at Mandy's nose. "I know what you're thinking. You're wrong. He loves you. He's never been the kind of dom to fuck his submissives. Why would he start now?"

Good question.

Sarah gave Mandy a little nudge.

"Okay." This time Mandy's hand made contact with the gold-toned doorknob. She grasped it.

"Have fun." Sarah gave her another nudge. "You'll thank me later."

Mandy turned the knob and pushed. She stepped into the room as the door swung wider. Her gaze locked onto Zane's tall figure. He was standing. Dressed head to toe in black, as usual. His back was facing the door. He didn't turn around right away.

His hips. He was moving. Was he...?

His head fell back.

Mandy stood frozen in place, unable to move.

Behind her, she heard Sarah mutter, "Oh, shit."

Her breath caught in her throat.

Zane's movements became jerky, uneven, as he drew nearer to completion.

Mandy clapped a hand over her mouth. She wanted to turn around, walk out, save her dignity. Why the fuck couldn't she move?

"Yes, harder. Please harder," a man said. The partner hidden from Mandy's view.

So that was why he couldn't make a commitment to her.

Zane was fucking another man.

A man. Mandy didn't know if that made it easier or harder for her. Neither, probably. He was still fucking somebody else.

"That's how you like it. Rough. Hard," Zane said, his voice raw, breathy. "You can't ever get it hard enough."

"Yessss," the man said.

"Mandy, come on," Sarah whispered.

Mandy felt a tug at her arm. She didn't move.

Who was he fucking? Did they know each other well?

Why did she care?

"Mandy, honey. Let's go," Sarah urged.

Mandy jerked her arm out of Sarah's grasp. She dragged the back of her hand across her face. It was wet. Tears. She was crying. She sniffed.

Still, Zane didn't stop. He kept on fucking. His narrow hips ramming back and forth. Although Mandy couldn't see anything, she could imagine a man bent at the waist, Zane's cock pistoning in and out. Zane's beautiful face darkened, his eyes glimmering with sexual hunger.

And she'd been stupid enough to think he only looked at her that way.

"Mandy," Sarah said, louder.

The sounds of male moans and groans of pleasure were building. They were both close to release now. Zane would hold off; he would wait for his lover to come first. Mandy knew it.

"You don't need to watch any more of this," Sarah hissed. "Come on."

Mandy was finally able to turn away, but as she walked through the doorway, she couldn't help glancing over her shoulder.

Sarah jerked harder on her arm.

"I'm coming already. You don't have to be so rough."

"Sorry." Sarah stopped when they reached the end of the hallway at the top of the stairs. She glared back in the general direction of Zane's suite. "I'm just so...angry. For you. Not at you."

"Don't be. He told me he couldn't make any kind of commitment."

"But—"

"Zane has always made it clear I shouldn't expect monogamy..."

"But—"

"I told him I was okay with it. I shouldn't have let myself get carried away, believing the fantasy. I'm such a fool."

"You're crying." Sarah wiped at Mandy's wet cheeks. She was doing a lot of blinking, too. And her eyes weren't exactly bone-dry.

"I'll be okay. I'm a big girl."

"It's my fault. I shouldn't have suggested he had feelings for you. I led you to believe things were more serious than they were."

"I'm not upset with you. Not at all."

The muffled sound of men's cries of release echoed down the hall. Both Mandy and Sarah followed the sound of the voices with their eyes. Then they looked at each other.

Mandy's eyes were burning again.

"Let's get out of here."

Mandy nodded. She wasn't in a party mood anymore. She was in the mood to get into some comfy sweats and snarf down a half gallon of chocolate fudge brownie ice cream.

They clacked down the stone stairs. Mandy tried to hold her head high. Sarah was in front of her. Mandy couldn't help noticing how stiffly she was walking.

Now, that was a good friend.

At the bottom of the staircase, a familiar man strolled up to Sarah. Eric. Sarah's bisexual ex-boyfriend. He caught her elbow, cradling it in his palm. Sarah gave Mandy a guilty look. "There you are. I've been looking for you. Waiting for you. I need to talk."

"Shit, Eric," Sarah grumbled. "Now?"

"Please."

Mandy waved her off. "Go ahead."

"I'll only be a minute. I swear to God."

Mandy stepped to the side to wait. She spent the time trying to hide behind a huge indoor tree, while running her index fingers under her lashes, hoping to wipe away what had to be terrible raccoon eyes.

Eric pulled Sarah toward a quiet corner where they chatted intimately.

"Amanda."

Oh, shit, Zane.

With a great deal of reluctance, she turned to face him. She saw the surprise in his eyes as their gazes met.

"Did you just arrive?" He extended his arms to hug her.

She struggled with how to respond. Let him hold her and make things even more painful? Or let him know she was upset? If he knew she was upset, he would probably reiterate what he'd said before, and then she'd probably feel even worse.

She leaned into him and closed her eyes. Sadly, the image of him fucking that man was burned into her memory and it played the instant her eyelids fell closed. She squeezed them harder, trying to trap the tears that were burning to be released.

Quit being such a crybaby. You've always known what kind of man Zane is.

One of his hands cupped the back of her head. His slow, steady heartbeat thumped in her ear as she flattened it against his chest. She inhaled, drawing in the scent of him, his cologne and the slightest hint of sex.

"Is something wrong?" he asked.

A man strolled up to Zane before Mandy could answer. "Heya, Zane." The man's gaze slid to Mandy. "Thanks for the invite."

"Not a problem." Zane cupped Mandy's elbow in his palm and steered her toward the stairs.

Mandy's gaze snapped to Sarah.

Sarah was still talking to Eric, head bent, expression serious. Whatever they were discussing, it was something intense. Mandy didn't want to interrupt to let her know Zane was escorting her up the stairs. Mandy didn't necessarily want to go upstairs with him either. But when another guest bounced up to him, a female this time, wearing a dress that looked like blue shrink wrap, Mandy knew she wasn't going to be able to hold a private conversation with Zane out in the foyer. Better to take it somewhere quiet.

Up the stairs they went and into Zane's suite. Zane shut the door, then turned to face her, arms crossed over his chest. "You were crying."

Lie? Or tell the truth?

"I was. But I'm okay now."

Something flickered in his eyes. "Why?"

Lie? Or tell the truth?

She opened her mouth. Nothing came out.

Dammit.

She tried again. "Zane..." That's all she could manage to force out. *Don't cry. Don't cry. Don't cry.*

"What is it?" He came to her, slid a flattened hand against the side of her head. The touch made it ten times worse.

She backed away. "I think I need to take a break."

"From...? Me?"

She nodded.

"Why?"

She crossed her arms over her chest, mirroring him. "I have to be honest with you. I'm starting to have feelings for you. It's making it hard for me to—"

Realization spread over his face. "It was you, wasn't it? You came up here earlier."

Mandy's eyes were practically on fire. Her nose, too. She nodded.

"Shit," he said.

"You don't have to explain. You've made it clear from the start that you weren't offering a committed, monogamous relationship of any sort." Her damn eyes were leaking. Her nose too. She sniffled and dragged her hand under her eyelashes. "Dammit."

He pulled her into an embrace. "I'm sorry, Amanda. I never wanted to hurt you."

"I know." She relaxed against him. Her arms slid around his waist. It was so unfair. She felt warm and safe here, with this man, in his arms. If only he could give her more.

If only he could love her.

That isn't fair. You knew who he was. You can't expect him to change just so you can be happy.

* * *

You fucked up this time, asshole.

Zane was so frustrated and lost, he didn't know what to say. He ached to comfort Amanda. She had trusted him. She had let herself be vulnerable. Wasn't that what he'd expected?

But the consequences...the fucking consequences.

He'd been vaguely aware that someone had come into the room when he'd been fucking Bruce. But he'd been concentrating so hard on what Bruce needed, that he hadn't let himself become distracted.

You should've known it was her.

To be fair, Amanda had told him she wouldn't be arriving until later. When Bruce had come to him, pleading with him to feed, he'd figured he'd have plenty of time to do what he had to before she'd arrive.

How could he explain so she'd understand—without having to tell her *everything?*

"I'm being such a baby about this," she mumbled into his chest.

"Amanda."

She didn't look at him.

He hooked his finger under her chin and forced her to raise her head. He waited until her gaze had finally found his before he continued. Dammit, her eyes were so red, so full of pain. "What I have with Bruce is nothing like what we have together."

"You don't have to say that."

"Of course I do. It's the truth. And I want you to know it. To *believe* it."

"O-okay." She sounded so small and meek, nothing like the headstrong bulldog he knew she was. He'd done that to her, crushed her.

You bastard.

Someone knocked on the door.

Of all the fucking times…

Amanda turned from him. "I should go."

He caught her elbow. "Wait."

The door swung open. Of course it was Bruce. Who else would it be?

Fuck.

"Zane, I need to speak with you," he said.

Amanda left without saying another word. Zane knew there was no sense trying to stop her.

21

Sarah was lounging in Mandy's office the next morning when Mandy dragged herself into work. The second Mandy stepped through the door, Sarah jumped to her feet. "Tell me everything."

"There's nothing to tell." Mandy dropped her purse onto her desk.

"You talked to him, right?"

"Sure, I talked to him." She circled the desk.

"And you told him how you feel...?"

She slumped into her chair. "Not in so many words. But he knows."

"And...?"

"And all he had to say was that what he shares with Brent—or Bob or whatever his name is—is different from what we share."

Sarah plopped her tush onto Mandy's desk. "That's something."

"That's not enough, dammit." Mandy rubbed her palms

over her face, totally smearing her makeup. She didn't give a damn. "Shit. I thought I was okay with this."

Sarah sighed as she swung one leg over the other. "I completely understand. Look at me and Eric."

"Yeah, speaking of you and Eric, what happened? It looked like your conversation was getting pretty intense."

"It was." She started avoiding eye contact and fiddling with the file sitting on Mandy's desk.

"Tell me."

Sarah sighed. "He got married."

Mandy actually smacked her hands over her mouth. That was the last thing she'd been expecting to hear. And, looking at Sarah, it must have been the last thing she'd expected to hear, too. "Married? To a *woman*?"

"Yeah, a woman. That fucking bitch."

"Ohmygod. When?"

"Last weekend. They went to Vegas. Said he wanted to tell me himself, before I heard about it from someone else. I was this close to kicking him in the nuts when he told me." Sarah indicated a tiny fraction of an inch with her finger and thumb.

"I would be, too."

"I still can't believe he married her. After he held me off all those years, telling me he couldn't commit because he loved Christopher..." Sarah stared down at the desk again. "That was after I found out Valdez is married."

"No!"

"Yes. Bastards. Both of them." Looking broken, defeated, Sarah slumped her shoulders. "I'm getting sick and tired of men. Maybe I should turn lesbian."

"Can you 'turn' lesbian?" Mandy absentmindedly shuffled through the reports Sarah had stacked on her desk.

"I don't know." Sarah's gaze slowly dragged up to Mandy's. Her eyes were watery now and red.

"Oh, hon. I'm sorry. Men suck." Mandy took Sarah's hand in hers. It was small, delicate, fragile. Oddly, Mandy had always seen her friend as a strong woman, the mistress she played in the dungeons.

Sarah gave Mandy a watery half smile. "I think we should both turn lesbian. I'd do you."

Mandy felt her face go colorless. She remembered all too well how those three women had made her feel a couple weeks ago. Could she actually go there with Sarah? *No way.* With her free hand, she grabbed the tissue box out of her desk drawer and set it within Sarah's reach.

"I was just kidding," Sarah said, a humorless laugh hiding her pain. She dabbed at her eyes with a scented tissue.

The chime on the agency's front door tinkled.

Saved by the bell.

Sarah hopped up. "I'll go see who that is. Maybe it's a new client."

"Thanks." Mandy returned the tissue box to the drawer and rummaged in her purse for her cell phone. A tap sounded on her door. She glanced up and stood, prepared to open the door for her visitor.

The door opened. Zane.

"Amanda. I need to talk to you." Stepping inside, he pointed to the door. "May I?"

Mandy nodded. "Sure."

He closed it, then, after waiting for her to sit, took a seat in the chair in front of her desk. "I've been thinking about things. About what happened last night at the party."

Oh, shit, here we go.

Lie? Or tell the truth?

Truth.

"Zane, I'd be lying if I said I wasn't thinking about it, too. But, I don't want you to feel like you need to explain anything.

From the beginning you told me you couldn't get involved in a committed relationship. I agreed to your terms. I have no right to expect something else from you now."

Zane leaned forward, resting an arm on her desktop. "Maybe you feel you have no right, but I know I've led you to believe things were progressing that way."

"Did you intentionally try to mislead me?"

"No, but—"

"It's not your fault, then, is it?"

Zane stood. Mandy hoped he'd stay where he was. Keeping the desk between them would make it a whole lot easier to stay somewhat objective. Of course, he didn't.

She pushed to her feet as he came around to her side of the desk and crossed her arms over her chest, giving him the don't-come-too-close vibe.

As usual, he ignored it, crowding closer. "Amanda, I can't begin to describe my feelings for you. When I said what we share is different, special, I meant it. I've never felt this way about anyone."

"Okay, I understand." She tightened her arms.

"No, you don't." Looking intense, Zane jammed his fingers through his hair. "I can't stop thinking about you, wondering what you're doing, where you are, if you're safe...." He lifted her chin, staring into her eyes. "I can't get enough of you. I can't kiss you enough. I can't touch you enough. I can't hear that sweet little voice of yours enough."

She really, really liked what she was hearing. But what exactly was he trying to tell her?

"And I can't fathom the thought of losing you."

"What makes you think you might?" she asked.

Zane didn't speak for a handful of tense moments. Mandy waited, watched, as he visibly thought through whatever he was about to say next. Finally, his gaze found hers. "I need to tell you something. I've never cared so much for a woman that I've felt the need to tell her this."

Was he Married? "Okay, Zane."

"What you saw last night wasn't exactly what you think."

He'd been fucking someone, a male. Was he trying to tell her he hadn't been fucking? Had he not penetrated his partner? Where was this going?

"Fucking is part of a practice, a procedure," he explained.

He wasn't even trying to deny the fact that he was fucking someone else. But why call it a "procedure"? That was a very odd term to use. Clinical.

"Was it some kind of...therapy?" she asked, intentionally revealing her confusion.

"No, not exactly. It's more like foreplay."

"Foreplay?" she echoed, feeling more confused than ever. How was this conversation supposed to make her feel better about things? It was having the exact opposite effect. "Foreplay to *what?*"

"To pain," Zane said.

Lightbulb. "Okay, I get it now. It's part of the whole S and M thing."

"No, not in Bruce's case. It's part of a relationship we've shared for over forty years." *Forty years?* "A mutually beneficial one, in which we both get something we need." *Sex.* "In my case, it's sustenance. Blood."

Blood?

"Huh?"

"You don't know this, but there are beings walking among you that aren't mortal. Beings like me."

Beings?

She realized midstride that she was taking a step backward. "What do you think you are?"

"We're *Dejenen.* Vampires."

Oh, God. He was one of those people—the ones who thought they were vampires. She'd read about vampirism online. There were folks who actually drank blood. It was one of the creepiest things she'd ever read about. Right up there with people who had sex with animals.

She should've known he had some ugly skeletons in his closet. He'd earned a reputation among people who had very loose definitions of right and wrong. In a world of gray, he'd somehow become a black sheep. Now she understood why.

The question was, did this change how she felt about him? Would knowing that he drank blood make her heart ache less when she wasn't with him? Would she stop dreaming about him every freaking night?

She wished it would. But she had a sneaking suspicion it wouldn't.

"You know what, I'm not going to judge you. If you think you're a vampire, then...Wait a minute. You said 'forty years'?" When he nodded, she asked, "How old are you?"

"I'll be two hundred thirty-eight on my next birthday."

Two hundred thirty-eight. "Isn't that...fascinating."

"You don't believe me."

"Sure, I do." She took another step back. "So, let me get this straight. You were fucking some man before you bit him because you're a vampire and that's what you need to do?"

He nodded. Moved closer. "It sounds crazy."

She took a few more backward steps. "It sure does."

"But it's true," he said, closing the distance between them again.

She fingered her neck. How many times had he nibbled her there? Grazed her skin with his teeth. "And because you need sustenance, you must fuck this guy before you bite him."

"Yes."

What a convoluted way to justify his actions.

Mandy wondered if Zane wasn't a gay man trying to hide his true sexuality from himself. That was a distinct possibility.

Where would that leave her, though? She was a female. If Zane was indeed a gay guy trying to convince himself he was straight, she'd end up heartbroken sooner or later, when he finally accepted the truth about himself.

Zane stepped forward yet again, closing the gap between them. But this time he caught her arms in his fists, holding her in place. "I know it must be hard for you to believe this. But I'm telling you the truth. I couldn't go on keeping these secrets from you. Not when I could see I was hurting you."

"So you believe it'll hurt less, now that you've told me you can't help fucking your gay partner?"

Genuine pain flashed over his features. "You don't believe me."

"I believe you've convinced yourself that you're a vampire. But, no, I don't believe you are one. You're a man. A man who needs to work some things out."

Zane released her arms and sighed. "He said you probably wouldn't believe me, but I was hoping—"

"Who?"

"Rolf."

"Who's Rolf?"

"Yes. He's the guy who almost caught you with the camera at Twilight. He's one, too. I went to him for some advice after you left the party."

"Rolf's a vampire, too?"

"Yes. In fact, his brother, the owner of Twilight, is our king."

"King of the vampires?"

Zane's jaw clenched. "You're mocking me."

She was. "I'm sorry. That isn't nice of me." A very awkward, strained silence stretched between them. Mandy shifted her weight from one foot to the other. "Is that all you came to tell me?"

"Yes."

"Okay." More silence. "Thanks."

"Please don't tell anyone."

"Of course, I won't." That was a lie, of course. The minute he left, she was going to tell Sarah. Not because they'd share a good laugh. Right now, she was too confused and frustrated to see the humor in the situation.

"Thank you." He opened the door, stared at her for a long stretch. "Amanda, I . . ."

When he didn't finish his sentence, she waved. "Good-bye, Zane."

"Bye."

Mandy slumped into her chair, boneless.

Sarah shuffled in a couple of minutes later and took the chair Zane had occupied. "What was that all about?"

Mandy stared down at her desk, combing her fingers through her hair. "You're not going to believe it."

Sarah scooted the chair closer to the desk and leaned forward. "What?" She blinked wide eyes.

"He explained what he was doing with that guy last night."

Sarah waved a hand. "What's to explain? He was fucking him."

"That's what I thought, too. But actually, there's more. You see, he wasn't merely fucking him." This time Mandy leaned forward, as if she was about to tell Sarah some big, shocking, dark secret. "Zane was preparing him for pain."

"Sure, like S and M?"

"No, like a nasty bite on the neck." Mandy tapped the side of her neck to illustrate.

"Huh?" Sarah scrunched her brows.

"Zane thinks he's a vampire. And he said fucking that man was foreplay before he bites him. According to him, he's been feeding from Bob or Ben or whoever for forty years. Oh, and get this—he's over two hundred years old."

"Oh, gosh, and I thought I had it bad with Eric."

Mandy clapped her hands over her face. She didn't know if she should laugh or cry. Probably both.

"I'm telling you, we should become lesbians," Sarah said.

Mandy was beginning to think that sounded like a good idea.

22

Mandy checked the clock. Four-thirty.

It was Thursday night. Over the last couple of weeks, Mandy had started to get a feel for Nickerson's schedule. Lucky for her, he was the kind of man who lived and breathed by a schedule. After talking to Mrs. Nickerson about loosening the purse strings, her husband went back to his usual routine. Thursdays, he took the little mistress out for dinner. Afterward, they spent some quality time at a local motel.

Ready to nail him—she'd prepared everything in advance this time—Mandy swung her purse over her shoulder and headed out to Sarah's desk, expecting to find Sarah dressed and ready to go.

Sarah was wearing black, just like she had the last time she'd ridden along during a stakeout. However, instead of athletic pants and a sweatshirt, Sarah was sporting a little black fuck-me dress. And instead of the Shox, she was tottering on five-inch stilettos.

Mandy's mood soured. She'd sort of been looking forward

to having Sarah around on tonight's stakeout. "Big plans tonight?" Mandy asked.

"Yes," Sarah answered, blushing slightly.

Sarah was looking guilty.

"Tell me you aren't going out with Valdez."

Sarah averted her eyes. "Ummm..."

Mandy checked her watch. She had no time to engage in a conversation about the hazards of dating married men. Sarah knew firsthand what lengths some wives would go to to catch their husbands cheating.

How ironic, here she was chasing cheating men for wives and her best friend was sleeping with a married man.

"Mrs. Valdez had better not come strolling into the office someday."

"She won't." Sarah checked her lipstick with a compact. "We're being very careful. Thanks to working with you, I know what not to do."

"Great," Mandy said, giving Sarah a dose of disapproving mean-eyes. She hoped she'd eventually somehow talk her friend out of seeing that man. There was no time to get into it tonight.

After muttering a silent apology to an unsuspecting Mrs. Valdez out there somewhere, Mandy headed to her car. She cranked on the radio and motored off, zigzagging through early rush-hour traffic to get to Nickerson's office. Like clockwork, he came strolling out with his mistress at exactly 5:08. She followed them to a swanky restaurant a few miles away. She munched on a protein bar while she waited for them to eat, then took up the chase again when they left.

However, instead of heading straight to the hotel, as she'd anticipated, they drove twenty miles to a trendy nightclub. Fabulous, they were in the mood to party. The sun worked its way over the western horizon while she sat in the parking lot waiting for them to come out of the bar. Her phone rang just after sunset.

Sarah.

Mandy hit the receive button, answering with a, "Hey, what's up?"

Sarah was crying.

"Sarah, what's wrong?"

Sarah said something, but hell if Mandy could understand it.

"Where are you?" Mandy asked.

Once again, Sarah responded, but Mandy couldn't make out what she'd said, not one word.

Mandy's gut twisted. "Hon, take a few deep breaths and let's try it again."

"'Kay," Sarah blubbered. She sniffed and snarfed and sobbed. Then she said something that sounded like, "Mfr-rrghdababreglafled."

Of course, because Mandy was busy worrying about her best friend and trying to figure out what was going on, Nickerson and his mistress had to come strolling out of the bar, his arm slung over her shoulder.

Mandy pinched her cell phone between her shoulder and ear and started her car. "Sarah, I can't understand you. You've got to stop crying."

"I'm tryingggggg," Sarah said, the word trailing off into another long series of sobs and hiccups and snorts.

Listening to her friend bawl in her ear, Mandy followed Nickerson's car at a safe distance. After driving a few miles, it turned into the hotel parking lot. "That's it, get her drunk and then fuck her brains out. What a class act you are," Mandy said to herself.

"Huh?" Sarah responded.

"I'm on Nickerson's tail. He's at the Fairview Inn."

"Oh."

"Are you okay now?" Mandy asked, cutting off the engine. "Do you need me to come over? Where are you?"

"I'm okay," Sarah said, not sounding okay.

"If I left right now, I could be at your place in a half hour."

"No, don't. Go ahead and finish what you're doing. Call me when you're done." Sarah sounded worn out, both emotionally and physically.

"Are you sure?" Mandy climbed out of her car, heading toward the hotel.

"Yeah." More sniffles. Another snort. "I'll tell you later. I don't want you to miss the chance at nailing Nickerson."

"I'll get there as soon as I can. You're at home, right?"

"No, I'm at your apartment."

"Okay. I'll be home within an hour. Hang on. And if you need it, there's a carton of German chocolate ice cream in the freezer."

"Already found it. Thanks."

Standing at the hotel's main entrance, Mandy hesitated. "Are you sure?"

"Positive. Go. Nail the son of a bitch. Cheating husbands suck."

"Okay. I'll call you when I'm on my way."

"Okay, bye."

Mandy shoved her phone into her pocket and headed inside. Nickerson and his girlfriend were at the front counter, checking in. Mandy pretended to be a guest, strolling right through the lobby and heading down a corridor that led to the elevators. A couple of minutes later, Nickerson and his girlfriend joined her at the bank of elevators, along with a pretty nice-looking man. Mandy inched a little closer to the man, hoping they'd think she was with him. Truth of the matter was, it was probably unnecessary; they were too wrapped up in each other to care who was waiting with them. Mandy pulled out her pen camera and snapped a couple of photos of them pawing at each

other, then stepped into the elevator with them. The man followed her. Up they rode. The car stopped at the second floor.
The man got out. Mandy stayed in, riding it up to the third
floor with Nickerson and his grabby, horny mistress. Luckily
for her, Miss Handsonhiscrotch made it easy. Mandy snapped
shot after shot, then followed them down the corridor. They
stopped at room 316. She kept on going.

Once the door shut, she circled back, snapped a shot of the
room number placard, and headed back to the elevators. She
punched the DOWN button, and the elevator's doors instantly
slid open. To her surprise, the guy who'd rode up with her was
now riding down. She gave him a little nod of recognition, then
stepped into the car. It rumbled to a stop on the first floor. She
went into the lobby. He followed. Assuming he was going out
to his car for his luggage, Mandy headed outside. She rounded
the building's corner, her car in sight, when something big and
heavy barreled into her from behind. She went flying to the
ground, hitting it so hard the air blasted out of her body. Struggling to reinflate her lungs, she rolled onto her side. Something
smaller, harder, struck her back. Pain exploded through her.

What was happening?

She curled up as a second and a third impact struck her.
More pain. Blinding pain. The world was a swirling mass of
black and gray. She tried to see what was happening, who was
attacking her, but she couldn't. Every time she moved, she was
hit again.

Darkness.

Cold.

Unbearable pain.

Just let me go unconscious. Please.

Icy fingers clamped around her neck.

I'm going to die. Oh, God. I'm going to die!

Pressure.

Her heart pounded in her head. Loud, like a drum.

No air.

She struggled.

Need air.

She fought harder.

Tired. So tired. Can't fight anymore.

The fingers tightened.

Soon it'll be over. Just let it be over.

Pretty white stars glittered all around her. She felt her body grow heavier. *Almost over.*

The fingers disappeared.

She jerked in a huge lungful of air. Her throat ached. Her lungs burned. Pain. She pulled in another gasp. A third. A dull thump sounded close by. She dragged her eyelids open. A man was scrambling to his feet not far away. The man from the elevator. A second man was fighting with him.

That man...looked...familiar.

Zane?

Slowly, gritting her teeth against the pain, Mandy pushed herself upright. She was sitting in the middle of the parking lot, but she didn't care. All she could focus on was the sight of Zane and her attacker punching each other, hurling each other against parked cars and trucks. They were both fighting with everything they had. And both seemed inhumanly strong. Her attacker caught Zane by surprise, rammed him like a linebacker, and Zane sailed at least twenty feet through the air, landing on top of a Mercedes. The car's alarm screeched. Still the melee continued. Zane was back on his feet before the attacker reached him. They raced toward each other, met somewhere in the middle, and exchanged a round of bone-crushing blows.

Mandy wanted to stop them, wished the attacker would give up. She prayed someone would hear the car alarm and call the police. Time slowed as she watched Zane in horror. He took as many blows as he gave. And each time the attacker hit him, she was terrified it would be the final one, the one that would send

Zane falling to the ground. She tried to push to her feet, but the pain in her back and sides took her breath away. She tried to cry out, but her throat was too raw. Barely a whisper came out. Her eyes burned, and she dragged the back of her hand across her face. Tears. She was crying.

Zane bent at the waist and caught the attacker in the gut. Off the ground he flew. Zane raced after him as he sailed through the air. The man landed, and Zane hauled him up, smashing his face with his fist once, twice, three times. The man's legs folded, and he started to sink to the ground, but Zane grabbed him around the neck, holding him upright. He blasted him again and again. The sound of bones snapping echoed between the wail of the Mercedes's alarm, creating a morbid symphony. Mandy tried to stand again, but the pain sent a rush of nausea through her. She sank to her knees, doubled over.

A strange sound made her jerk her head up. She looked through watery eyes at Zane. His head was bent, his face buried in the crook of the attacker's neck. The sound was coming from the attacker. At least, that's what it seemed like. Mandy couldn't be sure. It was a high-pitched squeal, like the call of a seagull but creepier. Zane tipped his head back, and the halogen light overhead highlighted his face. It was covered in something dark.

The attacker's limp, lifeless body fell to the ground.

Zane rushed to her.

Mandy gasped in horror when he came closer.

His mouth, chin, and neck were covered in some slimy substance. Blood, but a darker shade, perhaps. He said something. Mandy didn't hear. She was too focused on how he looked, at the elongated fangs gleaming in the dim light. At the creepy red light seeming to glow from his pupils.

He was a monster.

She shrank away from his touch.

Someone shouted from the hotel's door.

She twisted her head to see who it was. When she turned back around a split second later, Zane was gone. So was the attacker's body.

Gone.

The Mercedes's alarm cut off.

A man walked up to her. "Are you okay?" he asked.

"I'm..." Mandy glanced around. "Someone attacked me." She wrapped her arm around her aching rib cage. "Please call nine-one-one."

The stranger pulled a cell phone out of his pocket and made the call.

What felt like a lifetime later, a stampede of police, fire, and rescue vehicles descended upon her, lights flashing red and blue and white. She was questioned by a police officer. She was lifted onto a gurney and questioned some more. She told the EMS guys where she was hurt, and while they fought to put in an IV, she told her story to yet another pack of police officers. She told them about being jumped. About a second stranger coming to her rescue. And about them both disappearing. She left out a few details, however, figuring the police officers would think she was either delusional or on drugs.

She didn't give them Zane's name. Not when telling them about the fight. Not when she was asked who she'd like them to contact. When asked for an emergency contact, she gave them Sarah's cell phone number without a second thought.

The area was cordoned off. She was put into an ambulance and was bumped and jostled to a nearby hospital.

Sarah was there, waiting for her, when she was wheeled into the ER. Sarah took one look at her and went ghostly white.

Mandy tried to reassure her. "I'm okay, Sarah."

Sarah white-knuckled the gurney's railing. "Ohmygod, Mandy. Oh my freaking God."

"I'll be fine."

The EMS guy pushing the bed gave it a nudge forward, and

Sarah dragged along. "Miss, I'm sorry but you're going to have to wait out here."

"But my friend—"

"She's stable. We need to get her in and have her looked at. They'll call you back as soon as they can."

Mandy grabbed Sarah's hand, gave it a squeeze. "Sarah, I'm not dying. I promise."

Sarah took a step back. Her eyes were very red, her face very white. It was a stark contrast. Shaking hands covered her mouth.

The gurney was wheeled into a room. Mandy was helped onto a hospital bed. The EMS guys wished her luck and off they went, leaving her to lie there in pain. Now she wished Sarah was there with her. At least her rapid-shot questions would have distracted her from the pain a little. Her side was killing her. Every time she inhaled, a sharp blade of pain sliced into her rib cage, nearly taking her breath away.

Why had that awful man attacked her?

A cheery nurse came in, asking her how she was feeling.

"Pain," was all Mandy said.

She did what she had to and left, promising a doctor would be in shortly.

Much to Mandy's surprise, a doctor did come into her room soon afterward. He was young. He was smiling. There was nothing to smile about.

"I need drugs," Mandy said to him before he'd spoken a word.

"Let me see what we have going on. If it's safe, we'll get you something. Now, what happened?"

Mandy went through the whole thing for the umpteenth time, this time focusing on where she'd been struck and where she hurt. He poked and prodded, finally saying, "We'll need to run some tests."

"Drugs?"

"I can give you a little something."

"Thank you."

Twenty minutes later, Mandy was feeling much better.

Sarah dashed in shortly after the drugs kicked in. She ran up to the bed and stared down at Mandy, looking as horrified as Mandy had ever seen her. "What happened? Ohmygod, this is my fault! I should've gone with you. Why didn't I? Because I wanted to have sex with a fucking married cop? That was no reason to abandon you!"

The words were coming too fast for Mandy's drug-hazed brain to register them. But she got the overall message. "Hon, it isn't your fault. I was doing what I always do. Some man I've never seen before decided to attack me."

"Why?"

"I have no idea."

"I don't understand it. Why would anyone attack you? Unless... Did he look familiar? Was he one of the husbands we've nailed?"

"No."

"Huh." Sarah dragged a wheeled stool to her bedside and plopped onto it. "So, what happened after he kicked your ass? Did he just leave?"

"Not exactly. Zane showed up and sort of kicked his ass for me."

"Zane?"

"It gets weirder. The fight was like nothing I'd ever seen. Zane and the bad guy were like... unnaturally strong. They were throwing each other twenty, thirty feet."

Sarah gave Mandy a strange look.

"I know what you're thinking. Yes, I had been unconscious at one point. Strangled." Mandy fingered her neck. "But I know what I saw wasn't a hallucination."

"Who won the fight?"

Mandy's eyelids were growing heavy. Tired. Very tired. She

let them shutter out the bright lights. "Zane. He bit the other guy. It was disgusting."

"I don't know. To me, it sounds like you might've had a near-death experience. And your brain probably created that whole scenario, based upon what Zane had told you recently. I've read some research about near-death experiences."

"I'm sure what I saw was real," Mandy mumbled, slipping into a shallow semisleep. "Enough about that. Why were you crying?"

"We can talk about it later. Rest." Sarah's hand settled on top of hers.

Mandy nodded. "Later." She let herself tumble into a deep sleep.

23

"Amanda, I'm going to take you home now."

Zane?

Was she dreaming?

"Amanda."

Zane again.

She opened her eyes.

No, she wasn't dreaming. It was him. He looked perfectly normal. No bruises. No swelling. No blood.

Had she been hallucinating after all? It was maybe possible. Her brain had been deprived of oxygen for over a minute. Maybe longer.

"Where's Sarah?" she croaked. Her throat was so sore. Dry.

"It's okay, baby. I'm going to take care of you."

She tried to move. It hurt like hell. She quickly decided she was better off staying right where she was. "Hurts." She gently placed her flattened hand on her side. It was bandaged. When had they done that?

"You have a couple of broken ribs. I can give you some more pain medication when we get home." He clicked the side rail down and carefully scooped her into his arms to transfer her to the wheelchair sitting next to the bed.

The world spun. She groaned. "Sick. Hurt."

"Sorry, baby. I'll try to make this as painless as I can."

She was wheeled to the exit, where she waited inside with a security guard while Zane ran out to get his car. He pulled up to the entry, and she was helped into the car's comfy leather seat. A few minutes later, she was reclined, eyes closed, while the vehicle prowled the quiet, empty streets. She woke up to discover Zane had brought her to his house.

"You'll be safer here," he explained as he pulled the car into the attached garage.

"Am I in danger?"

He cut off the engine. "Not from the bastard who attacked you. He won't be hurting anyone ever again. But I didn't find out who hired him."

"Someone hired him?"

"He's been on our Most Wanted list for centuries. Damn good at his job."

In other words, she had probably used up a lifetime's worth of good luck tonight, just by surviving.

"What were you doing at the hotel?" she asked him after he walked around the car and opened her door.

"Let's get you inside first. Then we can talk." He helped her out of the car, supporting her as she walked—she insisted he not carry her. Her rib cage hurt less when she walked. He took her upstairs, to the guest room where she'd stayed before. He pulled some cozy pajamas out of the dresser, set them on the bed, and told her he'd go down to get her something to wash down her pills.

It was not easy, but she finally exchanged her dirty, torn clothes for the pajamas. She also stumbled her way into the bathroom, brushed her teeth with the toothbrush that she'd left there the last time she'd stayed, and went to the bathroom. By the time she was finished with all that, Zane was waiting for her with a tall glass of ginger ale and a bottle of pills.

Of course, he rushed to her side the minute she opened the bathroom door. He helped her to the bed, treating her like she was made of delicate china. Once she was settled in, he handed her the glass and two pills.

"Thank you," she said, searching his face for any sign of injury. He hadn't denied being there, in the parking lot. So she knew that much had truly happened.

But what about . . . ?

"I'll explain everything once you're feeling better," he said. He leaned close, arms extended, hands braced on either side of her body. He pressed a kiss to her forehead.

She palmed his cheek. "You weren't hurt?"

"I'm fine."

She let her hand fall to the bed. Her gaze followed it. "I need to know. Was what I saw real?"

He pinched her chin and lifted it, not speaking until she'd met his gaze again. "What did you see?"

"You and the attacker fighting. Throwing each other impossible distances. Tossing each other like you were both weightless." She hesitated to say more. Her gaze drifted back to the bed.

"What else did you see?"

"I saw you bite him. The blood."

He said, "It was real." Her insides twisted. "I was hoping you hadn't seen that. You're afraid of me now."

"Not afraid. Uneasy."

He backed away. When she lifted her gaze to his face, she saw his expression had turned a little distant, a little cool. He was pulling back, no doubt because of what she'd said.

"You saved my life," she said. He nodded but he didn't respond. "I'll always remember."

"I don't want your gratitude." He turned and left the room.

*   *   *

The next two days passed by in a blur. Part of it was the painkillers. They tended to keep Mandy in a cloud. She slept a lot, spending her waking moments taking care of basic essentials like using the bathroom, eating, calling Sarah to check on her.

Zane was a kind and generous host. He brought her food, he brought her clean clothes, he showed her how to operate the flat-screen television, and he bought her books. During the day, he would check on her hourly. At night, he let her sleep. Mandy asked nothing more about the attack. Zane offered no more information. Nor did he tell her when it would be safe for her to return home. On the third day, she woke up feeling much better. The pain had subsided enough that she didn't need to take the heavy-duty medication. As a result, her mind was clearer.

She needed to get out of this room.

After taking a long, almost scalding-hot shower, she changed into clean clothes. Following the mouthwatering scent of cooking food and freshly brewed coffee, she barefooted it down to the kitchen.

Zane was standing at the counter, watching the news on the little flat-screen television suspended from the cabinets and cutting up a melon. He was wearing that silly apron again. One day, she'd have to take a picture....

Her camera! She needed to find out if it was still in her pocket. For all she knew, it had fallen out in the parking lot.

Zane glanced over his shoulder. "Good morning. You're up."

"Yes. Up and clean. I took a shower."

"Feeling better?"

"I am. Thanks." Mandy settled onto one of the raised stools lining the breakfast counter while Zane poured a glass of orange juice. "Thank you."

"You're welcome."

"For everything."

His smile was distant.

"I know, you don't want my gratitude," she said, remembering his parting words the night she'd been attacked.

Zane placed the melon chunks into a bowl and set them on the breakfast bar. "That's right. No gratitude."

"What do you want?" she asked.

Zane went to the stove, stirring whatever was cooking in the cast-iron skillet. "I want you to heal." He poured what looked like scrambled eggs onto a plate. "I want you to be safe." He added a couple of slices of buttered toast to the plate and set it down in front of her.

"I think I'm well on my way to being healed."

"Good."

"But I don't know about the other. Have you found out anything about the attacker? What about the police? You haven't said a word about the attack since you brought me here."

"The police have nothing. I'm not doing much better. All I know is that the bastard was hired to kill you. And in case you were wondering, he is one of us."

"*Us?* As in a vampire?"

"That's right."

Mandy tried to piece it together while she ate. Zane cleaned the kitchen.

Someone wanted her dead. Who? Why?

The most obvious answer to that question was an angry ex-husband. Revenge being the reason why. Oddly, despite the fact that she'd made a living digging up dirt on cheating spouses, she'd never expected anyone to go this far. Vandalize her car, maybe. Break a window or make a phone threat, sure. But hire a hit man to kill her?

She mentally ran through the list of her former clients' husbands. She couldn't imagine any of them doing such a thing.

None of them had violent criminal backgrounds. The first thing she did when she took on a new client was look at the husband's criminal record, if he had one. The worst had been Mr. Travis. He'd collected hundreds of unpaid speeding tickets and landed in jail for driving on a suspended license.

Maybe one of them had become violent after the divorce?

Or maybe it was that bitch who'd punched her.

By the time she was finished with her breakfast, Zane had left to tackle some other chore. He was definitely not himself today. But that was a whole nother problem.

First things first. She located her cell phone upstairs in the guest room and called Sarah.

"Mandy!" Sarah screeched.

Mandy yanked the phone away from her ear to protect her eardrum. When the squealing ended, she reluctantly placed the phone to her ear again. "Wow, that was some greeting."

"I am so relieved to talk to you. You have no idea how much I've been worrying."

"Didn't Zane tell you he was bringing me to his place?"

"Sure, but that doesn't mean I wasn't going to worry. After everything that man has put you through, I have good reason."

So true. "I'm fine. Feeling better. I could probably head into work, but I doubt Zane would like that idea very much."

"Don't do it. Zane may be a lot of things—heartless and insanely stubborn, for instance—but when it comes to keeping people safe, I have no doubt he's more than capable."

Easing onto the bed, Mandy sighed. "I don't like being cooped up like this."

"I hear you. But would you rather be dead?"

"Of course not."

"Well, then..."

"Fine. Listen. I need you to do something for me."

"Anything."

"Do a criminal record check for all the cases we've taken in the last six months or so. See if any of the husbands have been arrested for any violent crimes. Also, dig up what you can on Clark's neighbor, the one with the mean left hook."

"Will do."

"Also, could you go over to the hotel where I was attacked and take a look around the parking lot? See if the police missed anything?"

"How likely is that?"

"Extremely unlikely, but I want to find out who wants me dead sooner rather than later. If I have to hide out for more than a few days, I may go insane." After a beat, she asked, "Hey, you never told me, what happened with Valdez?"

Sarah sighed. "He's an ass, not worth talking about. You'll be glad to hear it's over. I learned my lesson. Never again."

"I'm sorry, hon."

"Don't be. I'm not. I'd better get going if you want me to get all this research done so you can get out of the Bat Cave."

"Okay. But only if you're sure you're all right."

"I'm fine. Don't worry."

"Okay. I'll talk to you later then." She ended the call, then went in search of Zane to ask him about her clothes. She checked the most obvious places for him first, like the kitchen, the family room, the home office. Finally, she headed back upstairs and pressed her ear to his bedroom door. It was closed.

She heard the distant sound of running water.

Assuming he'd be occupied for at least twenty minutes or so, she went in search of the laundry facilities. In most houses, they were in the basement. In fancy houses like this, they could be anywhere. After checking all the doors up on the second level and coming up with nothing, she went down to the first floor. In searching for a laundry room, she discovered a nicely furnished home office, a sparsely stocked walk-in pantry, the basement stairs, two half baths, and a coatroom full of very nice wool and leather coats and expensive men's shoes. No laundry room.

The next stop: the basement. She flipped on the light and descended. The main space was set up as a home theater, complete with reclining seats set onto shallow risers. The doors leading out were painted to match the wall, making them blend in. Mandy tried one, found it led to an empty storage area. She tried the other.

Success. At last.

She checked the basket of dirty laundry sitting in front of the washer. It was full of black clothes. She'd been wearing black that night. She bent over and grabbed a piece of clothing.

"Amanda?"

Zane.

She whirled around. "I was looking for my clothes. The ones I wore the night of the attack."

"That's not what you're holding."

"Oh." Mandy glanced at the garment. "Ohhhh." Men's boxer-briefs. Cotton. Black. She let them slip from her fingertips. They landed back in the basket. "Do you know where my clothes are?"

He moved closer. His eyes glimmered in the semidarkness. Like a cat's. "They're in the dryer."

Mandy clamped her arms around herself. "I don't suppose you checked the pockets before you put them in the wash?"

"I did. They were empty." He loomed over her.

"Dammit." She stepped to one side, thinking he might want to get to the washing machine.

He didn't move that way. He moved closer to her instead. "What's wrong?"

She shifted positions again, this time stepping toward the dryer. "I had taken some pictures with a pen camera. The camera was in my pocket when I was attacked. It must've fallen out."

Once again, he followed her. "You need to consider a career change."

"I know."

Awkward silence.

"The job I told you about is still available."

Mandy nodded. "I'll think about it." Despite the fact that she believed Zane, she still visually searched the laundry room for her camera. Better to look at a washing machine and dryer than into those dark eyes.

"Amanda." He crowded her.

She backed against the wall. Trapped. "What?"

His expression darkened. He caged her head between his outstretched arms. "You *are* afraid of me."

"Not afraid." She sounded petrified, even to her own ears. "Uneasy."

"Why?"

"Because." She shivered. Her gaze locked onto his. Those eyes. They were so dark right now. She could hardly make out the pupils. Her heart started bouncing against her breastbone.

Zane tipped his head down and audibly inhaled. "I can smell your fear."

"Dammit, you bit a man. His blood was all over your face. It was a gruesome, shocking sight. What do you expect me to feel?" She sniffled. A fat tear dropped off her lashes, plopping onto her cheek.

"Would you like me to make you forget?" His teeth grazed her neck.

Ohmygod, is he going to bite me? She stiffened. "No."

"I could." He did it again, scraped his teeth against her neck.

This time, she lifted her shoulder and tipped her head to fend him off. "I have no doubt about that."

"Have you forgotten how I make you feel?" Undeterred, Zane turned his attention to the other side of her neck. "You used to beg me to touch you, to kiss you, to fuck you."

"I remember." A prickly cold swept through her body, immediately followed by a wave of sensual heat. Whoa boy, did she remember. Her nerve endings started sizzling, even as a ripple of fear coursed up her spine.

Zane curled his fingers around a fistful of hair and tugged gently to the side. Her head tipped, exposing her neck to him. A wave of dread swept through her, making her tremble.

"Please, Zane."

"Please what, Amanda?" He flicked his tongue up and down her neck.

"Please let me go."

"Are you sure that's what you want?" He gave up teasing her and suckled her earlobe instead.

Dammit, he knew what that did to her.

She practically melted. Her body softened beneath his. Her breathing grew shallow, ragged. She gripped his steel-hard upper arms in her hands and fought against the carnal need building inside her. "Zane..."

How could she feel so freaking turned on with this man? After what she'd seen? After watching him practically tear another man to pieces? He was a monster. A freakish being she didn't understand. She tried to push him away, but he didn't budge.

He forced his knee between her legs, angling his thigh so it rubbed against her burning pussy. "Isn't this what you crave? The thrill of the unknown. Erotic hunger blended with genuine fear. It makes your blood pump hard and hot through your body." He pressed his thigh against her pussy. "Makes your pussy warm and wet." He dragged a hand up her side, his fingers trailing little wakes of pleasure up, up, up.

He was right. Maybe.

"You could never be content with your average Joe. He'd be safe. Boring. Dull." Zane moved the wandering hand to more sensitive territory. His palm warmed her breast. Her nipple hardened. Tingled. She felt her spine stretching, her body arching into him. "I could never be dull. I'm a mystery. Full of terrible secrets. That's what draws you to me, those shadows you see in my eyes."

He had her there.

While he kneaded one breast through her clothes, he used the free one to slowly drag her shirt up until her breasts were bare. Shifting back, he cupped a breast, lifting it, and pulled the nipple into the sweet, warm depth of his mouth.

She heard herself sigh. Her pussy clenched.

God help her, she wanted him. Maybe not for forever. She was too hazy-headed to think that far down the road. But she wanted him for now. She wanted to feel his weight resting on her, his hips wedged between her spread legs. His cock stroking in and out of her slick heat.

"Zane . . . ," she said on a sigh as she arched her spine more, pushing her breast into his face.

He nipped, sending a blade of pleasure-pain slicing through her. A gush of liquid heat followed, flowing to her core. "Say the words, Amanda."

"Take me. Please. My master. My king."

He carefully undressed her before gently cradling her in his arms. With an arm looped around his neck, she let him carry her into the home theater. He set her on one of the reclining chairs, then angled over her to kiss her.

This kiss wasn't like any they'd shared before. It was full of raw emotion, not only hunger and need, but also something else, something she couldn't name. His tongue stroked hers until she was seeing stars, breathless and squirming beneath him. Blindly, she reached out, found his zipper, and yanked it down. Her hand found hard cock covered in cotton. She rubbed up and down while he plunged his tongue in and out of her mouth.

When he growled, a quiver of excitement raced through her. He backed up slightly and jerked his shirt over his head. She traced the lines of his abs with a fingertip while he yanked down his pants. In a heartbeat, he was standing before her, nude, glorious. Hard. The look in his eye was feral, dangerous. Utterly devastating.

She leaned back, sliding her bottom to the edge of the seat. He lifted her knees, draping them over the chair's arms, then angled over her, using his arms to hold his weight.

"Say it, Amanda. Tell me you need me. Tell me...you love me."

She couldn't say those words, could she? What the hell did he want to hear her say that for?

Tears seeped from her eyes. "What are you trying to do, Zane? You want me to love you and yet you don't. What the fuck? Sometimes I think I hate you."

Zane's cock thrust forward, filling her. She closed her eyes, wrapped her arms around his neck, and clung to him as he fucked her hard and fast. This was no gentle coupling. No sweet lovemaking. It was fierce. It was a possession. It was un-restrained. And it brought her to a quick, soul-shattering climax.

24

Ten minutes later, Mandy was still caged in Zane's arms, her body wedged beneath his, her pussy full of his cock. She still hadn't caught her breath. That had been one hell of a quickie.

Her rib cage ached a little. She didn't care.

"Are you all right?" Zane asked, nuzzling her neck. His hand was splayed over her broken ribs, his fingers prodding gently.

"It hurts a little. Not much at all."

"Hmmm. Do you still hate me?"

"I do."

"Good. You should. I've been an ass."

She couldn't help smiling. "Glad to hear you say that."

"I'm not the kind to deny my own failings. Never have been." He kissed her. "Will you forgive me?"

"If you ask nice." She kissed him back.

"Please." He pinched her nipple.

She sighed. "Forgiven."

He sat upright and stared down into her eyes. "It can't be that easy."

"Sure it can. If you're genuinely sorry. You are, aren't you? Sorry that you've led me on, messed with my head, and then continued to keep me at arm's length. Tell me you're finally going to let me in, let me know who you really are, and you will be forgiven. Wholeheartedly."

Zane hesitated.

This was it, the moment she'd been waiting so long for. Either they would move forward or it would be the end. She couldn't breathe. "Why is it so hard for you?"

He looked away. His jaw clenched. "You've seen what I am."

She traced the line of that jaw with an index finger. "A very passionate man. A very sensual man. And very protective, generous—"

"Violent," he added, his gaze snapping to hers again. His mouth was tight as he said, "I can just as easily rip out another man's throat."

"A man who is hurting someone you *love*," Mandy said. She held her breath. Would he admit it?

"Yes, someone I love." Zane rammed his fingers through his hair. "That's why this is so hard. I'm . . . I can't lose you."

"The only way you'll lose me is if you keep pushing me away."

He motioned toward the laundry room. "You were afraid. You can't deny it."

"No, you're right. I was afraid of you after seeing what you did to the attacker. But he had his hands around my neck. He almost killed me. And he would have killed both of us if you hadn't killed him first." She reached for him, slid her hand over his. "Tell me the truth—have you killed more people? Children? Defenseless women?"

"Yes. I did. One woman. Many years ago. But not intentionally. It was because of her that I've been afraid to love you."

Silence.

"Will you tell me about it?" Mandy asked.

"I loved her." The love he still felt shone in his eyes. "She was my world. My light. My everything. But that kind of love takes on a life of its own. I smothered her. Not physically. Emotionally. Mentally. She couldn't take it. And as I watched, she withered. I tightened my grasp, too overcome with fear to realize what I was doing to her." He curled his hands into fists. "She hung herself. I found her." He scrubbed his face with his palms and curled his fingers into his hair and pulled. "And I cannot ever erase the image of her face from my memory. It's burned in, branded into my soul."

He'd driven a woman to suicide. That was one hell of a story. Warning lights blinked. Clearly he was the kind of man who controlled his woman's every move.

"I'm so sorry, Zane."

He didn't speak.

"Would you be that way with me? Is that what you're afraid of?"

"I am. I would be. I can see the signs."

She set a hand on his shoulder. "We can work on this together, if you'll let me. If you'll try. I want to try."

A single tear slipped from his eye. "I've been pushing people away for so long I don't know how to be any other way."

"You took a step today. That's all we have to do—take one step at a time, together."

He enfolded her in his arms. He kissed her eyelids, her cheeks, her hair, and finally her mouth. Against her lips, he whispered, "I want to give you the love you deserve, a kind, gentle, sweet love."

"But that doesn't mean we can't have dirty, naughty sex, right? Because I kinda like that part."

His laughter reverberated through her body, finding its way to her soul. She felt so happy, so overwhelmingly joyful. And hopeful.

But then he said, "Now, about your job..."

She slanted her mouth over his, grabbed a handful of hair, and shoved her tongue into his mouth.

That'll shut him up for a while.

"This time we're gonna get him," Sarah whispered the next evening. Decked out head to toe in black, Sarah looked like a ninja. Very fitting, in more than one way. They were sitting in Sarah's car—they'd both agreed it was wise to avoid using Mandy's car after the last stakeout—outside of Clark's mistress's kung fu studio. Turned out JoAnn Hackner wasn't a paranormal creature with superhuman strength. She was merely a human being with a black belt in at least three different forms of martial arts.

Mandy wasn't particularly happy to be messing with this woman. And Zane wasn't happy about it either. But he hadn't stopped Mandy.

She had a sneaking suspicion he wasn't far away—keeping a close eye on her. The thought made her feel safe.

"There she goes," Sarah said excitedly, bouncing in her seat. "I am *so* ready to take that bitch down."

"We're not 'taking' anyone down. We're going to hopefully get some pictures and call this case closed."

"Yeah, yeah. Party pooper." Sarah stuck out her fat lower lip.

Mandy laughed. She grabbed her ribs, grimacing. "I'm wondering if I wasn't better off doing this on my own. You're looking to pick a fight, aren't you?"

"Hey, she picked a fight with us when she clocked you. Besides, you're in no condition to be doing much of anything on your own yet."

"Fine. Just do me a favor."

"What?" Sarah dug into her bag while Mandy started the car.

Mandy shifted the vehicle into drive and began following Hackner's car at a distance. "Forget about getting revenge. She'll get what's coming to her sooner or later."

"You take all the fun out of this job."

"Whatever." Mandy took a corner. Hackner's white SUV was an easy vehicle to tail. Not too many people drove snow-white SUVs. It took a meandering path to an apartment complex, then parked in a lot in front of a town house. Hacker entered the building.

"I bet you're right. Loverboy *is* renting this place so they have somewhere safe to meet," Sarah said. "It's smarter than hiding out in the pool house."

"It is. But I'm not convinced. Yet."

"What's to doubt? You were the one who found out about the lease."

"Actually, it was his wife who told me," Mandy corrected.

Hackner exited the building, walked to her truck, and opened the back. She pulled out a large cardboard box.

"Then again...maybe...," Mandy said.

They waited an hour. No movement. Outside, that was. Inside the car, Sarah had done plenty of moving. And griping. And eating. She even took a quick cat nap. "Let's go peek in some windows." Not waiting for Mandy, Sarah opened the door.

Mandy watched Sarah dash around the side of the building and disappear into the heavy shadows. She decided to hold off. Someone needed to keep an eye out for Clark.

A half hour later, Sarah came back. "She's cooking dinner. The table's set for two. Why didn't you come with me?" She pulled open the passenger side door.

"Wanted to watch for Clark."

"Good idea. Not here yet?" Sarah flung herself onto the seat.

"Nope."

Sarah jerked the door closed. "He'll come."

"I hope you're right. I'm so ready to be done with this case. This work just isn't giving me the same sense of satisfaction it once did. I think I'm getting burned out."

"Which is why you're going to make me a full-time PI. I'll do the dirty work. You'll just get the credit. You can do all the computer stuff. The background checks. Internet research. I'm bored with it."

Mandy checked the road behind them. "Zane would be happy to hear I wasn't going out in the field anymore."

"Yeah, I bet he would. I don't have a man to answer to. Another reason why I should be doing this stuff."

"I'll think about it."

Sarah nudged Mandy's arm. "Isn't that Clark's car?"

"Yes, it is."

"Oh, yeah. We're going to get him. I have a good feeling about this."

They waited for Clark to go inside before they tiptoed around the back of the building. A wide set of sliding glass doors opened into the living room. The shades were closed, but there were some convenient gaps between the vertical blinds. Mandy and Sarah huddled on the back porch watching the two eat dinner. A half hour later, they moved to the living room. Mandy snapped a few shots of them cuddling on the couch. Then a few more of them kissing. And a few of them petting. Clark was the first to undress.

"Look at that man's abs. Wow," Sarah said, echoing Mandy's thoughts. Mandy had seen those abs before. "And his butt is so round and cute and firm." Mandy had seen that butt, too.

JoAnn pulled off her top.

"Fake boobs," Sarah murmured.

JoAnn pulled off her jeans.

"What the hell is that lump in her panties?" Sarah whispered.

"I think I can answer that," Mandy whispered back.

JoAnn pulled down her panties, and sure enough, her—his—thick seven-incher sprang free.

"Holy shit!" Sarah said.

Mandy clapped her hand over Sarah's mouth and shushed her.

Sarah nodded.

Mandy snapped some more photos while JoAnn gave Clark a blow job, then fucked him in the ass. After getting roughly fifty shots, she motioned to Sarah, who was watching in silence.

When they got back in the car, Sarah laughed. "JoAnn is a dude. I so did *not* see that coming."

"At least I have the evidence we need now. This case is officially closed."

They did a fist-bump.

Sarah pumped her hands in the air. "Let's go celebrate."

Mandy checked the camera. "After I get these to Mrs. Clark. I don't want to take any chances that something will happen to them."

"Fine."

Mandy drove them back to the office. They went inside, locking themselves in and setting the alarm. Mandy went to her office, hooked up her camera, and waited for the pictures to download. Meanwhile, Sarah slumped into one of the chairs and stared at the ceiling.

"I want to get laid," Sarah announced. "Watching those two made me horny. I don't have a man. And you aren't going to become a lesbian now that you've worked things out with Zane. What am I supposed to do?"

"I'm sorry, hon."

"Let's go to Twilight."

"There's no penetration. You can't get laid there."

"In the main dungeon. Anything goes in the private suites."

Sarah waggled her eyebrows. "I'm thinking a couple of hot young submissives might take my mind off of Whatshisname."

"A couple, eh?" Mandy maneuvered her mouse, clicking on one of the shots to check the resolution.

"Yeah. Two's better than one. Most definitely."

"Why's that?" Mandy asked, scrutinizing the picture.

"You don't know what full is until you've been double penetrated. Let me tell you, it's divine."

Mandy wasn't sure *divine* was the right adjective.

The disk drive stopped. A little notification popped up on her screen.

She hit the button, and the disk she'd burned the pictures onto slid out. She checked the clock. It was after ten P.M. Probably too late to go to the Clarks'. "I need to put this somewhere for safekeeping until tomorrow morning. Bank's closed."

"You can lock it up in my apartment. We can run over there and change before we head to Twilight. I need something sexier. You can borrow something, too."

"I don't know . . ."

"Hey." Sarah grabbed Mandy's left hand, lifting it. "Do I see a ring on this finger?"

"No, but—"

"Has he said anything about a commitment yet?"

"No."

"You're a free woman. Have some fun. Besides, if you stick with the main dungeon, there isn't any penetration. You said so yourself."

"If I go with you, I'm not going to scene with anyone. I'm good with Zane. He's the only dom for me."

"Ah, it must be true love." Sarah patted Mandy's cheek. "There's a bar on the main level. And a restaurant. If we take separate cars, you can leave if you get bored."

That was the first suggestion that made sense. "Okay. Fine. I'll go."

*   *   *

They rolled into Twilight's parking lot a little before eleven. Sporting a miniskirt that barely covered her ass, Sarah walked with a sway-hipped swagger into the club. Mandy felt a little plain standing beside her at the check-in desk. Wearing a simple black dress and cute high heels, she was dressed for a nice dinner, not a bondage club. The guy at the counter wished them a good evening and buzzed the locked door behind him to let them in.

Sarah led the way, grabbing Mandy's hand and dragging her through the doorway. "There's a bar down here, too, serving nonalcoholic drinks. Can't drink and play here."

"That's a good rule."

"Yeah. Alcohol and bondage gear don't mix." Sarah made a beeline for the juice bar. She ordered some guava berry concoction that smelled good. Mandy decided she'd try one, too. Sarah handed Mandy hers and ordered a second one from the bartender for herself.

Sipping, they turned to watch the action going on in the main dungeon.

Mandy grimaced. "This stuff tastes awful. Salty. Nothing like what I thought. What's in it?"

"I don't know. A bunch of herbs that are supposed to be healthy. Oh, and some pheromones. You know, to heighten your pleasure."

"Pheromones, you say?" Mandy took another taste. The second wasn't quite as bad as the first. "Do you see any promising submissives yet?"

"No. I'll give it another ten minutes, and then if nothing shakes out, we can go up to the bar." Something caught Sarah's eye.

Mandy looked. Zane.

Her heart jumped.

"Hi, Zane," Sarah said.

"Hello, Sarah, Amanda." He had a wicked look in his eye as he leaned into Mandy. "What are you drinking?" he asked, reaching for her glass. "Is it alcohol?"

"No, it's not." She handed him the glass.

He sniffed, smiled, and returned it to her. "Excellent. Come with me."

Mandy glanced at Sarah.

Sarah shooed her away. "Go, have fun. I'll be fine. I think I may call it a night. Nothing's doing it for me tonight."

"Call me tomorrow."

"Will do." Sarah waved.

Mandy slid her hand into Zane's, following his lead around the perimeter of the dungeon. "Where are we headed?"

"To my private suite. There's someone I want you to meet."

"Oh." Clearly, he didn't have what she'd assumed in mind— a cozy scene with just the two of them. She didn't want to let on that she was disappointed, so she pasted on a smile. "Who is this person?"

"You'll find out soon enough." Zane walked the rest of the way in silence. He was playing the mysterious dom card. Mandy kind of liked it. She was intrigued. He opened the very last door and motioned Mandy into the suite, closing the door behind them.

As Mandy had become accustomed to seeing, there was a nude man kneeling in the middle of the room. And, as usual, he was beautiful, with a body that would make any girl breathe a little fast and heavy.

"Amanda, this is Bruce. I don't know if you recognize him, but he is the one I was fucking the day you surprised me at my house."

"Oh." That day, she hadn't gotten a good look at Zane's partner's face. In fact, she hadn't gotten a good look at much of any of him. She had to say, Zane had excellent taste in men. This one could inspire some serious wet dreams.

Bruce stood and extended a hand, his gaze meeting Mandy's. Oh, yes, wet dreams. Most definitely. "Hello, Amanda. It's nice to meet you at last."

Not sure how to respond, Mandy shook his hand. "Nice to meet you, too." When he released her hand, Mandy took a step backward, bumping into Zane. Why'd he bring her back here? What was he up to? She glanced over her shoulder.

"Do you remember what I told you about our relationship—Bruce's and mine?" Zane set his hands on Mandy's shoulders.

"I remember the basics." She recalled him telling her they'd been together a long time. And it had something to do with his being a vampire. Feeding.

"We've been talking and we've had a thought."

"What thought?" Her gaze ping-ponged back and forth between Zane and Bruce. She was feeling cornered. It wasn't a pleasant feeling.

"Bruce has had some trouble finding another situation. And because I've been feeding from him for so long, he's become dependent upon my venom. It's not common—"

"Addicted to vampire venom?" she echoed.

"You could say that." Zane nodded. He eased Mandy around to face him. "I need you to understand how dangerous this is for him. If he doesn't have a regular dose, he'll die."

Mandy knew Zane wanted her to take this situation seriously, but it was so over-the-top melodramatic that she was having a very hard time. "He'll die?"

"Yes. And he's discovered that it isn't good enough if he finds a new . . . partner. Our venom is unique to each individual. I knew this. What I didn't know is that the substance he's addicted to within my venom isn't common to other Dejenen's venom. In other words, another's venom won't stop his withdrawal."

"What about medicine? Can't he take something? Like methadone?"

"There is no medicine. I wish that was an option."

Ugh. "So there's no getting around it. You'll have to fuck him indefinitely, right? That's what this is leading to."

"No, *I* won't have to fuck him." Zane smiled, and a few parts of her body got warm and tingly. Here they were, talking about Zane screwing someone else, a guy, and she was getting hot. "I can let someone else do that for me."

"Okay." Mandy tried to imagine how that would work. She pictured Bruce bent over, some man fucking his ass while Zane chomped on his neck. It wasn't a totally off-putting image. In fact, it was quite pleasant. "So... where is this leading?"

"I was thinking, because I need to feed two to three times per week, that I'd like to offer you the chance to be a part of the process."

Was he asking what she thought he was asking? Was he asking her to be the third of his kinky vampire-feeding trio?

"Um..." She swallowed a huge lump. What exactly was she feeling about this? Zane was doing what she'd asked him to do. He was opening up, letting her see all the secret sides of himself. Wouldn't she be a bitch if she freaked out about this now? He might shut down. She might never earn his trust again.

Oh, shit, but he was asking her to be part of a threesome. Much more shocking, he was asking her to watch him drink a man's blood. She hadn't seen that coming. Maybe she should have, but she hadn't. When she'd asked him to open up, let her see who he truly was, she was thinking he might tell her some more stories about the past, about what it felt like to be a vampire.

Zane motioned Bruce away and took Mandy's upper arms in his hands. His expression was darker than she'd ever seen it. "Amanda, I won't be upset if you're not ready for this."

"It is a bit much," she admitted. Zane nodded. "But we just talked about how I wanted to know you, to understand you. If I don't—"

"You're afraid I'll be upset," he finished for her.

"Of course."

"Don't let that pressure you into making a decision you'll regret. When I told you I love you, I meant it. And loving you means I'll do anything for your sake. It also means I cannot allow you to do anything you'll regret. Do you understand?"

"Sure. What you're saying is I've got to go into this full steam ahead, ready, willing, and able, with a huge smile on my face. Or I need to reconsider sharing a future with you."

"I'm not saying that."

"No, you're not. But that's the bottom line."

"You need time to sort this out."

"Yes. I think I do." Mandy glanced at Bruce, who was silently waiting at the far end of the room. He'd pulled on a robe and was sitting on the couch, acting like he wasn't listening. Of course, Mandy knew he was. At the door, Mandy gnawed on her lip as she looked into Zane's eyes. He was the most amazing man she'd ever met. And she couldn't stop thinking about him. But was that enough? Or would they both be better off if she walked away? Was their relationship destined to fail because they were so different? "Dammit, Zane." She palmed his cheek. His stubble scratched. Her fingertip traced the graceful curve of his jaw. "Why do things with you have to be so freaking complicated?"

"I'm sorry, Amanda. I tried."

"You did more than try, Zane. I guess I just wasn't prepared for reality. It's me who's sorry."

He placed his hand over hers and blinked. His eyes glistened. Tears? "Call me when you're ready to talk. I won't pressure you."

"Okay."

"In the meantime, I'll ask an associate to keep an eye on you. We still don't know who wants you dead or why."

"Thank you." Swallowing a sob, Mandy let her hand drop to her side. She felt Zane's gaze on her until she reached the end of the corridor. The hollow echo of a door closing behind her sounded just as she turned the corner.

Feeling like crap, certainly not in the mood to party anymore, Mandy headed out to the main dungeon. Assuming Sarah'd gone home, Mandy headed out to her car.

In the dark parking lot, two sets of footsteps *click-clacked* in the quiet. Mandy's. And someone else's. Not sure if that someone else was Zane's hired help or another hit man or just someone leaving the dungeon, Mandy spun around to take a look.

25

At the rear of the parking lot, Sarah stepped out from behind an SUV, beaming. "Well, this is a pleasant surprise. What happened with Zane?"

"Long story." Feeling worn out, both physically and emotionally, Mandy kicked off her shoes and barefooted it the rest of the way to her car.

"Want to talk about it?" Sarah asked as Mandy slumped into the driver's seat.

Mandy powered down the window.

Sarah peered through the opening. "Hmmm, you don't look so good. Are you okay?"

Mandy shoved the key into the ignition. "Yeah. I'm fine. I'm just worn out. I need to get home and go to bed. I think I could sleep for days."

"I hear that. Okay, I'll let you get going." Sarah smacked the car door.

"Thanks. I'll call you tomorrow. What're you doing here anyway? I thought you left."

"I ran into an old friend and we were talking."

"That's good." Instead of pulling out of the parking spot, Mandy let her head fall back against the headrest. She was starting to feel a little woozy. Could be exhaustion. She hoped she wasn't coming down with something. The flu, maybe.

"Yeah, it was nice to see him again." Sarah shooed her. "Anyway, we can talk about it tomorrow. After you've had some sleep."

Mandy's head swam when she nodded. "Okay. G'night." She shifted her car into reverse and twisted to look over her shoulder. The world tipped back and forth, like she was sitting on a ship, rolling over a huge wave. "Shit." Holding her head very still, she maneuvered her car out of the parking spot. Once again, the world swooped when she turned around to face forward. She'd never been so dizzy. She shifted into drive and inched her car to the road. She tried looking for traffic, but this time when she turned her head, little stars flickered over her vision, obscuring it. She shoved the gear shift into park and started digging blindly through her purse.

Someone knocked.

She blinked, trying to clear her vision. "Sorry, I'm not feeling well."

"It's me, Sarah. What's wrong?"

"I don't know. I feel like..." She broke out in a head-to-toe sweat. "I think I'm going to..." Her vision dimmed.

"Mandy! What's wrong?" Sarah said, sounding far away.

Silence.

Mandy couldn't move her arms. She strained to open her eyes. Her eyelids were so freaking heavy. It took herculean effort to lift them at all. When she managed, she saw she was lying on a bed in a bedroom she didn't recognize. She was on her side, facing a wall covered with tattered 1980s blue and yellow flowered wallpaper. She tried moving her arms again. They were secured behind her back.

Sarah scurried into the room and, seeming unaware that Mandy was awake, started digging through the contents of Mandy's purse.

"Sarah?" Mandy said. Her voice was raspy, her throat dry.

"Oh!" Sarah jerked her head up. "You're awake?"

"What's going on?"

"You're sick."

"Where are we?"

"At a friend's house. Where's your phone?"

"I don't know." Mandy tugged on her arms. "Why am I tied up?"

"Oh, um, well, when you were asleep, you were thrashing around. I was afraid you'd hurt yourself."

Even though her brain was in a thick fog, Mandy wasn't buying Sarah's explanation. "I'm awake now. You can untie me."

"I'll get to it in a minute. I need to find your phone first."

"Why?"

"Because . . . I need to look up a phone number."

"Whose?"

"You're not feeling well. Why don't you close your eyes and go back to sleep?" What Sarah had probably intended to be a reassuring smile came off as an empty one.

What the hell was going on?

A distant knock echoed through the house.

Sarah jerked upright. "Be right back."

"Sarah, what's going on?"

"I'll explain everything in a minute." Sarah rushed out of the room, pulling the door closed behind her.

Mandy tried to think. She couldn't. Her brain wasn't working. She wormed and wriggled until she was sitting upright. Everything threatened to go black again. She waited out the spell, wishing she knew what was happening. Once her vision cleared somewhat, she slowly eased to her feet. The floor beneath her pitched back and forth as she staggered to the door. Turning her back to it, she twisted the knob and pulled. The hinges groaned as the door slowly swung open. Mandy headed into a narrow, dim hallway that led to a steep staircase. She gripped the railing with both hands, leaned into the wall, and prayed she'd make it down the staircase without falling.

She was lucky. She had a couple of close calls and once had to sit down and rest, but she made it to the foot of the stairs without breaking her neck. She followed the sound of voices, coming from around the corner.

"I don't care," Sarah said. "You have to do it now. Today. I need her dead within the hour." *Dead? Who? What the hell?*

"This is all fucked up," a man said.

Mandy couldn't see him. Who was he? What was going on?

"You shouldn't have brought her here," he said.

Please tell me I'm not the "her" they're talking about.

"Make it work. It's the best I could do under the circumstances," Sarah snapped. "I couldn't very well take her home. And I didn't think taking her to my place was a good idea either."

"What happened to our original plans?" the man asked.

"I couldn't get her out of the bar earlier. Dammit, you're wasting time. The drugs are already wearing off."

Holy shit, they are *talking about me.*

Drugs. That was why she was feeling so fucked up.

Sarah wanted her dead? Dead! Her best friend? Why?

Mandy leaned back against the wall and tried to think. What should she do? Where could she go? She had no idea where she was. She was still very unsteady on her feet. She'd kill herself if she tried to run.

"Lady, if you want the bitch dead, you're gonna hafta do it yourself. Take her the hell out of here. I don't want no part of this."

Thank God for small miracles.

"Listen, you asshole, I already paid you. You'll do what I say—"

The sound of scuffling ensued. Mandy guessed Sarah was being set straight. Mandy's first inclination was to charge in there and try to protect her friend. But then she remembered that bitch had hired someone to kill her.

She walked in the opposite direction, staggering from one piece of furniture to another until she reached the front door. Out she went, into a dark and moonless night.

Praying to every god she'd heard of, she stumbled and rambled down the sidewalk. Little 1930s bungalows and mature oak trees lined the narrow street. Front yards were cluttered with toys, trash, and in some cases, discarded furniture. To say this wasn't the best neighborhood was an understatement. She sent up some more prayers and continued down the street. Two blocks later, three encounters with mutant rats that were the size of a beagle, and one nearly fatal fall, she was standing at the intersection of the residential street and a main road. The squatty buildings on the road, most of them industrial, were all dark. Outside of the occasional car rolling past, the area looked deserted.

Just her luck. Her homicidal best friend had hauled her unconscious body to the bad side of town. But at least she'd been able to use the rough edge of a mangled metal fence post to cut the ropes and free her arms.

If her luck continued, she'd find an open party store. There were generally lots of those in areas like this.

She made it one block up before a car rolled to the curb. She knew that car. And there was no way in hell she was getting into it.

"Mandy," her former best friend called to her through the open passenger window. "What are you doing out here?"

Mandy didn't say a word. As tempting as it was to tell Sarah what she thought of her diabolical plans to have her killed,

Mandy knew that was the wrong thing to do right now. She couldn't afford to tip her friend off that she knew what was going on.

Sarah pulled the car into a parking lot a few buildings up and jumped out. The two former friends met in the middle. "It isn't safe out here, especially with someone out to kill you."

Yeah, isn't that the truth. Mandy decided to play the too-drugged-up-to-know-what-she-was-doing card. "I was thirsty. Need a drink," she slurred. "Where's my car?"

"It's in the bar parking lot. You passed out."

Mandy eyed Sarah's running car. She thought about her wobbly legs, her blurry vision, and her delayed reflexes. It was one hell of a long shot, but why not? "What the hell, I can walk." Mandy tossed a casual wave over her shoulder and continued up the road, her sights set on Sarah's car.

"Mandy, how about I drive you to the store?" Sarah called, shuffling after her. "It's a half mile up the road. You wouldn't want to walk that far."

"I dunno." Mandy stopped at the car's rear bumper. She squinted at nothing down the street, behind Sarah. "Hey, who's that? I think that man's running this way."

Just like she hoped, Sarah whirled around. Mandy scrambled into the car and threw it into reverse just as Sarah dashed up to the driver's door. Sarah jerked the door open, but Mandy slammed on the gas. The car zoomed backward. Mandy stomped on the brake, shifted into drive, and hit the gas again. Ten seconds later, she waved at a shrinking Sarah in the rearview mirror.

"So long, bitch."

Knowing she was in no condition to drive all the way home from wherever the hell she was, she pulled into the first full parking lot she came across. It was a bowling alley. Never more thankful for the built-in phone in Sarah's car, she called Zane, explained everything, did some crying, and thanked him when he said he'd be there in fifteen minutes to pick her up. After cutting off the call, she did some more crying.

Her best friend, her employee, her confidant, and her companion had hired someone to kill her. Why?

By the time Zane's fierce black car prowled up, she was almost completely cried out, or so she thought. Turned out she had a few more tears to expend when he hauled her into his arms and held her. She sobbed like a baby, making a mess of his shirt. Thankfully, he couldn't care less. He merely asked, after she'd stopped, "Are you okay? Do I need to take you to the hospital?"

"I'm okay, but do you think we need proof that she drugged me?"

Zane's expression changed. Mandy decided she didn't like what she was seeing.

"I believe in the legal system," Mandy told him. "You aren't going to go vigilante vampire on me, are you?"

"I want to."

"Please don't. I'd rather do this the right way."

"Very well." His tone was clipped. "I suppose, in that case, a trip to the hospital would be wise."

"Thank you."

"But if you change your mind..." He let the rest trail off.

She knew what he meant.

Several hours, a blood test, a pee test, and a police report later, Mandy was safe and sound in Zane's bed. Being a god, he was kneeling, his legs straddling her unclad upper body, rubbing her back and spoiling her rotten.

After letting loose a long moan, Mandy murmured, "I could seriously get used to this."

"You deserve it." He angled over her, kissing her shoulder.

"Are you for real?"

"I think we've already established that."

"Yeah." Recalling the difficult conversation they'd had at the bondage club, Mandy's happy, floaty mood dampened slightly. "That's right."

"Let's not talk about that until later, after you've had some rest."

"That's probably wise." She turned her head to the side, resting it on her raised, crossed arms. "Since I just found out my BFF wants me dead, I might not be thinking too clearly."

"Exactly." His hands worked lower, kneading the knots out of her lower back. "Close your eyes. Relax. Don't think about any of that right now."

She squeezed her eyelids shut. She could do that much. But shutting down the brain wasn't quite so easy.

She tried thinking about work.

Her stupid brain switched gears, going right back to Sarah.

She tried thinking about Zane, naked.

Once again, her thoughts shifted back to her bitch of a former best friend.

Finally, she sighed. "I can't stop thinking about it. I don't understand. Why would Sarah want me dead? I sign her paychecks, not to mention I've been a true, trustworthy friend for ages. This makes no sense. None whatsoever." She felt her body tensing up, even as Zane worked her muscles with his sure, strong hands. A few minutes later, he slid those hands down over her buttocks. An oil-slicked finger dipped between the globes, teasing her anus. "I can make you forget about her." The finger slid inside.

Nothing.

"Sorry," Mandy said. "I don't think even sex is going to do it tonight. I need answers. I need the truth." Pause. "I need to talk to her."

"No."

"Alone."

"*Hell* no." Zane swung off her.

Mandy logrolled over, then sat up. "I don't believe she could kill me herself. That's why she hired someone. I'll be safe."

Zane crossed his arms over his chest. "She could plan an ambush."

"We'll prepare for that possibility."

He shook his head. His eyes were like ice. "This is a bad idea."

"But you'll help me, right?" She turned on the charm, tilting her head to display her sad puppy eyes. "Please?"

"Oh, hell."

Mandy flung herself at him, knowing he'd catch her. Together, they tumbled onto the mattress, Mandy landing on top. "I love you, Zane."

Zane's hard eyes softened. "I love you, too."

26

Twelve-oh-one.

Sarah was late.

Zane was looking tense. "Something's not right."

Mandy was feeling tense. "Sarah's always late." That much was true. "She'll be here." That much Mandy was beginning to doubt.

"I still think this is a bad idea."

"You've prepared for every possibility imaginable, including a few that are beyond imagining." Mandy leaned over and slid her arms around his big, hard, stressed-out bulk. "Thank you."

"You're welcome," he grumbled as he pushed to his feet. "I'll be right over there if you need me."

Mandy tried to hide her anxiety. She figured she failed. "Thanks."

The bell above the coffee shop's door tinkled, signaling the arrival of another customer. As it had the last thirty times, Mandy's gaze jerked to the entry. This time, she saw Sarah, looking nervous as she scanned the room.

Mandy waved.

Zane was long gone and out of sight by the time Sarah had reached the table. They'd selected that particular spot for a reason. It was located in the back, easy to protect. Zane was hiding in the hallway that led to the bathrooms, wearing an earpiece. He would hear every word Sarah said.

So would the hidden video camera Mandy had placed in the table's centerpiece.

"Where have you been?" Sarah exclaimed, playing the part of worried best friend to perfection. This girl should win an Oscar. She had some skills. "I was so worried about you after you took off with my car."

"I didn't total it, if that's what you're worried about. I left it at a bowling alley."

"I know. I had it tracked. GPS." Sarah pulled a face. "Of course, I wasn't worried about the car. I was concerned about you."

"Of course you were." The sarcasm in her voice couldn't be clearer.

"What's that supposed to mean?"

"It means, there's a reason why I ran away. I heard what you said."

Sarah's face took on the pasty shade of uncooked bread dough. It wasn't a good look for her. She shifted in her chair. Her gaze lurched away, then bounced back. "What did you hear?"

"Oh, something about wanting me dead—"

"I wasn't talking about you. Why would I want you dead? You're my best friend."

"Exactly." Mandy didn't say anything for a while. She let her former best friend squirm. Finally, she raised her eyebrows. "So, what's the story?"

"I don't know what you mean. I didn't say anything about wanting anyone dead. I think you must've been hallucinating or something. Maybe it was the drugs—"

Hah! "How did you know I'd been drugged?" Mandy snapped.

"It was...just a guess. I mean, you were acting like you were on something. I thought Zane had dosed you when you went to his suite."

"Zane." Mandy shook her head, a humorless laugh filling the awkward silence. "I ate nothing that night. Drank nothing, other than that fucking berry concoction you handed me. It tasted like shit, but you'd convinced me it was awful because it was healthy."

"There was nothing wrong with that drink. He could've injected you—"

"I had no needle marks."

"Perhaps they were hidden."

"I went to the hospital. What do you think the doctors found in my blood and urine tests?"

Sarah's lips were becoming mighty thin. "I wouldn't know."

"GHB."

"If you were dosed, it wasn't by me."

Mandy slapped her hands onto the table. The sound echoed through the entire shop. Heads turned. Curious eyes shifted to them. Mandy said, "Bullshit. I know it was you. If you don't want me to go to the cops, you'd better tell me what the hell is going on."

Sarah glanced over her shoulder, toward the door.

"Looking for someone?"

"No," Sarah snapped.

"Dammit, you owe me an explanation."

Sarah stared at her for one, two, three seconds. "I can't..." Her eyes blinked. The whites were turning red. Quickly.

This was not the behavior of a woman who was capable of planning a murder for her own selfish reasons.

Then again, Mandy couldn't deny Sarah's acting talent. Was this teary-eyed scene an act? Or was it real?

"Okay." Sarah nodded. "You're right." She grabbed a paper napkin and wiped her watery eyes. "I did hire someone to kill you. But it got all fucked up."

Mandy's heart sank. "Why?"

Sarah's jaw clenched. "Because...I was jealous. Of you and Zane. You know, I've wanted him. For ages."

"Wanted *him*? For what? He's a dom. You're a dom."

"He's a man. I'm a woman. And I've been in love with him since the moment I met him."

"Really." Why didn't this make sense?

Sarah was doing a lot of sniffling now. And she was not keeping up with the tear flowage. Her face was getting wetter by the second. "I'm a bitch. I deserve to go to prison."

"Then you'll get what you having coming, I guess."

Sarah nodded. Stood. "Okay. I suppose I should make some arrangements."

"As long as they don't involve vacation plans in, say, Mexico."

"I won't run. There's no use. They'll find me." Sarah stood. Turned around. Walked out the door.

Mandy knew she was going to cry again. She grabbed Zane and rushed from the building just as the first sob tore up her throat. Zane held her. Stroked her back, her head. When she was done, she looked up into his dark eyes. "She said it was because of you."

"I heard." He looked genuinely confused.

"She said she's been in love with you for a long time. That she was jealous because you love me."

"Do you believe her?" he asked.

"I don't know."

"I think she's lying," he said.

Mandy was having her own doubts.

This wasn't making sense. None of it did, actually. But Mandy figured that was because she was an emotional basket case, and how could any of it make sense when her world was all ajumble? "But I told her I'd be pressing charges. She knows she'll go to prison. She didn't try to talk me out of it."

"Okay, so if she's lying, why? Why would she be willing to go to prison for a crime she didn't commit?"

"I wish I knew."

Three weeks later, Mandy still didn't know if Sarah had lied or not. She'd given everything she had to the police, including the recorded confession. They'd taken things from there, issuing formal charges. Sarah was now sitting in jail, awaiting a trial that wouldn't take place for months.

Mandy did what she could to move on. She hired a new receptionist. His name was Max. He was young. He was enthusiastic. He did his job well...but he wasn't Sarah. Regardless, Mandy pushed on, pretty much throwing herself into her work. At night, she fell into bed, too exhausted to think about Sarah—for more than a few minutes. And during the day, she was too busy to think about much of anything.

Things with Zane progressed slowly. He didn't pressure her into making a decision about Bruce. She was grateful for that fact. Still, she knew they continued with their relationship, spending time together when Mandy wasn't around. It was a simple case of necessity. She knew that. But a part of her wondered if she was losing Zane because of what the two of them shared.

This week, she decided she'd see if she could handle being with them. Just this once. If it didn't work out, she'd go back to the way it was before—the boys doing their thing while she *tried* to pretend it wasn't happening.

God, she hoped she could handle it.

She called Zane on Wednesday. They made plans for Friday. Today was Friday.

Mandy was ready...well, as ready as she was ever going to

be. She was dressed to kill. She'd waxed, plucked, and buffed her skin to smooth perfection. She'd curled her hair into a mass of bouncy ringlets, just the way Zane liked it. And she'd carefully applied her makeup to accentuate her eyes and mouth. The overall effects, she'd have to admit, were more than impressive.

Still, she was nervous as hell as she *click-clacked* up Zane's front steps. Zane greeted her at the door, sweeping her into an embrace that melted away the worst of her anxiety.

"How are you?" he asked, pressing a kiss to the top of her head.

"I'm better now."

"Good. This way." He led her to the dining room, an arm looped around her back. Bruce was sitting at the table. He was wearing clothes. That set Mandy somewhat at ease. He smiled. Mandy made her best effort at smiling back. Zane pulled out the chair opposite Bruce's. "I hope you're hungry."

"A little." Mandy settled into the chair, giving Zane a "Thanks," over her shoulder after he pushed it in for her.

Zane took his seat at the head of the table.

Mandy glanced at Bruce, then focused her attention on Zane during the appetizers. Zane didn't eat. Not a bite.

It was quiet. Eerily so.

Finally, Zane broke the silence. "Bruce, Amanda is a private detective. She runs her own agency."

Strained small talk ensued. Mandy told Bruce about her work. He told her about his—he was a librarian. She discovered they had two things in common—Zane, of course, and loving the challenge of uncovering a hidden truth.

Outside of those two things, they lived very different lifestyles. Bruce had fathered five children, all of whom were fully grown. He looked like he couldn't be a day over thirty. Zane explained the slower aging was a side effect of his venom.

Mandy began to wonder if being a vampire's food source had other perks as well.

By the time dessert had been served, Mandy was feeling slightly more at ease. Of course, her nerves became all jumpy and jerky the minute the meal was over and Zane suggested they head up to his suite.

Upstairs, he offered Mandy a drink. She decided one little wine cooler wouldn't hurt. She sat on the couch, flung one leg over the other, and gulped the alcohol, hoping the big meal she'd just eaten wouldn't keep her from catching a little buzz. At the moment, she needed some liquid courage.

Zane sat beside her, resting one hand on her thigh. Bruce took the seat on her other side. When he placed his hand on her other knee, she bristled.

How the hell would she get through this?

"Relax, Amanda. You've enjoyed having other men touch you before."

"I know. But this is different somehow." She glanced at the half-empty bottle. The fruity beverage was almost sickly sweet. It wasn't sitting so good. She set it down.

"I have an idea." Zane went to his closet of toys and returned with a blindfold. "You won't know whose hand is where."

"Maybe. Maybe not," she said.

"Trust me."

She indicated he could go ahead with a nod. What the hell? It was worth a shot. The alcohol wasn't working. She really wanted to enjoy this experience. Zane was one of the most beautiful men she'd ever seen. Bruce came in a close second. If she could get past her anxiety, she might have fun with this.

Zane tied the blindfold on and her world went dark.

Her heart, which had already been thumping heavily, started racing. Her mouth went dry.

"I'm your king," Zane whispered in her ear. He nipped her earlobe. "You'll do as I wish." How she loved it when Zane took charge like that. A little shiver of excitement raced through her body. Two hands skimmed up her thighs. "Your body is mine. Always mine." Her knees were drawn apart. Heat rushed to her core. "Mmmm. You smell good. Woman. Need." A fingertip flicked over her pussy, covered by a thin layer of satin. She slid down until her bottom rested on the very edge of the cushion. Her back arched, tilting her hips up. "Patience, Amanda. You'll get my cock soon. But not yet."

Her wet pussy clenched. She was definitely getting into this. *Thank God for blindfolds.*

Someone lifted her ass off the couch. Her panties were tugged down over her hips. Little nibbles and kisses were trailed along both legs as the garment was slowly pulled lower, lower. Then they were gone, and her pussy was aching to be filled. A steady throb of moist heat pulsed through her groin. Her nipples were tingling, their points pushing at the thin material of her dress.

"Are you getting warm, Amanda?" Zane asked.

He knew the answer. "Touch me and you'll find out for yourself."

His chuckle reverberated through her whole system. "We're going to make you burn."

"Promises, promises," she said on a contented sigh. Someone had decided she didn't need to wear her dress any longer. That someone was a god. Now fully nude, she was lounging on the couch while two sets of hands and two mouths explored and teased and nipped and tasted. She was quickly racing toward orgasm. And just as fast concluding that the threesome thing was not a bad idea at all.

Rather than recline there, languishing in decadent indulgence, she put her hands to work, yanking shirts over heads, tugging pants down long, lean, muscular legs. She mapped two broad chests with her fingertips. She traced the deep lines crossing two defined stomachs. She sighed and moaned as images of two glorious male bodies played through her mind. And when one hard cock landed in her palm, she happily gave it a few long, slow strokes. In return, she received a deep, husky male groan.

She felt a smile spreading across her face.

"What are you smiling about, minx?" Zane asked.

"Nothing in particular." She shivered as a finger or tongue flicked over her labia. "Oh, does that feel goooood..."

"What?" Again, Zane.

"Everything."

"We're going to move to the bedroom now," Zane told her.

Someone swept her up into his thick arms. All Mandy had to do is lean into him and inhale and she knew it was Zane. His scent was unique, intoxicating. He set her on the bed. "Have you ever thought about being penetrated by two men at once?" Zane asked. A finger slid into her pussy. Her slick passage clamped tightly around it. "Here," he said. A second finger circled her anus. "And here."

"I have...but...I'm not sure." Instantly, she thought of his piercing. Would it hurt if he was the one fucking her anus?

"I promise, we'll go slowly. And we'll stop if it becomes uncomfortable. Every woman I've done this with has enjoyed it. A great deal."

She hoped he wasn't exaggerating. "I'll try it."

Zane kissed her to oblivion before murmuring against her mouth, "You won't regret it."

"If I don't, I guarantee it'll be the last time."

Once again, his low, rumbling laughter vibrated through her body. In its wake, little blazes of erotic heat simmered everywhere, from the soles of her feet to the top of her head.

The bed shifted as male bodies took their positions, and

Mandy, still blindfolded, was set on her hands and knees over one of them.

"I'll be fucking your ass, Amanda," Zane said behind her as someone smoothed lube over her clit with slow circles. His words, coupled with the heaviness in his voice and the waves of spiraling pleasure crashing through her, nearly sent her over the edge.

"Zane...," she said. A thick cock slid inside her pussy and she jerked upright. "Ohmygod." Her flesh gripped the invading member. Her body tightened. Her heart rate kicked up into overdrive. "Ohmygod," she said again when two fingers plunged into her ass.

So full.

So good.

Beneath her, Bruce rocked his hips up and down, driving his cock deep inside her wet pussy. Behind her, Zane scissored his fingers, preparing her anus for his rod.

Any moment now he'd drive his cock inside. Would it hurt? Would it feel as good as his fingers did now?

Zane gripped her ass cheeks, pulling them apart. His cock breached her entry easily enough, but he didn't force himself deeper quickly. Instead he inched in, which amplified her pleasure.

Unbelievably full now, she was tense all over, burning with fever and barely able to register what was going on around her. In the distance, she heard Bruce's heavy breaths huffing from his chest as he slammed into her. His fucking was rough and raw and delicious. Different from Zane's but nearly as mind-blowing. Zane, on the other hand, was in complete control as he drove home and withdrew with smooth, long strokes.

"We can feel each other," Zane said. "We can feel every inch."

The best Mandy could manage was, "Ahhhhh..."

Beneath her, Bruce's body was heating up and tightening.

The warmth seemed to be soaking into her body, too, amplifying her pleasure.

Almost there.

So close.

She trembled. She quaked. Her body tightened all over. Her toes curled. A storm surge of erotic pleasure tumbled over her and she was lost. Her body spasmed. She cried out. Zane leaned over her, his weight pushing her down onto Bruce. Bruce trembled. A low, drawn-out cry of pleasure cut through the thick air. Mandy's body rhythmically contracted around both cocks, milking them. Zane withdrew first, kissing her shoulder, her mouth before brushing past her. She knew the minute he bit Bruce. Bruce's cock instantly grew enormous inside her. And a low guttural sound vibrated in his chest.

Somehow, Mandy was swept up in a second orgasm. Her body spasmed. Fierce flames blazed up and down. Throbbing pleasure pulsed through her veins. She heard herself cry out. Felt her lungs deflate and then, burning with the need for air, she gulped in huge mouthfuls.

This was insane.

This was intense.

This was everything Zane had promised.

And more.

Yes, oh, yes, she'd do this again. Soon. Very soon.

Five minutes later, she was no longer blindfolded, feeling tingly and happy and good all over as she lay, panting, between Zane and Bruce.

"Amanda," Zane said, giving her a very serious look, "a friend down at the police department told me Sarah's being bonded out. She'll be walking the streets tomorrow. I want you to stay here with me. Until the trial."

So much for the tingly, happy, good-all-over feeling.

27

Mandy rushed into the office the next morning, her brain a jumble of mixed-up thoughts.

Sarah was out of jail.

Zane wanted her to move in for the next six months or more. Her life would be very different if she moved in with him—much more complicated.

"Good morning!" Max said, his voice a cheery invasion as she zoomed past his desk on the way to her office.

"Good morning." She stopped. Looked at him. "Can you do something for me?"

"Sure, anything."

She motioned to the pad of stickies sitting on his desk. She scribbled her former best friend's name on the top one and handed it back to him. "Dig up everything you can find on that woman. Everything. I need to know her darkest secrets."

"Will do." Max set to work immediately, his slim fingers flying over his keyboard. The kid was a genius, able to find stuff even Sarah hadn't been able to get. Mandy figured she didn't need to ask how he did it. Some things were better left unexplored.

In her office, she slumped into her chair and checked messages. Thankfully, her caseload was light this week. If she did decide to move in with Zane, now was probably the best time to do it.

But...

Was she ready to take such a huge leap with Zane? Their relationship was far from stable. There were so many issues that hadn't been hammered out yet. Hell, they hadn't even agreed to any kind of exclusive sexual relationship. How weird would it be if she was living there and Zane brought home some other woman?

I can't do this.

That other issue aside, there was a part of her that had always believed it was better to get married than live with a boyfriend. She'd watched so many of her friends' relationships fail when they'd gone the living-together route.

Of course, this situation was unique. Moving in with him was a matter of security, safety. Her life was in jeopardy. She needed protection.

What the hell was the judge thinking, letting Sarah out of prison? Gah! This was all his fault.

Mandy paced back and forth, accomplishing nothing for over an hour. She made lists, pros and cons. She thought about the situation, looking at it from every angle she could imagine.

What if she stayed somewhere else for a while, like a hotel?

She thought about her strained bank account.

No, that wasn't going to work.

Her phone rang. She checked the number. Zane.

She answered with a cheery, "Hello." She didn't want him to know how stressed out she was about moving in with him. She didn't want to hurt his feelings. In his mind, he was doing the right thing—protecting her. "What's up?"

"Hi," he said in that sexy bedroom voice. "I hired a moving company. They'll be at your place at six. I hope that's okay."

"Six o'clock? Today?"

"Yes. I figured you'd want your things sooner rather than later. Was I wrong?"

"No...but..." She plopped into her chair, shoving her fingers through her hair.

"Amanda, what's the matter?"

"Nothing. I just...haven't had time to pack."

"The movers will pack it all for you. You don't have to lift a finger. And don't worry, they're very trustworthy. I've used them before."

She wasn't going to ask.

"Amanda?"

"I'm here." She dropped her head. Her forehead struck the desktop. *Thunk.*

"Do we need to talk about this again?"

"No. Yes. Maybe."

"I'll be there in fifteen. Where are you?"

"Work. But—"

"Fifteen." He cut off the call before she could tell him not to bother. She stared at the phone.

Was this what her life would be like? Would he take over, leaving her with absolutely no control? Could she handle this?

She tried to accomplish a few things before Zane came in. She failed. Exactly fifteen minutes later, Zane strolled into her office, looking as devastatingly handsome as always. In his hands he carried a coat, hat, sunglasses, and umbrella. He closed the door. "Now, tell me what's going on." He set his things down on the floor.

"Nothing's 'going on.' It's just...this is all happening so fast."

He settled his hot body into the chair across from her desk. "Yes, of course it is. But I don't see another option. I won't have you staying at your apartment with that...woman...on the loose."

"But moving in with you for such an extended period of time is a big step. It's not like I'll be a temporary houseguest. I'll be living with you." *Maybe sleeping with you...?*

"What are you worried about? Losing your independence?"

"That's one issue that's come to mind."

His expression darkened.

She sighed. Dammit, his feelings were hurt. She reached for him. "Zane, I appreciate the thought. You're so generous. Protective. Caring—"

"Controlling, overbearing. Manipulative—"

"No."

He lifted his brows.

"Okay, maybe a *little* controlling. I like that. Sometimes." She blushed.

He nodded. "In the bedroom."

"Yes."

"But outside."

She shrugged. "That's not my only concern."

"Tell me."

How she hated difficult discussions like this one. She gnawed on her lip. She shifted in her chair.

"Amanda, what is it?"

"I don't think I can live with you without having some kind of understanding between us."

"You're talking about sex?"

"Yeah. I can't sleep in the room next to you while you're fucking someone else."

Zane sighed. "I understand. Dammit." He stood. He paced. "It isn't that I don't care for you. I do."

"I know you love me, Zane. I'm in danger and of course you want to keep me safe."

His expression brightened a little. "Yeah."

She looked at him for a moment. "Here's the other thing. I told myself a long time ago that I'd *never* live with a man."

"Uh…"

"If I loved a man enough to make that kind of commitment, I'd marry him."

"Oh." His face went bread-dough white. It was almost comical. Vampire or not, it seemed Zane reacted like any other red-blooded man when it came to the big M-word. "I see."

"So, you understand where I'm coming from?"

"I do. I mean…yeah." He paced some more. "Maybe I can come up with another alternative."

"Thank you." That went better than she'd expected.

He walked around the desk and pulled her to her feet. He gathered her into his arms. After kissing her sweetly, he headed for the door. "Do you want me to help you?"

"Yes. Please. If you think of something, by all means, tell me."

"I'll see what I can do." He shrugged into his coat, pulled his hat down low to shade his face, and put on his sunglasses; then he left.

Breathing much easier, she flopped into her chair and tried to get back to work. Three hours later, she'd accomplished absolutely nothing. She glanced at her calendar.

Shit, it was the fifteenth. She had to pay Grandma's rent. She'd almost forgotten. It was a good excuse to run over and see that sweet old lady anyway. Lately she'd been too busy to make regular visits like she used to. Quickly, she wrote a check, sealed it in an envelope, and dashed out, waving at Max as she zipped past. Twenty minutes later, she was at Grandma's assisted-living complex, handing the secretary the payment. Five minutes later, she was knocking on Grandma's door.

Grandma answered, took one look at Mandy, and scowled. "It's about fucking time."

Mandy gave her angry grandmother a hug. "I'm sorry, Grandma."

"You should be." Grandma stepped aside to let Mandy into her tiny studio apartment. It was basically a bedroom with an attached bath and a kitchenette. It looked like a hospital room. It smelled like one, too. "Do you know how long it's been since I've had a visitor?"

"Yes—"

"I was beginning to think you'd forgotten about me." Grandma plopped into her recliner, the ratty old piece of furniture a vestige from the life she'd once led. "What the hell is so important that you can't take an hour or two out of your week to come and visit?"

"There's been a lot of stuff going on."

"Tell me." Gran waved at the little refrigerator. "Get me a juice first. I'm thirsty."

Mandy opened a bottle of apple juice, shoved a straw into the top, and handed it to her grandmother; then she spent the next hour telling her everything that had happened, right down to Sarah's arrest. Well, not quite everything. She left out the juicy parts. Like the stuff that happened at the bondage club. And the things she'd done with Zane at his house. And the threesome she'd had with Zane and Bruce. She also left out the bit about how Zane was a vampire and needed to suck Bruce's blood every couple of days. She was pretty sure those stories would put her dear old grandma in cardiac arrest.

Gran handed Mandy the empty juice bottle just as Mandy finished. "Well, I guess you have been busy." She motioned to the cabinet. "Now I'm hungry. Could you get me a doughnut? They're in the cupboard above the sink."

"Sure." Mandy found the box and, using a napkin, selected one of the powdered sugar–covered pastries. She handed it over and returned to her seat.

"So what's next?" Gran asked.

"I don't know. I agree with Zane. Staying at my place is probably not the best idea. But where else could I go?"

"I suppose you could sleep here. On the floor. If they tried to kick you out, I'd let them have it." Grandma shook a fist at the door. "I'll tell those bastards what to do with their rules."

Mandy swallowed a chuckle. Grandma had never appreciated people laughing at her. "No, that's okay. Besides, I wouldn't want to put you in danger."

"So why not stay with Zane? He sounds like a nice man."

"He is...nice." *Looking. He smells nice, too. Kisses nice.*

"Then what's the problem? Don't you like him?"

"I do. Very much." Mandy fidgeted in her seat. This was awkward. What had made her think it was a good idea talking about Zane?

"Is he sexy?" Mandy's face must've turned ten shades of red because Grandma grinned. "Sexy. Nice. You like him. If it were me, I'd have my stuff packed and would be sitting on his front porch by now."

"Yeah, I'm sure if it was anyone else, they'd have their stuff sitting on his porch." Mandy's eyes burned. Was she going to cry? Now? Why?

Grandma leaned forward. "You love him, right?"

"Yes, I love him. But...I'm afraid. This isn't exactly a simple situation. It's complicated."

Grandma waved a wrinkled hand. "Bah. Every situation is complicated."

"But not like this." She hesitated. Was she really considering telling her grandmother that Zane was a vampire? "Grandma, Zane isn't exactly human."

Grandma didn't look particularly shocked by that statement. *Could be dementia.* "What is he?"

"Vampire."

"Damn. You're one lucky girl," Grandma said, patting Mandy's knee. "You snagged a vampire. You'd be crazy to throw him back."

"What do you know about vampires?"

Grandma's eyes gleamed. "Plenty. Remember how I told you about that man I fell in love with before I married your grandfather?"

"Sure."

"He was a vampire. He was the sexiest man I'd ever met. Intelligent. Strong." Grandma's smile was wistful. "I've never forgotten him."

"What happened?"

"My father wouldn't let me marry him. So we broke up. What a fucking mistake that was. I've regretted it ever since. If only I could turn back time..." Grandma set one wrinkled hand on top of Mandy's. "Nobody's telling you what to do or not to do. I say trust your instincts. If you love Zane and know he loves you, all the other things can be worked through. I—"

A knock interrupted their conversation. Grandma glanced at the clock. She grinned. "Time for my shower." She shuffled to the door and opened it. A handsome man dressed in scrubs stepped inside. "Hello, Edna. Are you ready for your shower?"

"You betcha." Grandma winked at Mandy.

Having nowhere else to go, Mandy drove back to her office. That building, unlike her apartment, had a security system. It was far from perfect, but it was better than nothing. It was still daylight outside. The attack had happened at night. Mandy hoped that wasn't coincidental. If Sarah was hiring vampy hit men, perhaps they could only work after sunset. She knew Zane had to wear layer upon layer of clothing to protect himself from sunlight. Even then, he didn't expose himself any more than necessary.

She hurried inside, just in case Sarah decided to hire a living, breathing human being, and locked herself in. The suite was silent. She'd been here alone before. Plenty of times. But now the quiet was eerie. Spooky. Unsettling. She made a beeline for her office and hit the power button on her radio, filling the space with the sound of the B-52s' "Love Shack." Instantly, her mood lifted.

Feeling much less uneasy, she plopped into her chair and flipped open the file sitting on her desk. The tab on the file read SARAH GRAY. The sticky glued to the front was from Max. He said he'd found only the basics so far. She decided to flip through it anyway.

Right away, she was glad she did.

Name.
Date of birth.
Mother's name.
Father's name.

It was that last one that made Mandy's heart jump.

Father's name: Bruce Reeves.

That could be no coincidence.

Sarah had told her her father's name was Dave Gray. Supposedly, he'd died many years ago. Cancer. If what Max had found was true, Sarah had lied about her father's identity.

Some of the puzzle pieces seemed to fall into place.

Why would an innocent person lie about committing a crime? Mandy knew the answer—to protect someone else. Someone important. Someone you loved.

Sarah was willing to go to prison to protect her father.

Her father, the man Mandy had slept with.

Her gag reflex kicked in.

She rushed to the bathroom. To her relief, she didn't throw

up. But she came mighty close. After heaving for a few seconds, she doused her face in cold water. She stared at her reflection in the mirror.

Bruce Reeves wanted her dead. Why? Probably because of Zane.

Zane needed to know.

Mandy wobbled on still-shaky legs back to her office and dialed Zane's phone number. It rang once, twice, three times... six times, seven...

Mandy gave up, slamming the phone back onto the cradle.

It had to be true, she decided as she started pacing back and forth in her office. It made sense. In a sick, disturbing, shocking way, of course.

I need to tell Zane.

He won't believe me.

Oh, hell.

Mandy picked up her phone again. This time she dialed Max's cell. He answered on the second ring. It was decided— he'd get a raise...as soon as Mandy could afford to give him one. "Hey, Max. I need a huge favor," she said, skipping the whole "Hi, are you busy right now" thing.

"Sure. Anything."

"I need you to come into the office and dig up some dirt on someone."

"I don't need to do that at the office. I can access my computer remotely from home. Go to my desk."

This man was a freaking genius. Mandy sprinted to his desk and sat.

"Power up my computer," he told her.

She poked the power button. "Done."

"Hit the Okay button that pops up on the screen."

A little box popped up. Mandy clicked the mouse on the button in its center. "Done."

"Now the magic begins..." Screens flashed. The mouse

curser moved on its own, opening windows. Letters typed, filling in log-in screens. And minutes later, she knew everything there was to know about Bruce Reeves, including the one thing that made every piece of the puzzle fit.

Mandy thanked her brilliant assistant for a job well done. He pshawed it off as "no biggie." She printed out everything, stuffed it into a tote, and checked outside—still a little daylight left.

It was worth the risk.

She broke a land-speed record—that is, her own personal record—running to her car. She broke a few laws driving to Zane's. The sky to the west was mostly purple with a few streaks of pink when she pulled up to Zane's house. She rang the bell, aware of a car rolling up the driveway behind her. *Please, don't let that be Bruce.* Her heart was pounding so hard she could hear every single beat in her ears as she twisted to look over her shoulder. *Dammit.* She poked the doorbell a second time.

Why wasn't anyone answering? Where was Zane?

Bruce parked his car next to Mandy's. His door swung open and his lean body emerged. He tossed her a casual wave, which she returned.

She pasted on a smile. She hoped to God she could pull this off.

"Hey," he said as he stepped onto the front porch.

"Hey back." She motioned to the door. "Nobody's answering."

"Oh, that's no problem. I have a key." Bruce produced a ring from his pocket, slid a key into the lock, and gave it a twist.

So much for Zane's place being her sanctuary. She'd be no safer here than in a deserted parking lot at midnight. "Great," she said, following him inside. The lights were off. The place was dark. Where was Zane? Mandy headed straight for the staircase.

"He isn't up there," Bruce said from the bottom of the staircase. "He spent the night at *my place* last night."

Mandy couldn't be certain, but she could swear Bruce had sneered as he'd said "my place."

That meant she was alone with the man who wanted her dead. The man who had stood by and watched his daughter take the blame for something he'd done.

Mandy did a one-eighty, trotting down the stairs. "Oh, okay. I guess I can wait for him in the family room...." She gave Bruce a wide berth as she turned down the hall that led to the back of the house.

"Good idea." Bruce's footfalls *click, click, clicked* on the stone-tiled floor behind her. "I could use a drink," he said, moving to the refrigerator. "Would you like something?"

Like she'd be so stupid, to accept a drink from him after being drugged by his daughter. "No thanks." She felt a dark energy coming off Bruce when their gazes met. It made her skin crawl. The corners of his mouth curved up, producing the slightest hint of a smile.

I need to get the hell out of here.

"You seem a little...jumpy tonight, Amanda." He uncorked a bottle of wine and poured himself a glass. It was red. Made her think of blood. "Is something wrong?"

"Nope. Work's just been a little crazy. I'm having a hard time unwinding."

"Mmmm. I could help you there. If you let me." He drained his glass, then set it down and came toward her.

She did a quick survey of her surroundings and decided the door to the attached garage was her best bet. Trying not to be too obvious (and no doubt failing miserably), Mandy strolled toward the door, which was at the opposite end of the kitchen. She'd have to get past Bruce to reach it. Would he try to stop her if he knew she was leaving?

"What did you have in mind?" she asked as she moved

closer. She aimed for a playful expression. She could tell from his reaction she'd missed her target.

"I think you have some notion."

"I don't know what you mean." She broke into a run, her gaze locked on the door. He didn't follow her. She yanked it open, and the odor of gasoline and mown grass hit her. Then a huge, dark form lunged at her, hauling her off her feet.

She screamed, but a gloved hand clapped over her mouth, muffling the sound. A thick arm, strong, snaked around her midsection. She kicked. She wriggled. She cried. The attacker carted her to a vehicle parked in the garage, a vehicle that didn't belong there. A delivery van. The closer she got to the van, the harder she fought. By the time she was being shoved through the open door, she felt like she was going to throw up.

Inside, a second man waited, with restraints ready. Despite Mandy's frenzied motion, her hands were bound behind her back. Her legs were tied at the knee and ankle. A gag was shoved into her mouth.

Tears streamed from her eyes, blurring her vision.

Bruce poked his head into the van. "I just wanted to tell you it's nothing personal. The time we shared was great. But I can't let you take him away."

She was willing to talk about this. She tried. The gag wouldn't let her.

Wait! You don't have to kill me. I'll let you have Zane. I'll walk away—for now. I'll let you think you won...

The garage door opened with a deep growl. The door lifted. A car's tires squealed nearby. A low rumbling engine roared up behind the van before it could move.

"What the hell is going on?"

Zane. *Thank God!*

"You're just in time!" Bruce said, sounding breathless. What the hell was he breathless for? He'd done nothing. His goons had done all the hard work. "She attacked me!"

"What? Who?" Zane said.

"Amanda. I let us both into the house, to wait for you, since you were sound asleep still. And she said some shit about not wanting to share you, and the next thing I knew, she clobbered me on the head with the fireplace poker."

What a fucking liar!

"Who are these guys? Where'd this van come from?"

Mandy jerked at the bindings holding her wrists. If only she could get the gag out, she'd tell Zane the truth. And the truth, unlike Bruce's lie, would make sense.

The van's rear door swung open. Mandy's heart took flight when Zane's worry-filled gaze met hers. He knew she'd never do such a thing.

"She said something about me attacking her and that's why she needed to get rid of me," Bruce said, sounding injured.

She'd give him reason to sound that way soon enough.

She worked her tongue around the gag, trying to push it out of the way. Zane helped her by removing it.

"Amanda?" was all he said.

"He's lying," Mandy said first. "Although he is right about me thinking he was the one who attacked me. That much is true. And I have proof!" Where the fuck was her tote bag? She'd had it when she'd gone into Zane's house.

Zane looked extremely torn and confused. "Untie her," he barked to the man in the van with her.

"You're going to let her go? After what she did to me?" Bruce's voice was low. "She tried to kill me."

"I need to figure out what the hell is going on here."

"I'm trying to tell you what's going on," Bruce snapped. "She's jealous because I need you. But I can't help that. I fucking tried!"

Zane's expression turned grim. Mandy could see the guilt and regret burning in his dark eyes. That bastard Bruce needed to shut the hell up now.

"He's twisting it all around, Zane," she said. "He's the one trying to get rid of me. And he almost succeeded. Twice."

"Look at the lump on my head. It's real." Bruce pointed to the back of his head.

"*If* there's a lump—which I highly doubt—he gave it to himself," Mandy said, unwilling to back down. Zane's gaze tangled with hers. "Please, Zane. Believe me."

Zane looked at the van, at the red stripes on her wrists, which she was just noticing, at Bruce's flushed, strained face. "Dammit. This is all my fault."

"Don't blame yourself," she said. "He's the one who's made these terrible choices."

"No, you're wrong. It is my fault. Whether it's you or him who's being the aggressor, the reason for the problem is me, the shitty decisions I've made. I shouldn't have let one person become my sole source of nourishment—"

"You had no choice!" Bruce yelled. "You were trapped. You would've died if you hadn't fed from me. Once that week had passed, it was too late. You didn't know I'd become addicted so quickly. You told me that yourself."

Zane turned his attention back to Mandy. "And I shouldn't have dragged you into this." When Mandy tried to interrupt him, he shushed her with a raised hand. "Bruce's addiction is so bad, he'd probably do anything to protect me. Including kill you. I should've realized that sooner."

"What's next?" Mandy asked. Clearly, Zane's idea, about the three of them being together, had to be thrown out. She could walk away, let Bruce have what he needed, and spare herself what was bound to be a complicated relationship. She'd probably save herself a lot of heartbreak. And grief. If only . . . if only she could drum up the strength to do it.

I'm weak.

Zane's eyes lifted to Mandy's once again. "He'll die without me, but I'll die without you. What the hell am I going to do?"

28

Zane had dialed the number. All he had to do was hit the button and it would be done. He would turn Bruce in to the authorities. He would protect the woman he loved.

And in the process, he would sentence him to death.

"You believe me, don't you?" Amanda asked for the fifth time. "His story makes no sense whatsoever."

They were all inside the house now, clustered around the kitchen island. Amanda was alternately glaring at Bruce and lifting pleading eyes to Zane.

He didn't doubt her. That wasn't the issue. It was more the notion that he'd created this problem in the first place, and now he was letting someone else clean up the mess if he turned Bruce in to the authorities.

You're the worst kind of chickenshit if you don't handle this yourself.

There was another issue to think about. Bruce's death wouldn't be swift. It would be slow. Excruciating. Doctors wouldn't be able to help him. Nobody would.

There's another solution.

Zane's gaze met Bruce's.

How many times had they looked each other in the eye? Thousands? More? This man hadn't been just a source of nourishment over the years. He'd also been a confidant. A companion. A friend.

"I know you'll do the right thing," Bruce said.

Zane had to take some of the blame for him becoming a would-be murderer. It wasn't entirely Bruce's fault.

Bruce didn't deserve to suffer.

Zane knew what he had to do.

"Yes, the right thing." Zane set down the phone.

"What are you doing?" Amanda asked, sounding slightly panicked.

"It's okay." Zane took Bruce's hand. To Amanda he said, "Wait here." He and Bruce walked out of the room.

"I knew you'd see through her lies," Bruce said, his voice laced with confidence as they went upstairs to Zane's suite.

Zane made no comment about Bruce's continued lies, recognizing them for what they were—a desperate attempt at preserving his life. Perhaps Zane had become jaded over the years, but he figured most people would lie to save their own ass. Perhaps even Amanda.

Once he had the two of them inside his room, he locked the door. He didn't want to risk Amanda getting in the way.

"So, are you going to call the police?" Bruce asked, motioning toward the cordless phone sitting on Zane's dresser. He made himself comfortable on the couch, flinging an arm over the back.

"No, I don't think that's the best way to handle this situation." Zane sat next to Bruce.

Bruce, looking convinced of his own lies, shook his head. "I tell you what, she shocked the hell out of me. She's so sweet, so innocent. Who would've thought she'd attack me out of the blue like that?"

Zane nodded. "You never know what people are capable of."

"So true."

"Everyone struggles with the light and dark sides of themselves. The animal within."

"Sure," Bruce agreed.

"I do."

"Yeah?" Bruce looked surprised. "I've never seen it, if you have."

"Sure I have. You have, too."

Bruce shrugged nonchalantly. "I think I'm okay."

Zane leaned in, cupped Bruce's face. That was the chin he'd kissed and nipped a million times over the years. Those were the eyes he'd stared into when he'd been swept into climax. He wove the fingers of his other hand between Bruce's. Looked down. That was the hand he'd held in times of joy and pain.

Fuck, could he do this?

"Zane, I love you," Bruce said. "More than my next breath. More than life."

Get it done. Quickly. Don't give him time to be afraid. To suffer. You owe him that much.

Zane kissed him. It was a gentle kiss, full of tender emotions. "I love you, too." He kissed Bruce once more, drawing in his flavor, committing it to memory.

This would be their last kiss. Bruce's final moment of life. They'd share it, and Zane would do his damnedest to make it sweet.

"I can't live without you."

"You won't have to." Zane kissed Bruce's eyelids.

Bruce lifted his free hand to Zane's face. "Thank you."

"You're welcome."

Moving swiftly, Zane released Bruce's hand, cupped the other side of his head, and jerked it to the side, snapping Bruce's neck.

Zane caught his body as it collapsed, lifeless. He kissed

Bruce one last time and looked into eyes that stared blindly but reflected Bruce's emotions during that final second of life.

There was no fear in their depths. No pain. No anguish. Only love.

Tears of sorrow and guilt blurred Zane's vision as he sat, cradling the man he'd killed. He didn't hold back. He let the tears come. The awful, gut-wrenching sadness blasted over him in a series of waves. Vaguely, he heard the knock at the door. But he lacked the strength to walk. With Bruce's upper body lying over his legs, Zane curled over him and rode out the storm.

Mandy pressed her ear to the door again. Someone was crying. Was it Zane? Or was it Bruce? Maybe Bruce had decided to kill Zane? If he was capable of doing what he had to her, might he be capable of that?

Remember, he hired someone else to do the dirty work.

Mandy knocked. No answer. She pounded harder. "Zane?" she called several times. "Are you okay?" Still no answer. She listened, holding her breath so she could hear better. If that was Zane, he was sobbing harder than she'd ever heard a man cry before. He was in agony. She ran to the nearest bathroom, the guest bathroom. There were hairpins in that one. She grabbed one and ran back to Zane's door. It was still closed. Locked. She straightened the pin, and within seconds she had the door open.

Zane was sitting on the couch, curled over a limp-looking Bruce. Zane was crying, unaware she was there. Mandy clapped her hands over her mouth to keep from making any sudden loud noises and crept over to him. She set a hand on his shoulder.

He looked up. His eyes were bloodred. His face was blotchy and wet. "He's gone," he said.

Mandy wanted to ask what happened, but she couldn't. "Are you okay? Can I do something?"

He didn't answer right away. Instead, he stared down at Bruce's white face. A long minute later, he said, "Tell me you love me, Amanda. Tell me you'll always love me."

"I love you, Zane. I'll always love you."

He lifted those grief-filled eyes to Mandy's. It was hard to look into them, to witness such horrible anguish. "I killed him."

Mandy's heart jerked in her chest. She felt her lungs squeezing tight, pushing the air out. "You...?"

"It was the only way. He would've died in prison. A slow death. So much pain. Too much. It was better this way."

"Oh, God." Mandy's knees were like jelly. She crumpled onto a nearby chair. She had just witnessed Zane's second killing in a short period of time. The first had been pure and simple self-preservation. This one was different.

A mercy killing.

She would have never believed it, but she respected him more for doing what he had.

"I loved him," he said. "If there'd been a way for me to die instead, to suffer for him... Fuck. I have no right to live, no right to love. I have no right to your love." Zane covered his face with his hands. "I'm a fucking animal. A beast. Look what I've done." He gently moved out from under Bruce, standing. He tugged her to her feet and pulled her toward the door. "You need to leave. Now."

"But—"

"I don't want you to see any more." He escorted her down the stairs, to the door. "You're safe now. Go."

Oh, hell no. Somehow, Mandy knew that if she walked out of his house now, she'd never be let inside again.

"You're wrong." Mandy took his hands in hers and turned to face him. "You love fiercely. With your heart and soul. I know now, after seeing you like this, grieving for a man you had no choice but to kill, that you aren't a bloodthirsty beast.

You will protect me, yes. But you'll always think of me first. Just like you did for Bruce. I could never love and respect a man more than I do you. So please tell me...please..." A sob tore up her throat.

"Tell you what?"

She took a second to catch her breath. She was on the verge of losing this man, of having her heart ripped from her chest.

"Tell me I can spend the rest of my life in your arms, the rest of my nights at your side."

Zane groaned. "Amanda—"

"Goddamnit, I love you."

His gaze dropped. He pulled his hands free and shoved his fingers through his hair.

"You can shove me out the door, Zane, but I'll be right there, waiting for you to let me back in. I'm not going anywhere. Period. I love you. You need me. You need love. You deserve love." She blinked. Dammit, she was crying. "I need you."

"But you deserve so much more—"

"Okay, you're not the kind of man I'd once pictured myself spending the rest of my life with. I mean, you're the epitome of the controlling alpha male, and I'm a headstrong, stubborn female. We're bound to butt heads from time to time. And you're not even technically a human. But after doing some soul searching, some talking to someone I trust, and even a little crying, I can't deny the truth. I love you, dark secrets and all. There's nothing you can say to change that."

His gaze lifted to hers. He blinked. Then, moving so quickly she was caught off guard, he jerked her to him, gathered her into his arms, and kissed her.

So glad to be in his embrace, to feel his hard length against her, she flung her arms around his neck and kissed him back. She let her lips, her tongue, her body tell him exactly how much she loved him. The message he sent back was just as emotion-filled and heart-touching. He loved her. There was no doubt.

When the kiss was over, he cupped her face and looked down into her eyes. "Be my wife. I want you. Only you. Forever."

Her heart felt like it had taken flight. Those were the words she'd ached to hear. It was almost too wonderful to believe. She laughed and cried at the same time.

"So, is that a yes or a no?" he asked when she still hadn't answered after several moments.

"One question."

"Sure."

"If I marry you, will you be snacking on me? Or will you be unleashing those fierce-looking fangs on someone else?"

"That is entirely up to you."

"Good answer." She flung her arms around his neck and gave him a great big kiss. "My answer is most definitely yes." This amazing, mysterious, complicated vampire was hers. For the rest of her life. Her master. Her lover. Her fantasy-come-true.

Turn the page
for a sizzling preview
of Anne Rainey's
PLEASURE BOUND

An Aphrodisia trade paperback
coming November 2011.

1

Present day...

She had sweet, gentle curves that the tight black skirt and light pink tank top couldn't even begin to hide. Short blond hair framed a cute oval-shaped face. Pretty. Flirty too. Her smiles should've been pulling him across the room. *Do it, dumbass. Walk over to her, whisper some lame shit in her ear, and get laid.* Great fucking advice. So, why wasn't he listening to it? Easy. His dick wanted only one woman—and she was nowhere in sight.

Jonas slammed back the last of his light beer and stepped away from the bar. The neon lights, crowded room, and booming bass should've been exactly what he needed to get his mind off one Deanna Harrison. He had a feeling an earthquake couldn't even manage to accomplish that goal.

After giving the little blonde a parting grin, Jonas headed out of the bar into the cold winter night. As he slid behind the wheel of his new black Dodge Charger, he felt marginally better, but not enough. Not nearly enough. He sighed and stared out at the darkness. Friday night and more than enough honeys to fill his bed for a week, and where was he? Alone. Again. "Christ, I'm an idiot."

Shoving the key into the ignition, Jonas started the car. Listening to the hum of the engine as the beautiful machine came to life sent a shot of pride through him. He loved his car, but as he drove out of the parking lot and headed toward the highway, Jonas's mind turned toward another beauty, Deanna. The way her eyes lit with mischief whenever she saw him. Only Deanna could make a smart-ass comment sound sexy. What would it take to slip past that exterior? To reach the passionate woman beneath? And she would be passionate; Jonas felt it in his gut. A woman like Deanna would burn him alive in bed. If he could ever get her to stop rejecting him.

Without thinking, Jonas automatically took the on ramp, which brought him in the direction of Deanna's house. "Ah, hell. Clearly my dick is now in complete control." The part of his brain that controlled rational thought seemed to switch off the minute the woman's image slipped through the cracks.

As he approached her house, Jonas stiffened. There weren't any lights on, which meant she was out. "It's Friday night—of course she's out." With a guy? "Now that's a hell of an ugly thought."

Jonas drove up the street a little ways, then parked along the curb. No reason why he couldn't wait for her to return home. He needed to be sure she was safe, didn't he? Jonas got out of the car and locked it. Jogging the short distance to her front porch gave him a chance to think about his actions. Deanna was a grown woman. She had every right to date whomever she chose. To come home late. Hell, stay out all night. None of his business, of course. The logical discussion didn't stop him from selecting the chair situated in the shadows of her porch. Dropping into it, Jonas pulled his leather coat around him tighter and relaxed, waited. His head started swirling with images of Deanna and some faceless stranger. Kissing. Touching. Another man's hands stroking her alabaster skin. Another man's tongue teasing her plump lips. His temper flared.

Please, for both their sakes, let her be out with friends.

When a car pulled into her drive, Jonas stiffened. Definitely not Deanna's red coupe. The big, silver Lexus looked expensive, fancy. Is that the type Deanna went for? The clean-shaven, suit-wearing type? Jonas rubbed his jaw, then cursed when he felt the rough stubble there. Watching from the shadows, he saw Deanna lean toward the driver. He couldn't make out any more than their shapes. Was she kissing him? Was the asshole staying the night?

"Not damn likely."

When she opened the passenger door and stepped out, Jonas breathed a sigh of relief. She waved and the car started a slow glide back out of the driveway. Jonas waited. When she stepped onto the porch, he got a better look at her. She wore a pair of red heels and a matching slip dress with a little black shawl wrap. The dress hit above the knee. Classy, but sexy—and too freaking revealing for his peace of mind.

"Even though it's winter and that dress is clearly not designed to keep a body warm, you sure are heating me up pretty damn fast."

At his words, Deanna jumped and screamed. Jonas shot out of the chair and grabbed her by the shoulders in time to keep her from tumbling off the porch. "What the hell, Jonas? You scared the crap out of me!"

Feeling like an idiot, he mumbled, "Sorry. I didn't mean to startle you."

She shoved out of his arms and slapped his chest. "Why are you lurking in the dark? Are you spying on me?"

Her eyes flashed fire and ice at the same time. How did she do that? It captivated the hell out of him. "Who's spying? I just came for a friendly visit."

"You know very well you're spying." She bit the words out between clenched teeth.

He leaned close, inhaling her floral scent. Lilacs. She always smelled like lilacs. Delicate and gentle. Two things Jonas didn't know shit about. If he had any decency at all, he'd leave.

"A visit, Deanna." He stepped back and let her pass. "I'm not allowed to visit?"

She pulled open the screen door and shoved her key into the dead bolt. "No, you aren't. Now go away. I'm tired."

Her voice had lowered to a quiet, husky tone. It snaked up Jonas's chest like a caress. It pissed him off that she could get to him so easily. "Is that why you sent your date home? Because you're tired?"

She pushed her door open, then turned to him. "That's none of your business." She crossed her arms over her chest. "Go home, Jonas."

Jonas closed the distance separating them. "Let me come inside, Deanna. We need to talk."

"No, we don't," she gritted out, her voice not quite as steady as before. "You need to go home and I need to sleep."

His temper flared. "Why won't you give me the time of day?"

Deanna shook her head and looked away.

Jonas cupped her cheek and forced her back around. He wouldn't let her hide from him. Not ever. "This isn't all one-sided," he whispered. "This desire, you feel it too. I know you do."

On a sigh, Deanna closed her eyes tight. "Just because there's an itch doesn't mean we should scratch it."

Damn, her skin was as soft as flower petals. He stroked his thumb over her lower lip and found it plump, inviting. His dick hardened beneath his jeans as he imagined those full pink lips wrapped snug around his cock.

"An itch, huh?" he growled. "Is that the way you see it?"

She opened her eyes and stared up at him. The angry glare she shot him wasn't at all what he expected. "You had your chance once. You blew it."

Genuinely confused, Jonas dropped his hand. "Chance? You've shot me down at every turn, Deanna."

She squinted and pointed her finger at his chest. "You took my brother's side."

He shoved a hand through his hair and prayed for patience. "Wade?"

"Yes. At Gracie's apartment. When we were there helping clean up the mess that freak left behind. You sided with Wade. Some stupid nonsense about the sister code. Remember?"

Ah, it was all coming together finally. Gracie had been a client of his and Wade's investigation business, but she'd quickly become the love of Wade's life. Unfortunately, she'd been having trouble with a deranged stalker. When the creep had broken into Gracie's apartment and tore it all to hell, they'd all rallied together to help Gracie put things back in order. Once again, Jonas had seen a chance to ask Deanna out, but she'd shot him down. Then Dean and Wade, her two over-protective brothers, had gotten involved. Jonas and Wade were not only business partners but also friends—an annoying little fact that forced Jonas to back off in his pursuit.

"Wade is like a brother to me," he explained, "and he re-minded me of that. It's not cool to chase after your friend's baby sister, Deanna."

She quirked a brow at him. "And yet here you are."

"Yes, smart-ass, here I am," he said softly. "I talked to Wade. He's still not crazy about the fact that I'm hot for you, but he's not going to stand in my way either."

If anything, her frown turned darker. "You asked for his blessing?"

"Uh, something like that, yeah."

"He's not my father, Jonas. I'm a grown woman. Wade has no right to interfere in my personal life."

"Right or wrong, Deanna, Wade will always look out for you. Dean, too, for that matter."

She sighed. "And let me guess, Wade threatened to castrate you if you hurt me. Is that it?"

Jonas propped a fist against the doorjamb, then wrapped his other hand around her waist to keep her from bolting through the open door. "The last thing I want is to hurt you, Deanna."

Deanna's slender fingers gripped onto his forearm. "No," she whispered, "you just want to get me into bed."

He let his hand move lower, until he was mere inches from the sweet curve of her ass. "I want you like hell. Just looking at you makes my dick hard. But there's more than that between us."

She shook her head, maybe a little too vehemently, Jonas thought. "No, there isn't."

"There could be," he murmured as he dipped his head and brushed her lips with his. "If you'd stop playing so hard to get."

The hand she had on his forearm tightened, but she wasn't pushing him away. "I don't want to be another in a long line of conquests, Jonas. This isn't a game for me."

"If all I wanted was a few hours between the sheets with a warm, willing woman, I would've taken that cute little blonde up on her offer at the bar I went to tonight."

Her nails dug into his skin. "Cute little blonde?"

He nodded, enjoying the note of jealousy in her voice. It served her right, considering how jealous he'd been when he'd seen her in that Lexus. "She sent me all the right signals too. But the only woman I want isn't in some bar."

"She's not?"

"Uh-uh. She's standing right in front of me." He looked

down her body, his gaze snagging on the fullness of her breasts pressing so enticingly against the thin material of the dress. "And she's so pretty too."

Deanna dropped her hands and sighed. "I can't do this, Jonas. Please."

"Why? It's just a date. We can go real slow, I swear."

The satin skin over her cheekbones, the same skin he wanted to press his lips against, tautened. Jonas ached to take the starch right out of her. He wanted to watch her go all soft and rosy for him.

"It's not going to work," she said. "I've known guys like you. You're an oversexed playboy. You aren't the serious type, Jonas. You like to play, and I'm not willing to be your plaything."

He snorted at her description. "Plaything?"

Deanna stiffened and dropped her hands from his arms. Jonas instantly missed the warm touch. "Do you deny you're a player?"

Damn, she was serious. "That's what you think of me? That I'm a player?"

She pointed a finger at his chest. "I've watched you with women. None of them are ever around for long either."

Jonas felt his own anger rise. Only Deanna could get to him so quickly and with so little effort. "You think you have me all figured out, but you don't."

Her lips twitched. "Oh, really?"

Jonas scowled. "Really."

She crossed her arms over her chest, and Jonas's gaze shot to the plump swells. She might well be trying to hide them from his view, but Jonas could've told her not to waste her time. The woman put new meaning to the word *stacked*. A man would have to be blind not to notice Deanna's voluptuous curves. Jonas groaned. So fucking close, and yet he may as well be miles away.

"How long was your last relationship?"

Her question jarred Jonas back to the conversation. He had to think back quite a few months before he could answer. "Her name was Marissa, and it lasted two months."

She quirked a brow at him in that regal, slightly bitchy way she had. His dick, which always hardened the instant she came within view, perked right up. "Gee, a whole two months, huh?"

Jonas reached out and tweaked her nose. "Yeah, smart-ass, two months. Sweet lady, but not the one for me." He chose to leave off the part about not having had a serious relationship ever since the day he'd met one hardheaded, dark-haired vixen, who just happened to be his best friend's baby sister. "Now you," he murmured. "How long was your last relationship, Deanna?"

To his surprise, she looked away. As if uncomfortable with the conversation all of a sudden. "I've been busy with work lately. Dating has been the last thing on my mind."

"That doesn't answer my question. I was honest, sweetheart. Don't you think you owe me the same courtesy?"

"Fine. I haven't had a serious relationship since Roger and I broke up."

Jonas remembered Roger. Deanna had dated him for six months. It'd been six months of pure hell for Jonas as he imagined Roger touching Deanna. Touching, tasting, and loving. Jonas had gotten drunk more than once during those six months. Christ, just the thought sent Jonas's temperature into the red zone. "That was a year ago."

She rolled her eyes. "I'm well aware of that, but thanks for the reminder."

Jonas propped his hand against the doorjamb. "Did you love him?"

"I thought so at the time."

"Are you pining away for him, Deanna?"

She laughed. "*Pining?*"

At the sound of her quiet laughter, a dam inside Jonas burst and warmth flooded his system. "You're beautiful when you do that," he whispered as he lifted his hand and cupped her cheek in his palm.

"What?"

"Laugh. I love to hear you laugh."

"Jonas, don't." She shook her head and covered his hand with her own, but she didn't remove it. To his way of thinking, it was another step in the right direction.

Jonas dipped his head, slowly, afraid if he moved too fast she'd bolt through the open door. "Are you sure, Deanna?"

Her soft lips parted and Jonas swept in.